THE COUPLE NEXT DOOR

COLE BAXTER

INKUBATOR
BOOKS

Published by Inkubator Books
www.inkubatorbooks.com

Copyright © 2023 by Cole Baxter

Cole Baxter has asserted his right to be identified as the author of this work.

ISBN (eBook): 978-1-83756-164-3
ISBN (Paperback): 978-1-83756-165-0
ISBN (Hardback): 978-1-83756-166-7

1

THE PARTY

I couldn't stop smiling, and more importantly, I didn't want to. It was my party, after all.

I did it.

Everything was finally going my way, everything was slowly coming together, all my dreams were coming true. Well, not all of them, but I knew that eventually, they would, so of course I was happy.

"It is my honor to present Amber Dennis, the newest junior partner at Grant, Bryant, and Dawson," my boss said.

One day it will be Grant, Dawson, and Dennis, I thought. I really wanted my name added to the mix.

Mr. Grant had been giving his speech for the last couple of minutes, but I wasn't really paying close attention. I'd heard it all before. As always, he was doing this more to stroke his own ego than mine.

I didn't care. He'd helped me a great deal over the years and was the first person to notice what a brilliant asset I would become. For that, I tolerated his quirks. The enjoyment of hearing the sound of his own voice was definitely one of them.

The entire firm had gathered in an exclusive steakhouse conveniently located just a block away from the office. Lawyers were nothing if not practical. I knew at least half of them would return to the office after the party to do some work and clock a few more billing hours before calling it a night.

I had become the youngest junior partner in the firm at just thirty-six, and I deserved it. This wasn't me bragging. I really had worked my ass off to get here. It had taken a good chunk of money to meet the buy-in for the position too, but I'd done it because I wanted to become a partner in this firm. I wanted that and so much more.

I had been saving since college, putting aside chunks of each and every paycheck I received working as a lawyer, knowing this day would come. I was prepared for it, and still, my heart froze for a couple of seconds when receiving the stipulations of becoming a partner. Damn inflation was ruining everything.

It was time to stop focusing on the negative. *I am here now.* And the money given was an investment. And a pretty sound investment at that because our firm was one of the best, and I wasn't stopping at junior partner. In a matter of a few years I planned on becoming a senior partner. For that, I would have to replace one of the existing ones, and only then would I become a named partner.

I already knew whom I was going to replace. Phoebe Bryant. She was a named partner, so I would be killing two birds with one stone, purely metaphorically speaking.

My ticket in, the way to achieve all my plans, was precisely the man who was giving this long speech.

Michael Grant, a sixty-four-year-old senior partner, was the founder of the firm. Of course, back then it was simply called Grant and Associates. He was such a brilliant lawyer and savvy businessman who didn't mind getting his hands dirty every once in a while. He was also a power-hungry, driven workaholic, who was desperate to leave a significant mark on this city. Over the years he managed to achieve something great, and along the way, the firm grew as more equal-minded people joined in.

Today, Grant, Bryant, and Dawson law firm was one of the most successful companies on the west coast. And although all the senior partners were equal, some were more equal than others, and Grant had the most say.

So when he took me under his wing just over ten years ago, it was a sign to all the rest that I was the new shining star. Naturally, I had to back that up with hard work, an excellent record, and an impressive client list, but for me, that was the easiest part. I loved my job, and I was competitive enough to want to be one of the best.

"I remember the first time Amber came to us, fresh out of Harvard Law School and so green... we corrected that quickly," he continued, and that last comment raised a few chuckles.

The way he was speaking, it was as though he were singlehandedly responsible for all my successes. I hated when men did that. Especially since I was the only one responsible for my achievements. I stayed and worked overtime to learn as much as possible so I could hone my craft and be one of the best. It irked me this man was trying to take all the credit.

Still, I smiled like a good, obedient employee and pretended I was charmed by his condescending words, sucked it all up because I knew my time to rule, to shine, would come. That was how this game was played, and all the people present knew that.

Perhaps I should take his job and not Bryant's. I instantly banished that thought. The original plan was much better and easily achievable. I needed Grant. At least for now. Afterward, well, nobody could predict the future, and if he decided to retire at some point and focus on perfecting his golf, I would be absolutely all right with that.

Anyway, I was very much pleased to see that all the partners and associates had shown up to my party. And they had brought their partners, significant others, and even family members, which I was glad for, but everyone had someone, except me. There was nobody by my side, and although I tried not to focus on that, it was an ache in my heart.

Unfortunately, I only had one family member left, my mother. However, she couldn't be bothered to come to the party tonight. She couldn't be bothered with being happy with me or for me. She couldn't even pretend to feel such an emotion, so I was left all alone. Sadly, I'd learned to prefer it that way.

Banishing all thoughts of my selfish mother, I refocused on the here and now. I wasn't about to let my mother ruin this perfect moment for me. I'd managed this far without her; I didn't need her. Besides, what could a stay-at-home mom do for me anyway? She didn't possess any skills I found useful or desirable.

I'd left home right after high school and never looked back. If anything, she needed me more, relied on me because she was unable to move on and be her own person. And now she was punishing me for choosing myself. She was a selfish, spiteful woman.

Stop it, Amber, I warned myself.

I noticed that Grant was holding his champagne glass in his hand, which meant he was finally reaching his point, the end of the speech.

Finally.

"So join me now and raise your glass to our newest junior partner, our very own rising star, Amber Dennis."

Everyone raised their glasses and toasted.

I picked up my own glass of champagne and toasted firstly to Grant and then to everybody else. "Thank you, Michael, that was a very touching speech," I said humbly.

"I meant every word, kiddo," he said with a wink.

As expected, many joined in to offer their congratulations. A large portion of our job was establishing connections and keeping those relationships cordial. And I was happy to see that my colleagues valued my place in this very well-oiled machinery. Or so it appeared.

"If we're done, can we eat now? I am starving," Grant grumbled after a few minutes.

That was so typical of him. He gave the longest speech known to man, and then he complained it was taking too long. It was on the tip of my tongue to point out how that physique of his didn't really need another steak, but I held my tongue. Even I knew not to share that opinion among such a large group of people. It would come off as disrespectful. If we were alone, I could definitely tease him, so I saved that joke for some other time.

Michael Grant looked pretty typical for a lawyer in his sixties. It was obvious he'd stopped going to the gym a while back. He used to be a very handsome man, and he'd kept some of his ruggedness in his late years. However, he was definitely not in his prime. Another indicator of that was the fact he came to the office only when he absolutely had to. The rest of his time was spent between visiting golf courses and sailing.

Being a senior partner in a prestigious law firm is a taxing business, I joked. Most of the senior partners, except Phoebe, operated in a similar manner. Leaving the real work to the younger people, the junior partners, and the associates.

At the table I was sitting at, only the senior partners were seated with their respective others. The rest were seated around us since Grant had gracefully rented the whole place for the night. That must have cost him a fortune, but I knew he could afford it.

Phoebe Bryant, whose position in the firm I was gunning for, sat right across from me with her husband, Anthony, who was a judge. Peter Dawson was there with his wife, Susan, as well, and Grant came with his son, David, because he was currently between wives.

I'd forgotten how many times Grant had been married. At least three times. They all kind of blurred together because Grant definitely had a type. Young, good-looking, trophy wives whose only purpose was to look pretty on his arm while he attended all the social parties of the season. They meant nothing to him, and for them, he was a stepping stone, a way into the prestigious life they could only dream about before him.

I believe only David's mother stood out from that cliché, at least in Grant's life. They had met in college. Eveline was a successful writer, and he had been married to her the longest. The fact he had cheated on her with various assistants, secretaries, and even clients was what eventually broke them apart. That was typical too. No matter how powerful men were, they still needed to stroke their egos with meaningless affairs, as though that would elevate them in the eyes of others.

All the same, once Eveline learned about Grant's extra-marital relationships, she'd left the bastard. She'd had enough sense to leave with a very hefty settlement. In her place, I would do the same thing. An attitude like Grant's needed to be punished. In a manner that would hurt the most. And that meant taking as much money as was humanly possible. Eveline got herself a good divorce lawyer, a shark who made sure she got everything she deserved and then some.

The conversation around the restaurant stilled while everyone looked at their menus. The only exception to that was David. While I was perusing the menu, as though I hadn't already decided to order a salad and nothing else, I noticed his fingers were brushing against my thighs very coyly, underneath the table.

That was rather cheeky of him.

At first, the touch was so featherlight I wasn't even sure it actually happened until I discreetly looked, and sure enough, he was trying to get my attention.

Interesting.

David brushed against my thigh again, with the tips of his fingers, and this time his touch was more confident.

It was really hard not to laugh. Men his age, or should I say boys, since he was only twenty-six, thought very highly of themselves. They thought the world was their playground.

Sure, he had those youthful, good looks going for him. He was tall, fit, with thick black hair and wide, innocent green eyes, but that was it. Beyond that he was empty because he lacked experience; he lacked the wisdom that could only be gained through living life and going through rough patches.

And being the son of a millionaire kept him in a state of perpetual brattiness. Though, that didn't mean I was about to reject his advances. Quite the contrary. He was perfect for what I had in mind. A night of meaningless sex was what I wanted, needed, and David would be perfect to help me with that.

That was precisely why I took his hand and firmly placed it on my thigh, nudging it upward, silently congratulating myself for wearing a short skirt, since it made everything much easier. All the while I kept my eyes on my menu, but I could still see David's reaction.

It would be fun to have him in my bed. I figured I deserved a private celebration after this one. And the best way to do that was with a fit twenty-six-year-old.

Contemplating what kind of body he had underneath his casual black suit, I smiled at him, still coaxing his hand to caress me, and he didn't disappoint. The look of dazed astonishment I received in return was perfect.

Luckily, he recovered quickly, and I approved.

This is going to be so much fun...

2

THE AFTER-PARTY

I felt exhausted, but in a good way, as I drove home from the restaurant. The party was a huge success, everybody left happy, a little tipsy, especially Grant, and I hoped the way they felt tonight would stay with them when I had to deal with them at work tomorrow.

I was using GPS because I still hadn't fully gotten used to driving in this part of the city. I'd moved recently to my new condo, and I was still getting used to it all. Not that I was complaining. I was very proud to secure a place like that for myself.

The building I now lived in was called the Golden Sunrise. Despite its cheesy name, it was one of the most luxurious buildings in the city, and finding a vacant apartment was a rarity. Luckily, one had been up for sale six months ago, and I'd managed to snatch it. And now it was all mine. It had an amazing view and came with a private underground parking garage and a doorman.

Since returning to LA after college, I had dreamt of living in one of those buildings. Seeing all those beautiful, happy people coming out of them, pondering about their lives. I'd vowed to be one of them someday. Luckily, I'd managed to achieve that. Although, perhaps luck had nothing to do with it. I worked hard and had reached the levels of success that allowed me to purchase my dream condo.

Ever since I was little, I had a clear vision of what I wanted my life to look like. Actually, to be more precise, I knew what I didn't want. I didn't want to end up like my mother. So, in high school, my wish crystallized, and I knew I would become a lawyer. And not just any kind, a defense lawyer.

I wanted to be someone, somebody important, successful and rich, which was the opposite of what my mother was. She was a housewife who never strove to be anything else. And that was sad for me, her not having any kind of real goal in life.

Taking care of the house, of a man, all her life was all she lived for. And when my father died, she was left with nothing.

Pitiful.

She tried to refocus her energy on me while demanding everything in return, but I was having none of it. By that time, I was my own person, with clear goals in life and her way of living, her attitude toward me, toward life, was in conflict with it. So I knew I had to leave.

My father understood me. And my needs. At least, I had that.

Leaving and going to Harvard was the best decision I had ever made. Nonetheless, staying in Boston wasn't an option for me. It wasn't that I was homesick. It was simply that I preferred the sun, preferred the warm weather.

The fact this city had plenty of successful people

working in the entertainment industry who constantly needed legal services was a nice bonus as well.

After parking in the underground lot, I entered a private elevator and put in the specific code that would take me to my floor. I liked the level of security this place offered. It made me feel safer knowing not just anybody could waltz inside and raise trouble.

I was a lawyer, after all, and it was to be expected there would be people angry at me. That was part of the job. Still, I didn't want the job following me home.

Only when I got upstairs I realized I'd forgotten to stop at the lobby and ask Alex, the doorman who worked night shifts, if any packages had arrived for me.

I'll do that tomorrow.

Inside my apartment, I took my shoes off and sighed with relief. I liked wearing high heels, but like everything else in life, that had a price as well—sore feet.

Walking about in my new condo, I was as happy as I could be. This was a good night. And if I'd read the situation well, which I definitely did, it was about to get even better.

I couldn't believe the whole firm had decided to participate and come to my party. Then again, they probably thought it was mandatory considering I was Grant's protégé. It was fun seeing so much envy on some of their faces. I'd stood out among my peers right from the start, and some had a problem with that. Not that I really cared. As long as I had Grant on my side, none of it mattered.

While he was protecting me from all the backstabbing, I was practically untouchable. I still had to tread lightly among the senior partners, but that wasn't problematic for me.

And if I was extra careful, I could do some backstabbing

of my own. I didn't feel particularly guilty about that. This was a cutthroat kind of world. And I was sure Phoebe Bryant had ended up a named partner through doing the same thing to somebody else along her way to the top. That was just how things functioned, because if you did manage to take someone down, that was a clear indicator they didn't belong there in the first place.

Finally, becoming a junior partner meant it was obviously time for the next step of my plan. Becoming senior partner. That would definitely take some time, but I was nothing if not patient. And there was nothing I could not achieve if only I put my mind to it. I'd already proved that to myself time and time again, so this didn't feel any different to me.

I would get Phoebe's seat at the table. And not just because that was where the real money was. Senior partners had all the power, all the say around the firm, and that was what I wanted.

In truth, I could go after any partner, but there were a limited number of women in the firm, so I wanted it to be Phoebe. And there was a simple explanation for that. She was the only female named partner. And that was what I was aiming for in the end. I figured, with her out of the way, I could reach all my goals with a single stab in the back. *Simple.*

There was a chance other partners, especially seniors, would try to secure that spot for themselves, but I wasn't worried, because I had Grant on my side.

He was the one who had convinced Phoebe to vote me in for this promotion, and I was sure he would convince others when the time came for the next one as well. And with Phoebe gone, I would be the queen of the castle.

I could lie and say this was purely business for me. She was in my way, which meant I had to take her down. But it was personal as well. That bitch had had it in for me since I'd started at the firm. She didn't like me for some reason, and over time the sentiment became mutual.

Truth be told, I never understood her attitude toward me. I was nothing but nice to her, I tried to be helpful, assisted her many times in her cases, and still, she hated me. It was never an open thing; all the same, I knew the truth. That was why she was my biggest opponent when I was a nominee for junior partner.

And now, finally, I understood why she was behaving the way she did. She recognized I was a threat to her. She had been Grant's star before I arrived. She was the first African American female partner, and then I came along, and Grant started focusing on me, grooming me, and Phoebe realized there would come a day when I would replace her.

So she did everything in her power to make my life more difficult. She wasn't successful, of course. Her attitude only made me stronger and more determined that one day soon I would take her down.

I was much smarter than her. I was a better lawyer, and one day I would become more successful than her. And then it would be much easier to get her job. In the end, she had every right to fear for her job because I was going to take it from her, no matter what.

I will take everything from you, I thought with a smirk as I slipped out of my clothes. Everything on me reeked of cigars, and that made me feel sick to my stomach.

Unfortunately, Grant insisted on smoking those vile things, and naturally, since he was the alpha dog, all the men followed suit.

What's with powerful men always smoking those cigars and drinking whiskey? I pondered. *I will never understand that,* I thought with a shake of my head, looking at the pile of clothes underneath my feet. They'd cost a lot of money, but they reeked so bad I would much rather burn them than wear them ever again. Yet I would never do that. Not only because they were expensive, but it was one of my favorite ensembles.

I liked wearing this combination to court as well because the skirt was long enough not to be scandalous, but short enough to attract the men's attention, when they should be focused on the case. Judges included.

I would keep the clothes because I really liked them, I decided. Unfortunately, at times, I was sentimental like that.

As I was pondering my next course of action, not just about tonight but about life in general, there was a buzz on the intercom phone. I instantly knew what that meant, so I went to the door, still in my underwear, to answer.

I knew he wouldn't be able to resist me. "Yes?"

"Good evening, Miss Dennis," Alex greeted politely. "You have a visitor."

"Send him up," I interrupted because I knew who my visitor was and wanted to keep this conversation short.

Perhaps that sounded a bit eager from my side, but I still felt a little uncomfortable with a stranger knowing all my comings and goings, who was visiting me, and when. That was something I needed to overcome and fast because it didn't really matter if some doorman knew I had a booty call. This was what success looked like.

Besides, Alex and the rest of the staff working in a building like this knew how to be discreet. They had to, considering the kind of people who lived here, businessmen, celebrities.

It wouldn't be good for them if they had loose tongues. The residents would go berserk if their privacy was in jeopardy, even a little, and the person with a big mouth would not only lose their job, but much more. Their lives would be ruined, and I was sure all the employees knew that, so nobody tried to sell a story for a few bucks.

Of course, I would act in the exact same manner if my privacy was jeopardized. I would do everything in my power to destroy the person who tried to do that.

"All right, Miss Dennis," Alex replied, snapping me from my thoughts.

"Thanks." I didn't even have to think about whether I should cover my body or not. I remained in my black, lacy underwear. I knew why he was coming to see me this late at night.

He clearly knew it too, or at least he hoped so. Because it was always on the woman to say yes or no, and on men to beg for it.

That was why I opened my door when I heard the elevator stopping at my floor.

As expected, David came out, and his eyes practically bulged out of his head as he took in my appearance and gulped, loudly.

I knew I looked good. I took care of myself. Sure, genetics helped a little. I was tall, statuesque, tanned from spending time on the beach whenever I could, and blue-eyed. I was careful with what I ate, I worked out, I made sure my natural blonde hair was healthy, and I shopped for clothes that were complimentary to my physique.

So David's reaction completely made sense. That didn't.

mean it wasn't the best kind of compliment I received, especially because it was so natural.

I leaned against the door frame, watching him from beneath my eyelashes as he approached. "I hoped you would come," I said in my most seductive voice. At this point, I knew I didn't have to bother, he was already mine for the taking, but it was fun. I wanted to play with him a little longer.

He practically ran toward me. "I couldn't stop thinking about you. I would have come sooner—"

Apparently, there was more he wanted to say, explain, but I lost patience. I grabbed him by the lapels and pulled him against my body, locking our lips in a passionate kiss.

David responded immediately, letting his hands roam all over my body, grabbing at my ass.

Realizing Alex was probably watching us via the security cameras, I pulled him inside the apartment. David wasn't fighting me on it.

He might be young, but he wasn't entirely inexperienced. I approved.

The door was closed somehow, and we continued to kiss.

While he explored my body, I did the same with his and was pleasantly surprised to discover he was in excellent shape. Thank God everyone in LA was obsessed with their looks.

Everything about him was turning me on, which was a surprise. Then again, it had been a while since I'd had sex, and I was really looking forward to it.

But then he hesitated, breaking the kiss.

What the...? I looked at him in surprise. What was happening?

"I shouldn't be here," he admitted.

I could see how much it pained him to say that. He was really into me, wanted to be with me.

"My father would be furious if he found out about this."

I should have known he is afraid of Grant.

And he was probably right. Grant was very protective and serious when it came to his only child, his only son. Which was why I intended for him to never find out about this.

"It would probably cause problems for your work too," he added.

In that moment he truly showed his age. He was nothing but a boy scared of his father, which was a major turn-off. I had to do something before I lost my will for sex.

I offered my most reassuring smile, wrapping my arms around his neck and moving my body against his in the process. "Let me worry about your father," I said firmly as his pupils dilated at my proximity. It looked like he was high. And I had to admit I kind of liked the idea of being someone's drug of choice.

Without further delay, I leaned forward, demanding a kiss, and he responded immediately. All talk about his father or anything else was forgotten instantly, just the way I wanted.

He was a really good boy, really obedient.

I helped him get out of his clothes, and he didn't disappoint. He had a very nice, tanned body.

"Come with me," I commanded, reaching for him.

After a moment of hesitation, he took my hand, and together we went to the bedroom.

Being with him felt amazing. I let him fuck me three times that evening.

He might have been scared of his father, but he lusted for

me more, and that was a turn-on, such a head rush, it felt as good as the orgasms I had.

Overall, David was very good to me that night. He was a great ego boost, an amazing tension relief and workout. Everything a woman needed.

Got to love twenty-six-year-olds...

3

THE GOOD LIFE

I t felt good being me. I was finally a junior partner. I had an apartment many would envy. I had a great ride, a Tesla. And since I'd recently acquired a new lover who was great at keeping me occupied and satisfied during the night, my life was complete.

How could I possibly ask for more?

I could, but I was pretty satisfied with what I had.

For now.

So I decided to enjoy life and my current accomplishments before preparing for the next battle, because in my life, in my line of work, there was always a battle ahead.

That was guaranteed.

And I loved it.

Also, there was another thing that made me feel good. Or should I dare say, like a freaking rock star?

My new, very prestigious and highly coveted position came with a new office. And as was customary, I received a budget, complimentary from the firm, to decorate it if I saw fit.

I still hadn't decided about that. I liked my old office although it was on the small side. Also, I had personally acquired each and every piece of furniture that was in there, so there was a question, what to do with it all now? Although I tended to not get attached and wasn't too sentimental, there were a few pieces I wanted to keep. All the same, I would shelve that problem for another time. I needed to see the space first before making any decisions.

I waltzed into the firm feeling like a million dollars. I knew I should try to keep it humble, but it couldn't be helped. I was satisfied with myself and what I had accomplished. I didn't see anything wrong with that. Humility was for people who never did anything of importance in their lives. I had.

I helped a lot of people, good and bad, with my legal expertise, and I rose through the ranks at this firm. Life was good.

Bonnie, my legal secretary, was already at her new station in front of my new office, and I approved. She should always come in before me, to prepare for my day.

As I walked by her, she greeted me before rushing to prepare my tea. I patted myself on the back. *I taught her well.* I always drank green tea in the morning. Coffee was reserved for the nights I had to stay late at the office to prepare for a big case.

I stepped into my new office, taking it all in. It was a corner office that used to belong to Edward Cattley. I had no idea where he was now, nor did I care.

I was practically giddy that this was my new working space because the office definitely had the best view of the city. Apart from Grant's office, of course.

I was pleasantly surprised to see all my things had

already been moved here. And since all my books were already on the shelves, I figured Bonnie had taken care of the unpacking. That cheered me up.

I still hadn't decided what I was going to do with the space, but I liked how it looked. Although I felt like my desk should be moved to the other side of the room. Edward had kept it in that same spot, and I always thought that was a mistake.

Taking my shoes off, because I couldn't do manual labor in high heels, I slowly, painfully managed to move the desk right where I wanted it.

It looked much better in its new place, and I sat down in the chair, pondering what I should do next. Should I change everything? Should I make my mark?

It was true these things were mine, but were they worthy of my new station? What I meant was that everything in here had been bought while I was still just an associate. I was a partner now, and that should be plain to see all around me, not only in bold letters on my glass door.

I didn't want my clients to get the wrong idea. I needed all my clients, old and new, to know right from the moment they stepped into my office that I wasn't only one of the best, but pretty expensive as well. I wanted them to know what they would be getting. And I wasn't sure the image I had been trying to cultivate was represented in my current surroundings.

None of it screams—the youngest junior partner.

If the firm's clients demanded the best, I wanted them to be sent my way. And I was one of the best. I couldn't even pretend to be modest about that. My winning record in court was pretty impressive because when I had a court trial, I aimed to win, no matter what.

I managed to get away with murder, well, my clients had quite a few times, at any rate. And I never felt guilty about that because I was just doing my job to the best of my ability. It wasn't my fault the other side was never up to the task.

I should definitely remodel. These items had served me well while I was an associate. All the same, it was time for a new chapter in life. And that meant a different office as well.

Someone knocked on my door, snapping me from my thoughts. I turned to see Grant leaning against the door frame, smiling at me.

"I see you are settling in nicely," he commented, eyeing my high heels, which were still in the middle of the office.

"Yes, I am. Thank you."

"Here, I got you something for your new office." He approached to place a potted plant at the edge of my desk. "Welcome to the neighborhood."

I didn't care for such things per se, knew it would probably die if Bonnie didn't start taking care of it; however, I understood the importance of such a gesture. A named partner had come personally to welcome me and brought a gift. And that meant something around here. That meant everything. Sure, I would have a target on my back, because a lot of envious people worked here, but I was prepared for it all.

"That's very thoughtful of you."

I knew his secretary had picked it out for him. Honestly, Grant couldn't function without Millie. She had been with him for more than thirty years. In all ways that counted, she was his true wife.

And this wasn't me mocking. I hoped, one day, I would find the perfect legal secretary who would become such a vital part of my life, too, at least professionally speaking. Bonnie was definitely not that person.

"If you need anything, come straight to me. I am just down the corridor, after all," he added with a wink.

"Admit you did that on purpose," I replied with a smile.

"Of course I did," he said smugly. "I need you close by."

"Well, I appreciate it."

He was about to say something in return when his phone started ringing. He looked at the screen and frowned. "Got to go; see you later, kiddo." And with that, he rushed out of the office, answering his call.

Once he left, I fetched my shoes and asked Bonnie to come inside. I needed to start my day. But firstly, I needed to know whom to call about redecorating my office.

Later, I was caught up to speed on my day. As it turned out, I had meetings and consultations throughout the day. Old clients and new ones wanted to meet and greet as well, and I understood why. They all needed to be reassured everything was staying exactly the same with me in charge. That it would be business as usual. And I planned on honoring that. I wasn't planning on ruffling any feathers, at least not yet. At least not while I was settling into my new role.

On my way out for lunch, I saw a few of my colleagues and other junior partners exiting together. Although they nodded toward me in greeting, that was it. None of them came to see me or ask if I needed anything. And they certainly hadn't invited me to lunch with them.

I couldn't figure out why they'd never asked me to join them for lunch. Or go for drinks after hours. Even when I was an intern, other interns didn't like me. Of course, they were very professional toward me and worked alongside me just fine, but the social element was always missing. Not that I personally cared if the relationships evolved from being strictly professional. All the same, I found it strange that that kept happening.

Either way, it always worked to my advantage. I preferred to keep to myself, and since people left me alone, I could focus solely on myself and my career.

Attachments caused complications and distractions, and I didn't want those in my life. I had a plan to follow, and wasting my energy on anything else wasn't acceptable.

The afternoon hours turned out to be even busier. At some point even Dawson, a senior partner, came to visit me.

"Hello, what can I do for you, Dawson?"

"I need your help with this," he replied, throwing a stack of papers on my desk.

I picked them up to see what it was about.

"I need it done by tomorrow morning."

I skimmed through the contents. When I looked up, he was already gone. "Happy to help," I grumbled.

I received a couple of VIP clients as well. Since I was a junior partner now, Grant made sure I got a few of them as well. And since I was the new face, they all needed some special attention, some reassurance from me that all their needs would be taken care of.

It was tedious work, especially since they all acted like children, but it needed to be done, as it was part of the job.

At some point, Kelly, my best friend, texted to congratulate me on my promotion and to ask if I wanted to meet later for drinks. I said no because I was swamped. There were not enough hours in the day for all that needed to be done. And that had been before Dawson dumped that special assignment on me.

Still, she wouldn't let me go until I promised to see her soon. Kelly was like that at times, unaccustomed to hearing the word no from other people.

The fact I'd talked to her about my promotion last week meant nothing. Time wasn't a concept she was familiar with. That was what happened when you had a rich parent, could spend their money, and didn't have to work. Didn't have a care in the world.

To some people, that right there sounded like heaven. Truth be told, although she was a dear friend, I pitied her lack of direction in life. Not that I would ever tell her that. She was one of my only friends, and I loved her despite her many flaws.

It was strange how the two of us had become friends, considering how different we were. She was a party girl, and I was a career-oriented woman. Still, special circumstances had brought us closer together, and I really valued her, and I knew she felt the same way.

Give them hell, was her last text full of kiss emojis before finally leaving me alone to do what I loved best, work.

I smiled, thinking of her last message; Kelly really knew me the best. She knew about my plans as well, not specifics but enough to offer her two cents.

I allowed myself one bathroom break before returning to the job. While I was doing my business, I overheard two employees, clearly at the lower station, gossiping.

"I hope Phoebe has eyes in the back of her head because she's next," the first one said.

"That's true. Amber will stoop to anything to get what she wants," the other agreed.

I suppressed a gasp. They were speaking about me. More

accurately, they were gossiping about me in the worst possible way.

To be perfectly honest, they were not entirely wrong. Phoebe was in my way. I was only surprised that it wasn't as much of a secret as I'd hoped it was. Besides, what they were saying was rude.

They need to respect me more, not spread such vile gossip, I fumed. *Does Phoebe know about this too?* It really didn't matter. *My plan still stays the same no matter what.*

Though, these two needed to be dealt with. On one hand, I really shouldn't care what a pair of secretaries thought about me; on the other, they needed to be taught a lesson.

Unfortunately, by the time I got out of the stall, they were already gone. Rushing out of the bathroom, I didn't spot anyone in the corridor.

Damn it.

It could be anyone. How to find them? It was a pity I hadn't recognized their voices. Realizing I was obsessing over unimportant petty things, I stopped and returned to work.

I was close to finishing when my phone started ringing. That put a smile on my face.

"Hello?" I answered.

"When can I see you again? Tonight?" David said by way of greeting.

So eager. I snickered. He almost sounded like a true junky. It was kind of hot. I had to admit I took great pleasure in having this secret relationship right under Grant's nose.

"I'll have to let you know later. I am too busy now."

"Please, Amber. I miss you."

"I have to go. Talk to you later." I hung up then because

he was in danger of sounding pathetic, and I didn't want to hear that. That wasn't attractive, not one bit. Besides, it was imperative to always keep him wanting more.

I'd discovered a long time ago that that was the key to unlock every man's heart, or whatever. Never surrender; never give them everything they wanted. Only then would they be running back to you for more.

Like David.

I decided to check my emails one more time before calling it a night.

And then maybe I will give David a call. I smiled, thinking about all the things we'd done last time.

What the hell? I grumbled, stumbling upon something strange that erased my smile. I'd received an email from an unknown address.

That by itself wasn't the alarming part. It had no subject or personal information.

That is strange. All the same, I opened it.

It was a short message. Only a few lines, written all in capital letters.

YOUR LIFE AS YOU KNOW IT IS ABOUT TO END. I WILL RUIN EVERYTHING YOU HOLD DEAR. I WILL RUIN YOU.

4

MOTHERS AND DAUGHTERS

Closing the threatening email, I sighed. There were too many sick people running around the streets with nothing better to do than piss me off.

I hated when stuff like this, from some randos, some losers, managed to pass through.

This was clearly spam, so what was it doing in my inbox? I would have to speak with tech support because this was unacceptable.

After reporting that crazy email and reviewing my schedule for tomorrow, I turned my computer off. It was time to go home.

I started to think about David again. I decided to show him some mercy and let him come and see me that night. It had been a long day, and I deserved someone to worship me before going to sleep.

After I texted him and he replied that he'd come by later, I realized how the prospect of a booty call was rather exciting, especially with David. It wasn't that I was infatuated with him. It was the combination of all the elements—his good looks, solid sexual techniques, and the fact he was Grant's son—that actually worked for me and turned me on.

Once I got home, I showered quickly and went to my wardrobe to decide what to wear. Sexy lingerie had an effect on David, so I decided to stick to that.

Why change something that works, right?

I still had trouble picking the perfect lingerie. There was a possibility I was kind of obsessed with alluring underwear and had quite an impressive collection.

What could I say? It was empowering knowing I had something like that on underneath my regular clothes. It didn't matter if someone saw it or not, I felt the same.

Tonight, though, David was definitely in for a treat.

Should I wear a black lacy bra with matching panties, and if so, which ones? Or should I opt for the red one? What if I go with purple?

The poor boy is not going to know what hit him. I was certainly in a particular mood. Probably due to the fact I'd had such a good day at work.

Then again, if I planned on regularly sleeping with him, I would definitely have to teach him a trick or two. At the moment he was kind of a one-trick pony. It was an amazing trick, but repeating the same thing night after night could get boring. And I got bored pretty easily.

For some reason, I wanted David to stick around, which meant tonight he would receive his first lesson in how to properly satisfy a woman. And that was a pretty valuable lesson.

Those girls who faked orgasms and pretended their partners were the best lovers in the world, when in reality they could not even find a clitoris with a map, did all of us normal women a huge disfavor.

Firstly, because they were lying to those men, giving them false confidence, and secondly, because they made it more difficult for the rest of us when we tried to be honest. Not to mention we were all robbed of a good time, robbed of our orgasms.

I had been called a bitch a few times after not faking an orgasm and pointing out the sex encounter had been mediocre at best.

All my screams are earned. Always had been, and that was how it would remain until my last day on this earth. Perhaps that sounded too theatrical. All the same, it was true.

As I was lost in my thoughts, my phone started ringing. I made a face. *Why now?*

I instantly knew who was calling because there was only one person who preferred to use the landline and not my cell phone.

I have only myself to blame, I grumbled as the damn thing continued to ring. *Why, oh why did I give her the number in the first place?*

As I walked toward it, I wondered if I should answer or not. It wasn't like I couldn't let my answering machine handle it.

That woman hadn't bothered to be a part of my celebration. More to the point, she hadn't even congratulated me properly, so why should I care what she had to say now?

She probably had a million excuses for why she'd decided not to come, like always.

Unfortunately, despite knowing all that, I knew I would answer. I felt this pull, an almost uncontrollable urge to answer. Some would call it perverse curiosity, others madness, but despite my feelings or better judgment, I found myself picking up the phone.

"Hello?" I answered, having to work really hard not to sound as irritated as I was.

"Hello, Amber, it's your mother."

I rolled my eyes. She always said that, as though there could ever be a time I wouldn't recognize her voice.

"Hello, Mother," I greeted in return and then stopped because I didn't know what else to say. Besides, she'd called me.

What does she want now? I wondered. *She probably needs something. That's the only reason she calls anyways.*

"How was the party?" she asked after a long pause.

If you really cared about that, you would have been there.

"It was amazing. All my colleagues were there, and they brought their spouses and family members. It was a heart-warming thing to see how they'd all gathered for me and celebrated with me," I jibed instantly without missing a beat.

She needed to know she'd actually hurt my feelings with her behavior.

Although I'd learned a long time ago not to count on my mother, at times it still hurt, no matter how hard I tried not to let it.

"I'm sorry I couldn't be there to see it."

She wasn't sorry at all.

"And why couldn't you?" I asked, genuinely curious to hear her excuse. She was a true master at creating them.

"You know my new apartment is too far away from your law firm. I couldn't drive that far."

I rolled my eyes again, saddened she actually couldn't see it. *New apartment. What a joke.* She had lived in that apartment for more than fifteen years, yet she still acted as though she'd moved in yesterday. Not to mention how she had been bitching about it ever since.

However, that was my mother all right, unable to move on, let go of the past, always trying to make me feel guilty whenever we spoke, even though there was nothing for me to be guilty about. She was just a big baby, always whining about everything. She didn't know how to live her life any other way.

But I had to give her props. She always found new and creative ways to paint this very sad picture of herself and her life. No matter what, Maisie Dennis had the hardest life imaginable.

And according to her, I was the guilty party.

Ever since I'd decided to live my life the way I wanted and made my career a priority, she had turned against me. She never allowed me to forget I'd abandoned her.

At least that was what she believed, in her delusional mind. In my opinion, that was a coping mechanism. She had to have someone to blame, other than herself, for her failed life.

"You could have stayed with me," I said in return.

At this point, my mother and I shared this song and dance routine each time we spoke. I offered solutions; she offered excuses for why these solutions were bad. In her world, it was her way or no way, which was precisely why I was such a disappointment to her. I never listened.

"You know I had to work in the morning."

And the way she said work, it was a direct gibe at me. It was an accusation of sorts. I was at fault because she had to work after my father died.

I refused to take care of her, so now she had to work in her old days. And by old, I was being sarcastic. The woman was only sixty.

My mother was a very peculiar being. She had been a

housewife who never had ambitions to be anything else. So when my father died, although I was still in high school, my mother expected me to take care of her, as my father had.

She thought I would assume all his responsibilities, and that was something I couldn't agree to because I had plans of my own. I didn't want my father's life. I wanted to create something uniquely mine.

And I believed that over time my mother would see the wisdom of my ways. That she would snap out of her delusions and realize she'd gotten a second chance in life to become whoever she wanted.

That didn't happen, and for years she pestered me, tried to guilt me into doing what she wanted.

Eventually, lack of money forced her to start working for the first time in her life, and she never forgave me for that. It was irritating, among other things, that she acted that way. I wished she would get over certain things, stop living in the past and move on. Unfortunately, I wasn't holding my breath for that to ever happen.

"You only have one bedroom."

In my mother's language that meant *there is no room for me in your life. You don't care about me. You never cared about me.*

I forgot how exhausting it was to speak with her. And at times like this, I wondered why I went through all this trouble. We would never see eye to eye. My father knew that. That was why he'd gifted me my freedom before he died.

And she never forgave me for that either. That he'd chosen me over her.

"It was just for one evening," I pointed out. "Besides, I could have ordered you an Uber if you didn't feel like driving. If you'd only called and told me that."

"You know I don't like strangers."

Was she speaking about an Uber driver or me?

"Was there something you needed?" I decided to change the subject. "Why did you call me?"

"You know I don't need help." Now that was a joke. "I called to see how it all went."

And remind me what a huge disappointment I am to you. I filled in the blanks.

"As I said, it went well."

"I'm sorry I wasn't there."

Yeah, right. "So you say."

"Are you angry with me because I couldn't come? Amber, I told you I couldn't. I explained why. Don't make too big a deal out of it."

I am making too big a deal?

"It's fine, Mom, I really don't feel like arguing. If you say you couldn't come, then you couldn't come," I ranted, losing patience. "I am sure you'll be there when I become senior partner," I said before I could stop myself. And at that point, I couldn't tell if I was joking or not.

As always, she'd pushed all my buttons, irritating me to no end.

I knew relationships between mothers and daughters could be complicated, but I believed we could outgrow it eventually. Find a way to interact without all this baggage. I was wrong. The past was all my mother cared about. And that was just sad. As was the fact I pitied my mother, which was why I could never respect her.

She wasn't a parent. Not really. No wonder my relationship with her was all screwed up.

"Is that truly the only thing you care about?" she asked, snapping me from my thoughts.

"What do you mean?" I asked.

Of course I wanted to advance in life, to evolve. Unlike her, I couldn't settle for so little. I wanted more from my life. I wanted to be someone important. Someone who would leave her mark in this city.

I said as much, if not in so many words. "Of course that's important to me."

"Life is more than just having a career."

I made a face although she couldn't see me. "Coming from someone who hasn't had a real job her entire life, that sounds kind of stupid," I snapped in return.

How could she possibly know what it felt like to be elevated to a position solely based on hard work? How good it felt to accomplish something fully on your own. She couldn't, because everything she had, she'd got from my father. And before that, her parents took care of her. So my point was valid. My mother had been nothing more than a leech all her life, so getting career advice from her, life advice, was beyond ridiculous.

"I work," she rebelled.

Yeah, but not by choice. "I know, but it's not the same. I love my job. I love being a career woman."

"There was much I loved in life, but it was taken away from me. And now, at my age, I'm forced to work," she complained.

Here we go again. I was sick and tired of hearing that same old story.

"Um, you know what, Mom? I have to go. I have some work to do. Talk to you later."

And with that, I hung up. I had to before she said anything else that would make my blood boil. And this was definitely not the night to have a screaming match with my irritating mother.

That woman could make me so angry, it was beyond comprehension. Each time we spoke, I was convinced all over again that she was beyond help.

Completely irked and needing something to distract me, to stop thinking about her, I got dressed, grabbed my phone, my keys and left the apartment. I needed a drink, a good one, and I knew just the right bartender to help me with that.

One short Uber trip later, I was sitting at my favorite bar, drinking my favorite drink. And I had to admit it did wonders for my bad mood. And luckily, I knew someone who could further help with that.

I'd just finished texting David, telling him where to pick me up, when I noticed I had an email notification. I opened it up, figuring it was something work related.

It was not.

It was another threatening email, accusing me of being more evil than Hitler. I skimmed through the contents.

So unoriginal, I thought, unimpressed.

Looking at those sad lines, I could only shake my head. Those lunatics writing me day and night really needed to get a life.

Like my mother, they were beyond pathetic.

Maybe I should introduce them to one another. I am sure they would have plenty to talk about, like me being the biggest disappointment in their lives.

That thought almost made me laugh. Instead, I put the phone down and took a sip of my drink, waiting for my lover to arrive.

5

TROUBLE IN PARADISE

After a couple of martinis and two rounds with David, I finally managed to calm down and forget the exchange with my mother.

Sadly, no matter how many times I told myself not to get so riled up over her, over the things she said, I fell into the same trap over and over. It was like she lived to torment me.

That woman always tried to make me feel guilty, all the while painting herself as the victim, and I was a true idiot because here I was stressing about it.

I allowed her to stay in my life, and these were the consequences. And to be perfectly honest, I didn't even know why I did it. It was true she was my mother. She'd given birth to me, she had been there while I was growing up, but did that really give her the right to behave like this? To constantly drag me into the mud so she could feel better about herself.

Why was I trying to cling to a relationship that pretty much broke the day my father died?

Because that was definitely when all the troubles emerged.

Of course, my mother and I never had what one would call an easy relationship. We were too different to see eye to eye. We looked at things and life in general differently. When I was younger, while my father was still alive, we'd had a mediator who always managed to smooth any wrinkles in our relationship. Sadly, once he was gone, once all the problems re-emerged, we were unable to patch things back together on our own.

My mother should live her life the way she saw fit, and I should be able to do the same. Unfortunately, those words brought me no comfort because it was too idealistic.

My mother didn't see things that way though. She believed I was the reason she was unable to live her life the way she wanted to, which was staying home and doing nothing.

And it was frustrating that I couldn't reach her. I couldn't make her understand the simplest of truths. That she shouldn't rely on other people in the first place.

If my mother didn't like any aspect of her life, she could change it herself and not expect me, or anyone else for that matter, to change it for her.

Considering her way of thinking, I was surprised she hadn't decided to remarry. She'd remained a widow all these years, and I'd never even heard of a boyfriend. All the same, if that was her choice, I respected it. It was her life, after all.

Then again, if she had a new husband, that would make my life much easier.

I could just picture her if I dared to suggest that to her. It almost made me smile. Not that I would ever do such a thing.

My mother was a grown woman, in her sixties, for crying out loud, so it was actually time for her to get over herself and this notion she had been wronged in any way. It was time to live her life, to finally learn to stand on her own two feet, while she had time, while she was vital and in charge of all her faculties.

Stop it, Amber, I snapped. I needed to stop thinking about her; nothing good would come of it, anyway. Our relationship couldn't be mended. And I really needed to accept that, for my own peace of mind.

I also needed a distraction. And since David was with me, I decided to use that fortunate turn of events before kicking him out. I didn't like him staying the night. That would imply a deeper connection, but he was nothing more than a booty call.

"You awake?" I asked, loud enough to wake him if he had managed to doze off.

"Yes," he replied instantly.

"Are you ready for round three?" I asked flirtatiously. "Because there's something else I would like to show you."

To my utmost surprise, there was no reply.

What the hell?

I turned to look at him.

David was lying on his back, staring at the ceiling, wearing a strange expression on his face, clearly deep in thought, which wasn't a good sign.

I really didn't want to deal with this, whatever it was. Especially not tonight. Unfortunately, it didn't look like I had a choice, so I asked, "Is everything all right?"

He sighed, turning his head ever so slightly to look at me. "Yeah, I was just thinking."

So I was right, and I wasn't particularly happy about it, because I knew deep down that whatever he was thinking about, it couldn't be good for me.

"About what?" I forced myself to ask.

"About us," he replied, the sad expression on his face remaining.

I didn't like the sound of that, especially as he looked like a puppy that had been kicked too many times and expected another kick. I hated it.

"Us?" I repeated.

He nodded.

"What about us?"

It took him a moment to reply. "How I really like being with you. I like you," he corrected. "And how at times it's not enough to hang out around here, have sex... I want more."

And just like that, all the alarms blasted inside my head. All the code reds told me to run away as quickly and as far as possible. I remained perfectly still, though, while my mind raced.

It was too soon for this talk; couldn't he see that? Besides, this was never supposed to turn romantic. We'd only had sex a few times, nothing more.

And that was actually the only thing I wanted from him. So how come he had all those crazy ideas inside his head that this was more than strictly physical? I'd never encouraged such behavior, made sure he knew this was only a sexual thing.

When did I make a mistake? No matter how I looked at things, I couldn't find flaws in my plan except for one.

He was twenty-six years old.

It irked me his young mind was seeing our encounters as something more than they were.

It was true I wanted him, but that didn't mean I wanted more from him. I got everything I wanted, and it was infuriating to realize he'd had other notions all this time.

That had the potential to ruin everything.

I could not decide if his lack of experience or lack of intelligence was making him romanticize what was happening between us, but the bottom line stayed the same. I didn't like it one bit.

"I like being with you too." I decided to interrupt him before he said something else, something even more stupid. "And I like the sex."

He gave me a look, as though I was missing the point.

"I understand what you are saying, but can we not try to define things tonight, can we not overthink our relationship? It has been a really stressful day, and I merely want to have some fun with you." And that was one hundred percent true. Only not the entirety of it.

That was the lawyer in me, always looking for loopholes.

I tried to speak as delicately as I could, trying my best not to start an argument. The last thing I wanted was for him to storm out of my apartment in anger. A brat like him, there was no telling what kind of damage he could do. I didn't need him ratting me out to his father because he'd had his feelings hurt.

I couldn't believe he was doing this to me. Especially tonight.

What is it with the people in my life tonight? It was as though they'd all worked together to piss me off thoroughly.

First, I got that ridiculous email practically accusing me of being the biggest evil since Hitler, then my mother tried that passive-aggressive shit on me, and now David. His little antic was the cherry on top.

Can't a girl just have fun without having to deal with other people's bullshit?

Apparently, that was rhetorical, since the universe had

pretty much answered that for me.

"I was just saying I would like to do more with you rather than sneak over here in the middle of the night and have sex," David insisted.

I was starting to lose my patience with him. He was speaking nonsense, and the worst part was that he was totally unaware of that, which was maddening.

"Like what?" I asked instead.

I was still, despite my better judgment, trying to salvage this night. If I weren't, I would kick him out and be done with him. There were other men out there who would gladly share my bed and accept my terms without trying to turn it into something it wasn't.

So why was David still in my bed? That was a good question I wasn't prepared to ponder. Especially since he was speaking and I needed to concentrate on that.

"I don't know. Like, go on dates."

"You want to date me?" I asked incredulously.

"Yes. I want us to go places, to dinners, to movies, or whatever."

I groaned inwardly. Everything that came out of his mouth was beyond ridiculous. We shared no common interests, and I was sure that extended to culinary preferences and movies.

David looked like a guy who preferred hamburgers with fries, or pineapple pizzas, things I'd stopped eating a long time ago. And as for movies, I was sure he enjoyed watching those mind-numbing comedies I wouldn't be caught dead watching.

How to convey that to him without turning this into an argument? I had no idea. How to spell out that I wasn't his freaking girlfriend, nor had any desire to be? Still no clue.

"You know we can't do that." I opted for the safest path. Grant.

He looked like he wanted to argue, so I beat him to it. "Can you honestly tell me you would go to your father and tell him you want to date me?"

Although it was a cheap blow, it was the only card I could play and win. I knew firsthand how Grant treated his son. He was a complete control freak, and David was genuinely scared of him, of being cut off. I counted on the fact he would chicken out at the mention of his father because he'd done that many times in the past. He had to do everything Grant told him to do, like it or not, because he was nothing but a boy scared of disappointing his father.

"He doesn't have to know. At least not yet," David persisted.

"We both know that wouldn't work."

"I know. But there has to be a way. I want to be with you, for real."

I felt like banging my head against the wall. This wasn't what I wanted, at all. "Your father would never allow it," I reminded him. Then again, in retrospect, perhaps that was the wrong thing to say. The last thing I wanted was for him to find the will and courage to rebel. "We both know how he gets."

David shook his head, clearly frustrated that things were not going his way.

Join the club. "I work with him, and I have to say I can't predict how he would react. The last thing I want is to cause problems for you," I added with exaggerated deep concern. I was trying to create a narrative that would make him see he was speaking nonsense.

David sighed. "And I don't want to cause any problems

for you either," he replied, kissing the knuckles of my left hand.

Oh boy, he has it bad.

"I understand we have to keep it a secret."

Hallelujah, the choirs were singing.

"But..."

"It is what it is," I said before he could change his mind again.

"Yeah," he agreed, and it was clear he was deeply unhappy about it.

"That doesn't mean we can't have fun," I pointed out.

"Yeah," he agreed again before shaking his head. "I hate him at times."

"Don't speak like that."

"It's true. He is constantly in my face, trying to control everything."

"He is your father. He wants what's best for you," I pointed out.

"Please don't defend him. He has my whole life planned out. And I have no say in it. He is suffocating me."

That right there showed me how spoiled he really was. David had a successful father who did his best to secure a successful future for him as well.

David would never have to worry about mortgages, not having a well-paid job, or not having enough money for all his hobbies, because Grant took care of everything. He was already ahead in life because of his father, skipping all the struggles and insecurities. And still, all David saw was an overprotective, controlling father who wouldn't let him do what he wanted. Or in other words, ruin his life.

I would love to have had a father like that. Although I'd managed to achieve my potential on my own, having an encouraging father would have helped a great deal along the way.

"He picked a school for me. He picked a job for me. I do what he wants. I go where he tells me to go," he continued to whine.

Doesn't he know how lucky he is?

Apparently not.

"Do I have to love who he chooses for me as well?"

Wait, did he just say love? My skin actually crawled at hearing that. I really hoped, for my sake and his, that it was a slip of the tongue and nothing else.

I have to fix this and fast. "If you truly feel like that about your father, then you should definitely have your revenge."

David looked at me questioningly. "What do you mean?"

I grinned. "Me. You can have me, fuck me, here and now. He can't tell you what to do within these walls."

Only I could do that.

"And the best part? He will never know."

"You do know he wants to fuck you too?" David asked all seriously.

Of course I knew. I wasn't an idiot. But the key was to always keep him wanting, not giving him what he wanted.

I put a hand over David's mouth. "You know, I had an altercation with my mother this evening, so can we please stop speaking about parents? I want to focus on the here and now," I said, straddling him.

He immediately grabbed my hips, and I leaned down for a kiss.

"I want you, so kiss me," I commanded.

It took some coaxing, but eventually, he got with the program and did precisely what I wanted him to. After all, he was good at following orders.

6

DAY OF RECKONING

The next day at work I was pretty busy, having a case to try in court. I had tried to speak with my client and reason with him so it wouldn't come to that. I'd offered mediation, yet he'd declined. I'd offered to settle the matter, but the idiot was set on having his day in court.

There was nothing worse than a rich man with a bruised ego, so here I was, preparing for it, having to shift all my other responsibilities to another time so I could fully concentrate on this.

And the worst part was that it was a genuinely idiotic thing that should never have been presented in front of a judge. However, my VIP client wasn't prepared to hear reason, so I complied. Besides, considering I would be charging extra for that service on top of my rates, I really should not complain.

If he decided to sue everyone who'd wronged him in the slightest manner, I would be set for life.

Since I wasn't an idealistic novice who would die of

embarrassment having to present something so trivial in a court of law, I simply focused on what was important. Money. Because the more money I had, the more power I would accumulate.

As it turned out, I actually liked being a junior partner. That title came with a lot of perks. Of course, I had new responsibilities as well, the stakes were definitely higher now, but I was loving every second of it. I was born for it.

And I was sure I would love it even more after becoming a senior partner, because that was still the goal. It would be nice to have a genuine say around the firm for a change. I would definitely implement a lot of changes, starting with no frolicking among the employees.

I was sick and tired of people regarding the law firm as the perfect hunting ground for hooking up. That was beyond pathetic, in my opinion.

I understood lawyers worked an insane number of hours per week, which didn't leave much room for anything else, including romantic encounters, but that wasn't my problem.

Romantic relationships should be forbidden in the working environment, period. Men were less productive while chasing skirts, and the same could be said for women. Each moment they spent obsessing over their looks and whom to sleep with, they were wasting time and not doing what they were being paid to do.

But I had gone off track. That was a problem for another day. A day in the future. Still, it was nice to fantasize about these things and how I would run this firm if I was in charge.

When I'm in charge, things will definitely be different around here. Much different.

Sure, Grant listened to me now, but that wasn't the same. He only listened if and when it suited him, and only in regard to really small issues. That wasn't true power. At least not the kind I was craving, at any rate. I aimed higher.

And that was the constant drive that pushed me to excel at my work and do my best to achieve all my goals that much sooner.

Remembering what those women had said in the bathroom, I realized I really didn't mind them seeing me in such a light. If I gave my all to this job, I expected everyone else to act in the same manner.

Upon my return home, I stumbled across a girl on my floor, holding two huge boxes while fumbling with her keys, clearly struggling to enter the condo across the hall.

I had wondered who my new neighbor was, and now I had my answer. *Is she really an owner, or is she working for the apartment's owner?* I thought. It would be quite a surprise if I discovered this girl had enough money to pay for a condo in this building. She didn't look like the type, not that I was judging; looks could be deceiving.

"Do you need a hand?" I asked, feeling neighborly.

She looked startled as I approached. "Oh, yes, thank you."

She sounded like a little girl, although I was sure she was only a few years younger than me. She looked attractive in that messy, geeky kind of way.

My neighbor offered her keys to me. "If you could get the door for me, that would be great."

For a fraction of a second, I wondered if I should have pointed out she could have handled everything on her own if she'd merely put the boxes down before trying to unlock the door, but I ruled against it.

"Of course," I said, accepting the keys.

I opened the door for her, and she moved past me to

carry her load to the center of a very empty room, where she dropped them, not too carefully.

From the door, I could see the place was littered with unopened boxes labeled kitchen, bedroom, clothes, and so on. In the far corner of the room was a laptop and a couple of monitors, which were up and running.

I found that interesting. It all confirmed my previous thoughts; she was definitely new to the building.

It had taken me a great deal of time to score a place like this, so I couldn't help wondering how she'd managed to do the same. *Is she connected?* Was she the daughter of someone important? I knew the condo had been vacant for a while. She'd better not have gotten a better deal on it than I got on mine. Though she probably didn't. I couldn't see them giving this young woman a better deal, after all.

"Thank you," she said, turning to face me.

"No problem," I replied, offering the keys back.

"I'm Mercy, by the way."

"Amber."

We shook hands.

"Nice meeting you." She beamed.

"Just moving in?" I asked, looking about.

"Yeah, I know it's obvious. I moved a week ago."

Yet everything was still in boxes? I couldn't live like that. I needed order in my life to function properly.

"How do you like it so far?"

"I like it very much. Everyone is super nice, and Alex is really hot," she added, then giggled.

Mercy struck me as a bit of a frazzled girl. She certainly dressed for comfort because I didn't think overalls would impress anyone. And those doe eyes meant vulnerability. If she didn't change, vultures in the city would eat her alive.

"Where did you move from?" I asked conversationally. Usually, I wasn't so big on chitchat, but I was curious. She was my new neighbor, after all. I needed to know she wasn't some psycho.

"Kansas."

I should have known. "That is a big change."

"I know," she said, smiling.

"So why LA? You want to become an actress?"

"Oh, God, no," she replied, making a face. "I run a home-based computer business."

That would explain all the tech.

"And I needed a change," she explained.

"Well, that's great, and welcome to the building. To LA as well," I added as an afterthought.

I had to say I actually liked the idea of having a tech-savvy neighbor. I barely knew how to operate my computer beyond all the basics, things I needed for my work, so it would be nice having someone to turn to in case of emergencies. Also, it would be nice not having to worry about maintenance, viruses, and all that nonsense.

Sure, we had tech support at the firm, but I didn't like those people all up in my business, especially not rummaging through my personal laptop. That was a cringeworthy moment for me. Yet Mercy, looking so nonthreatening and innocent, was the perfect woman for the job.

"Thanks," she replied. "Being new in town, it sure feels nice to meet a friendly face."

I could only smile at that as I produced my business card.

Her eyes practically sparkled as she read it. "You are a lawyer, wow. That's so cool."

I thought so too. "Feel free to contact me once you've properly moved in," I said on my way out.

"You can count on it," Mercy said.

Inside my own apartment, I soon forgot about the new girl. I slipped into my most comfortable clothes, yoga pants and a tank top, and then went to the kitchen to prepare something to eat. I hadn't eaten anything since lunch, and I was starving.

Unfortunately, since it was late and all, I couldn't indulge. So I settled on a smoothie.

Feeling quite refreshed, I grabbed my laptop from the bag and carried it to my home office. I had to do some work before going to bed. I would have to go to court tomorrow morning, thanks to my idiot of a client, and I wanted to make sure I was fully prepared to argue my case, all the while making sure I was ready for the counterarguments as well.

It was tedious work, especially because I believed the case was so beneath me. Luckily, thinking about the gain managed to push me through.

Checking my emails, checking all the things my assistant sent me, I stumbled upon something that shouldn't have been there.

Although the email in question looked legit and was titled *Urgent*, I found it quite suspicious, especially since I didn't recognize the address from which it was sent.

I thought I'd reported all these fake emails, I grumbled as I opened it.

How many murderers have you set free while being a defense lawyer, Miss Junior Partner? How do you sleep at night knowing you defend the worst possible human beings from getting what they deserve? How do you live with yourself accepting blood money?

You are a disgusting human being, and the day of your reckoning is coming. You will have to pay for everything you did, for hurting so many innocent people with your actions.

I will make sure you suffer the way others suffered by your hand. That is a promise.

Spellbound, I read it again and again. Although I had received a fair share of rage-filled, threatening emails in my life, ever since practicing law, as did any other defense lawyer during their career, something about this email felt different.

Most of the time some frustrated illiterate imbecile would write to tell me how they wanted me to die. These were short messages, like *Die* or *I hope you rot in hell*, sprinkled with a few really graphic messages.

All the same, I never took those messages to heart. I viewed them as something that just happened. They came with the territory. I was a defense lawyer with a versatile clientele. It was to be expected my winning a case could rub someone the wrong way. And the fact I was a woman put me in even greater danger than my male counterparts.

I never thought much about any of it. I was aware of the risks, but I never let them govern me or the way I practiced law.

Unfortunately, reading this email, I felt something I hadn't felt before. It wasn't necessarily fear, but I was starting to worry. Because I felt an email like this had the potential to escalate into something else. And that was the last thing I wanted, of course.

Reading that email made me feel uneasy and uncomfortable, even in the comfort of my own home.

I started to wonder if I should share this with someone. *Should I report this?*

At our firm, we usually went to HR if we felt like someone had crossed the line. These were anonymous threats, though, so how to deal with them?

On one hand, I was worried, while on the other, I questioned my judgment. It was late at night, and I was stressed and worried. Was it possible I was reading too much into things? This email didn't differ from the others I'd received. And they'd all come to nothing. *Some coward wrote a few lines so they could feel better about themself, and that is that.*

Even with that in mind, all my reassurances, my question still remained the same. *Should I be worried about this email finding its way to my inbox?*

It was general enough so I couldn't decipher what it was referring to. If I knew, I could determine if the threat was real or not. And the fact I couldn't do that was adding to how I was already feeling.

Realizing I couldn't solve anything right then, I decided to call it a night. I turned my laptop off and went to bed.

I decided to sleep alone tonight. David was getting too attached, and I wanted to prevent that. I didn't need such a complication in my life. I was busy as it was.

As I was trying to force myself to fall asleep, those lines kept popping into my head.

You are a disgusting human being, and the day of your reckoning is coming.

Despite all my bravado, I didn't like the sound of that. Not one bit.

7

BUSINESS AS USUAL

The next day, after dealing with that idiotic case in court, I returned to the firm, only to be ambushed by Grant. He dumped Mr. Smith in my lap, promising him I was the best person for the job. I was flattered in part, but when I heard what the case actually was, I knew Grant had only done that because he didn't want to bother with it.

"I don't want any jail time," Mr. Smith said haughtily. "And I don't want to have to return the money."

I wasn't surprised that was all he cared about.

"This wasn't my fault. I did what I had to," my new client ranted.

"Don't worry, Mr. Smith. I will do everything in my power to keep you out of jail," I tried to reassure him, offering one of my dazzling smiles.

"And what about the money?" Mr. Smith insisted.

"Usually, the insurance company takes care of that; nevertheless, if the district attorney manages to ensure a guilty verdict—"

"I am not guilty," he interjected.

"If your boss has insurance, they will have to step in, especially if the money can't be recovered otherwise."

His answering smile was on the wry side. "I get what you are saying, Miss Dennis. And I have to tell you, to the best of my knowledge, that money has completely gone."

Probably stashed in some bogus account in the Cayman Islands or wherever powerful men hide their money these days. What a sleazebag.

Although it was a white-collar crime, this man was no different to other criminals.

Not that that was my concern. The only thing I cared about was preventing Mr. Smith from going to jail. Of course the man was guiltier than sin, but even guilty people were entitled to fair representation. Especially if they could afford me.

There was another reason Grant had dumped this guy on me, and that was Mr. Smith's appearance. He had some really ugly-looking moles all over his face and neck, and my boss had a phobia or something where those things were concerned. He'd confessed that at a Christmas party a few years ago while tipsy.

Grant was always complimenting me on how clear my skin was, and that was when I learned why it was such a big deal for him. He hated moles.

I had always wondered why he'd shared that with me. Perhaps he'd hoped it would bring us closer together because, as David so eloquently said, he wanted to fuck me.

However, that had never happened. *Not yet.*

All the same, Mr. Smith became my problem. And I had mixed feelings about that. I liked the idea of Grant coming to me when he wanted something done. At the same time, I wanted to be my own lawyer. I wanted to bring in my own clients, not be given someone else's hand-me-downs.

Mr. Smith coughed, snapping me from my thoughts.

I had to admit he was rather unappealing to look at, disgusting even. Yet I concentrated on the work, and that helped a great deal.

Perhaps that's why he had to steal the money, because he knew no woman would ever look at him if he wasn't rich.

"How long will this take? I have plans to go on a vacation with my family."

"I will ask for an expedited trial, but I wouldn't be packing my suitcases just yet," I replied.

"What a waste of time," he grumbled underneath his breath.

With every sentence that left his mouth, my first impression of him didn't improve. He was nothing but an embezzler who felt entitled to demand things because he had money, which was ridiculous, yet I held my tongue; he was a client, after all.

And the best part? His excuse for why he'd done this, as in, stolen a couple of million dollars, was beyond moronic.

Mr. Smith didn't see himself as guilty. He said he would never have gone to such extremes, stealing the money, if his boss had given him a big enough salary to begin with. He felt like his compensation was less than what he deserved, so he'd decided to take matters into his own hands and helped himself to someone else's money.

The way he saw it, he had been forced to steal. It was so preposterous that it made sense, in a weird way.

I could see his point. Nobody wanted to work for scraps when serious money was flying about, made at the company he was working at, for everyone apart from him. All the same, that didn't give him the right to steal it.

Naturally, the simplest solution would be to find a better job, work somewhere his hard work and effort would be not only appreciated but monetarily valued as well. Unfortunately, other than being good with numbers, Mr. Smith wasn't particularly bright.

The problem was, he was stupid enough to think he could easily take what he wanted and spend it excessively without anyone figuring out what he was doing. Naturally, the idiot got caught and landed himself in a world of problems. And left enough evidence for an easy guilty verdict.

Luckily for him, he was now my client, which meant I would do everything in my power to turn those hard pieces of evidence into shit. Not to brag but that was kind of my superpower.

I liked that part of my job. Trying to find new, creative ways to bend the law to my will, offer alternative narratives and other culprits, find loopholes. All in the hopes of creating reasonable doubt. If I managed to do that, my client would be off the hook.

I didn't view that as a way of cheating the system. Quite the contrary. Thanks to people like me, the laws written had the ability to change, evolve, and improve.

Thanks to me, the really guilty ones ended up in jail when concrete evidence was presented, just the way it was supposed to be. When the police did their job thoroughly, when the district attorney's office wasn't full of incompetent people, I was unable to win despite my best efforts.

Luckily, that hadn't happened yet.

Besides, not all men were equally guilty, guilty in the

same manner. My point was some crimes were far worse than others. Personally, I didn't like Mr. Smith, but it wasn't like the man had killed someone and needed to be thrown in jail for the rest of his life.

He'd taken some money. Granted, it wasn't his. Then again, so what?

Money was merely a medium of exchange, an entirely made-up concept civilizations agreed upon to prevent chaos and instill some order in life.

My point was, for that kind of offence, he deserved a slap on the wrist, not a jail sentence. He was a greedy bastard and a piece of shit, granted, and his punishment should reflect that. Although, considering I was on the case, there was a fair chance he would walk free, retire to an island of his choice, and enjoy the rest of his life spending the money he'd stolen.

Life isn't fair at times...

I just hoped he'd snatched enough money to pay for my services because if he hadn't, I would leave him to rot in jail myself.

We continued to talk while I tried to get as much information as possible before he asked, "So what's going to happen now?"

Mr. Smith had already gotten himself arrested but was fortunate that Grant had got him out on a fifty-thousand-dollar bail. In my opinion, he got out cheap, only because he was a first offender, and Grant knew the judge.

"I will look into your case, look at all the evidence the DA's office provided, then contact them; see what's going on."

"And then what?" he prompted.

Someone was desperate to go on vacation, and I wasn't

too broken up about having to burst his bubble. If he didn't want to become a fugitive, he would have to stay put, in LA, while I sorted out this mess.

"They will probably offer you some kind of plea deal." And it was my job to get as much out of it as possible.

"I don't want a plea deal. I am not guilty."

I gave him a look. "It is my advice, that if the terms are right, you should consider accepting it."

He crossed his arms over his chest. "What would they offer?"

I shook my head. "I can only speculate. Anything from a fine, to house arrest, to a couple of months in jail," I replied honestly, keeping something to myself.

There was a chance he wouldn't get a plea deal at all. If the DA in charge felt cocky and confident enough, he or she could try to win this case in court.

At this point, I had no idea who was on the case. That played a huge role in this as well. Some were more ambitious and liked to gamble, while others liked to play it safe and ensure a win for their office, no matter how small a win it was.

Luckily, I knew them and had battled against them all. I knew all their strengths and, more importantly, all their weaknesses. That gave me the confidence to believe I could win this, no matter what.

In my opinion, it would be best for both sides if we managed to reach an agreement and avoid a trial. To be perfectly honest, I didn't want to spend much time on this guy. It was true he was a paying customer, but even I had standards. If it were up to me, he would never have crossed my threshold, let alone be my client.

Sadly, it wasn't up to me.

Yet.

All the same, my time was coming. I could feel it. I merely had to take care of a few minor details first, like kicking Phoebe out, and then it would be my time to shine.

"No deal," Mr. Smith said adamantly. "I am not guilty, and I shouldn't be forced to spend a second in jail."

That was when I lost my patience. I couldn't listen to him whine a second longer. "May I be honest with you, Mr. Smith?" I asked politely.

He nodded.

"You are guilty. You took money that didn't belong to you. And you will have to sacrifice something if you want to stay free."

"But I had to," he was quick to defend. "I had no other choice."

"That's not true either. You had plenty of choices, yet you still chose a shortcut. And all your excuses will not matter in a court of law."

He made a face at that. He looked like a genuine brat; I knew he was.

Only really entitled men could master such an expression, expecting not to suffer consequences of breaking the law. I'd seen that many times before as a defense lawyer.

You have to be a special type of person to actually believe the rules never applied to you.

"I thought that by hiring you, I would not have to sacrifice anything," he jibed in return. "Grant assured me this would all go away. And if you are not up to the task..."

"Mr. Smith, please calm down. I was only giving you the reality check you needed."

It was obvious he didn't like hearing that either. Not that I cared. And before he could say anything else, I continued, "Besides, I wasn't hired to patronize you. I get things done."

"So can you do it?" he challenged.

"I will most definitely make this go away for you. The DA's office has been swamped with cases lately." That was a constant struggle they faced, too many cases, not enough personnel to deal with them, too small funds to ensure trials for all, which would work perfectly in my favor. "And they can't pay attention to each of them the way I can. If there was any kind of misconduct, I will find it and exploit it."

"That's more like it," he grumbled, raising his chin ever so slightly.

Naturally, I had to take him down a notch. "However, if all checks out, if they present enough evidence against you and offer a plea deal, in any kind of form, you will take it."

"I will not go to jail," he said stubbornly. "Or return the money."

"What about house arrest?"

It was obvious he was full of doubt. On one hand, he knew I was right; on the other, his pride was getting in the way. Luckily, the right side prevailed in the end, and he said, "Fine."

I smiled. "I will make it happen, then."

The DA's office was overjoyed when we managed to come to an agreement.

My client got five months of house arrest, and the DA's office got an admission of guilt. It was the best I could do considering the case against Mr. Smith was rock solid.

Mr. Smith wasn't too happy he would have to spend five months locked inside his home, as it would be the first time he'd be spending so much time with his wife and kids. But once I explained that was much better than going to jail or returning the millions of dollars he stole, he left my office with a smug smile on his face.

Another satisfied client, I thought, moving on to something else.

8

THE IMPORTANCE OF ART

I was really happy when my doorman, Alex, told me two packages were waiting for me when I returned home from work.

"Are they from the gallery?" I prompted, reaching his desk.

"Yes, Miss Dennis."

I felt like skipping from joy hearing that. Naturally, I didn't.

My paintings to complete my condo were finally here. That was the perfect ending to a perfect day.

But then I frowned. In their security packaging, the paintings looked much bigger and heavier than I expected. How was I to carry them all the way up to my apartment? *Will they fit in the elevator?*

"Don't worry, Miss Dennis, I will help you with them," Alex said, as though he could read my mind.

"Thank you."

With some finesse, patience, and ingenuity, we managed to put the two paintings in the elevator without damaging them. I was very relieved I didn't have to call around to find a handyman to do the heavy lifting for me at this hour.

I rode with the paintings while Alex took the other elevator. He was a tall and heavy man, so he helped me get them out of the elevator and carry them into my apartment.

We managed to do everything without a glitch.

"Thank you, Alex," I said, giving him a generous tip for doing this for me. That wasn't part of his job, so I was grateful he'd helped me out. I was of the opinion such actions should be rewarded, always.

"It was my pleasure, Miss Dennis."

Once he left, I took a pair of scissors and a knife and tried to take the protective packaging off my babies without damaging anything. I was pretty excited while I was removing the packaging, trying to get through to the artwork.

Finally, my apartment, which I had designed all by myself, was finished. I had carefully chosen each and every piece of furniture, and now it was complete with these two paintings.

I'd ordered them from a very prestigious art gallery a while ago. The instant I saw them hanging in the gallery, I fell in love. I'd managed to negotiate a fair price since I'd purchased both of them, which made me feel pretty proud of myself.

In reality, I was prepared to pay the full price for them, I liked them that much. The fact I'd managed to get them cheaper made owning them that much sweeter.

I got the same feeling looking at them now, in my house, as I'd had back at the gallery.

It was none of that abstract crap a lot of rich, especially nouveau rich, people liked to hang in their homes so they could pretend they appreciated and understood fine art. Simply to pretend they were refined and cultured.

Trying to impress others with such art only made those people look ridiculous. Not to mention they ended up with something that looked like splashes of human feces smeared against the canvas by a cat's tail. Too ugly to look at.

In my opinion, they were morons who'd missed the whole point of art.

Art's sole purpose was to entice and extract emotions. And I wanted to feel good while looking at them. I wanted those paintings to reflect how I felt about my apartment, about myself, about my whole life.

I was aware that sounded like a tall order, but I had succeeded. I'd found what I liked best and bought them. And now, I could enjoy them in the privacy of my home.

The paintings I'd procured depicted ballet dancers in graceful poses. For some reason, they had a rather soothing effect on me. Looking at them, I knew all would be well, all would be as I wanted.

Since it was late at night, I decided to hang them myself. They were not that heavy out of their packaging, and besides, I already had spots prepared for them.

It didn't take me long to accomplish my task.

My smile was short-lived. *This is not how I imagined it*, I thought glumly.

Once they were up there, hanging side by side on the wall opposing the huge window in the living room, I wasn't particularly happy with the end result.

The paintings themselves were still beautiful. They fit nicely in the enclaves made for them and complemented the furniture. Nonetheless, something was missing.

I stared at them, analyzing everything in the process,

trying to figure out the problem. It was bugging me that I couldn't figure this out, while I looked at them from each and every direction, changing angles and distance. Why didn't they look as breathtaking as they had at the gallery?

And then it hit me. *The lights.*

Basically, there wasn't enough light for them here. The canvasses were not illuminated enough. The paintings needed their own, special lights to shine fully, to let spectators get the full experience. Now I felt stupid for not thinking about this.

I need a professional to install display lights for me above the paintings, like the ones they had at the gallery, I mused.

Where to find a capable, reliable contractor? I'd had to fire quite a few contractors while remodeling my apartment, because they were such incompetent fools, acting as though they were the smartest people around. They were constantly trying to bully me, pushing their visions for my apartment instead of listening to what I wanted.

Condescending men were what I hated most in this world, so at the first whiff of it, I got rid of them. And now I found myself in quite a pickle. I didn't know whom to call.

Knowing I had a full schedule tomorrow, I decided to leave that problem for the next day and go to sleep.

I will have Bonnie deal with it tomorrow, and hoped she was capable of finding someone reliable for me. *If not, I will fire her.* I was only half joking thinking that.

She'd better not mess it up, because I need my apartment to be perfect, and for that, I needed someone smart and capable. Someone who could understand my vision and put it into action.

Was that really too much to ask? Apparently, it was. Especially since there was another issue I had to be mindful of. I didn't want just anyone roaming around my apartment. The contractor in question had to have great credentials and stellar recommendations.

Go to sleep, Amber. Yet despite the command, I couldn't.

Thinking about contractors inside my home, I started thinking about something else. More accurately, someone else.

Should I call David? I started debating with myself.

On one hand, he was starting to get too attached, which I hated. On the other, I would sleep better if I was sexually pleasured beforehand.

There was a chance my little talk with him had calmed him down, and that he'd realized he was getting way ahead of himself. I'd tried to explain to him sex was all he would get from me, without actually spelling it out, and I hoped the message was received.

David was fun and all, but he was definitely not someone I saw myself with in a real relationship.

I was far more successful than him, and I was making way more money. Perhaps, at some point in the future, that dynamic would change, especially if Grant had his way. Still, I wasn't planning on waiting for that to happen.

I was thirty-six years old. I needed a true partner now, not in ten years or whenever. He just wasn't bringing anything useful to the potential relationship, especially since his services as a lover could be outsourced to a fairly decent vibrator.

That was why he and I would never work as a couple. We were obviously not equal, and equality was the key to any successful relationship.

That didn't mean I didn't want to have fun, so I decided to call him. *I should take advantage of him while it lasts.*

Too lazy to text, I called. "I want to see you tonight," I said once he answered.

"I want that too, but my car broke down."

"Then take a cab."

"I can't."

"Why not?"

"I locked myself out of the car, and my wallet is inside."

I groaned inwardly. Was it possible he was that stupid? "Have you called Triple A?"

"Yes, they are on their way."

Can't anything go my way tonight? "I'll pick you up."

"Great, I appreciate you doing that for me, baby, but I'll have to wait for them before we go."

I hung up before he could say anything else. I couldn't believe I was going to such lengths just to get laid. What was wrong with me?

Deciding a light jacket over yoga pants and a T-shirt was decent enough to drive around, I grabbed my keys, phone and left the apartment.

As I stepped out of the elevator into the parking garage, I heard a huge crash.

Without thinking, I started walking toward the source of the noise and saw someone was vandalizing my car.

A skinny figure, in a gray hoodie that was covering their face, was breaking my car's window.

I was instantly enraged, outraged too. *How dare he?*

"Hey," I yelled. "What are you doing? Stop that."

The figure jerked as though startled, but he recovered quickly. I was sure it was a male based on his physique. He started running out of the underground parking garage as though his ass were on fire.

I was having none of it and started running after him.

Unfortunately, I was in high heels. I couldn't say what possessed me to wear them, but they were definitely not meant for running.

They were barely made for walking. So obviously, the hoodlum managed to get away.

"Son of a bitch," I screamed, thoroughly pissed off.

I returned to my car, and then I really wanted to rage. Two windows had been broken, the windshield was cracked, and all four tires were slashed.

"Son of a bitch," I repeated.

Enraged, I returned to the elevator and rode up to the lobby.

"Did you see what happened?" I yelled at Alex.

He looked at me, startled. "When?"

"Now! My car just got vandalized in the parking garage," I explained while waving my arms about. I gesticulate a lot when I'm this rattled.

"I am sorry, Miss Dennis, but our cameras went down fifteen minutes ago. I haven't seen anything. I was trying to sort that out."

"How convenient," I snapped back.

"Do you want me to call the police?"

"I am dialing as we speak," I said through gritted teeth.

I couldn't believe that this could happen in a building with its own underground parking, a doorman, and cameras everywhere. To say I was furious would be an understatement. I would definitely file a complaint to the managers of the building.

I remained in the lobby, waiting for the police to arrive. They took their sweet time coming. I would file a complaint about that as well. I was a law-abiding citizen. I paid all my taxes even though I believed the government didn't deserve such an insane amount of money from me, so I expected to be taken care of when in a crisis.

I spoke with the police officers and gave a description of the punk, and they spoke with Alex as well. Afterward, they looked at my car, took a few pictures, and left. The whole experience lasted about fifteen minutes.

That's it? I was rather underwhelmed by the whole experience, especially when the officers looked less than enthusiastic about finding the perp. Besides, nobody knew better than I how little a punishment he would get even if caught. All that was beyond frustrating.

After seeing them out, there was nothing else for me to do except return upstairs and call my insurance company. I had to deal with them as well before taking my baby to the shop.

I honestly hated how this night had turned out.

In the hallway, I stumbled upon Mercy. She looked like she was about to go out.

"What happened?" she asked immediately.

Clearly, my face revealed all the emotions I was experiencing.

"Someone just busted up my car," I explained, trying to remain calm and failing miserably.

"Are you all right?" she asked with concern.

"I am, but my Tesla is not." My beautiful car was ruined, defiled.

"I can't believe that happened here. I thought this was a secure building."

You and me both, sister. "Yeah."

"Do you know who would do that to you?"

Her question made me wonder. Was that a random act of

vandalism, as the officers believed? Or was someone intentionally targeting me?

I had no idea. And that was troubling.

"Some kid punk," I replied.

"I am really sorry you had to go through that."

Not as sorry as that punk is going to be when I catch him.

"Good night, Mercy," I said, going inside.

"Good night."

I immediately called my insurance company. As it was so late at night, I couldn't speak to whom I wished, which enraged me further. I hated when surrounded by incompetence. And I hated having to wait until morning when I wanted my problems fixed right now. That was why I paid them in the first place.

Once I'd managed to take care of everything, somewhat, and fully knowing those incompetent fools, the lazy officers, wouldn't help me catch the perp, I tried to figure out ways to do that on my own.

The police officers are too busy solving real crimes to help me, I mocked.

I could always hire a private investigator, but the problem was there wasn't much evidence apart from my ruined car. And I didn't want to bother with someone else.

It sounded like too much work for getting revenge because the insurance company would cover repairs for all the damages. So the question was, did mending my bruised pride really mean that much to me?

I decided to answer that tomorrow.

Getting into bed, I pulled the cover over my head and tried to force myself to sleep. In a matter of seconds, my perfect night had been ruined. Things were not supposed to end like this, with me all alone in bed.

Alone in bed... And then it dawned on me. In all this madness, my ruined Tesla, dealing with everybody, I had forgotten I'd promised to pick David up because he too had car problems.

Son of a bitch.

9

THE UBER EXPERIENCE

I was beyond furious, to put it mildly. All that security, all that money spent to ensure I lived in a place where this kind of thing could not happen, yet it still happened. Some scumbag had managed to weasel his way into the garage, or simply waltzed in as it turned out, and ruin the car without anyone lifting a finger to stop him.

I was the one who had to chase after him, in high heels. *Unbelievable.*

Honestly, I felt cheated. I felt like I hadn't received the services I had been promised. I hadn't gotten what I'd paid for, and that was security among other things.

I wanted to feel the promised assurance that when I entered the building I was residing in, I was protected. That my property was protected. But I didn't. Despite all the promises, my beautiful Tesla was still ruined, and I had to watch it being towed away.

I couldn't believe the cameras had gone down in the whole building at that precise moment, so now I didn't even have footage of the criminal in question who'd ruined my baby.

And the police proved pretty useless, unable to help me get justice. Overall, the whole experience had left a pretty sour taste in my mouth.

Since my car was at the shop, and I had no idea how long all the repairs would take, I was forced to travel around by Uber, which was beyond inconvenient.

I was reluctant to admit that my mother and I shared the same aversion for spending time with strangers while those strangers drove us around.

My skin crawled each time I was forced to get inside an unknown car and trust he would take me to the desired destination.

I wouldn't call that an unreasonable feeling. I knew what men were capable of, especially when they thought they wouldn't get caught. So I felt justifiable in my aversion. All the same, I sucked it up, because I had to get to work somehow, and I really didn't like the idea of renting a car either.

I hated standing outside, alone, while waiting for the driver to pick me up. I absolutely detested it.

That was precisely why I drove myself around.

I want my car back, I thought glumly, waiting on the street for yet another Uber to pick me up. I was dangerously close to being late for work, and that was something that could not happen.

Ever since I'd started at Grant, Bryant, and Dawson, I hadn't been late for work. And I wasn't going to blemish my perfect record now just because some punk had decided to trash my Tesla. Which was precisely why I waited on the street.

Sure, I could sit in the lobby and wait like a lady, but I

risked being late because the driver could decide to drive away if they didn't spot me immediately. It had happened before, and leaving a bad review didn't improve my mood or make up for the lost time. To make matters worse, I got a bad review as well, for not being there. It was maddening.

I want my car back. I stopped myself there because I was whining like a little girl. Things could not always go my way, and I needed to accept that and move on, like a grown-up.

To be fair, most of the drivers were pretty adequate, and I understood why they felt they were entitled to find another customer if you weren't there waiting. Time was money, after all. I could understand that, but I was still furious I had to go through that routine each morning to get to work. It was hard for me to rely on someone else.

I hadn't relied on anyone driving me around since high school. My father had bought me a car the instant I got my license at sixteen. He'd wanted me to be independent, and I always loved him for that.

I spotted my ride. *Finally*, I thought, going to the car.

Checking the time, I realized I was in danger of running late because this Uber driver had taken his time arriving.

I sat in the back, trying to discourage any kind of chitchat. Most honored that, but sadly, a few still felt compelled to strike up a conversation.

"Please hurry," I stressed as I double-checked I had everything I needed for the day. The most important thing was my laptop. I had some files I wanted to review on the drive as well, so I took them out.

"Of course," my driver replied.

Despite me being occupied with something else, it was hard not to notice him staring at me in the rearview mirror each opportunity he had. That was as frustrating as it was concerning. His eyes should always be on the road. The last thing I needed was to be involved in a car accident.

It took a great deal to make me feel uncomfortable in any way. All the same, I was definitely annoyed by his behavior. So I decided to do the only thing I could in this situation. Nip it in the bud.

"Is something the matter?" I asked, with a frown on my face, letting him see how displeased I was.

"No, no," he was quick to reassure me, clearly embarrassed he'd been caught salivating.

"You keep staring at me," I insisted.

Unfortunately, that seemed to encourage him, and he smiled. "I am sorry. It's just that you are so beautiful."

I rolled my eyes. "This is LA. The city is brimming with beautiful people."

"Are you an actress?"

As if I would ever sleep around for my fifteen minutes of fame. "No."

"Model?"

The idea of being treated like a thing held no appeal either. "No."

"That's a shame."

"Not from my perspective."

"Are you single?" he asked next.

I was really getting sick and tired of this forced conversation, especially since I had work to do. Besides, I couldn't believe he'd dared to ask such a personal question. He'd picked the wrong woman to mess with.

"That's crossing the line, so I'm ending this conversation," I snapped in return.

"Don't get mad. I was just wondering," he continued.

"You must have a boyfriend. Such a beautiful woman like you must be taken."

Must be taken? Was he even aware of his language? And the worst part? I was sure that in his mind he believed he was super charming.

Disgusting. Men like him should be prohibited from speaking with women until taking a class or something that would cure them of all this creepiness.

The idiot took his mobile phone out and, while he drove, turned to look at me. "I have to have a photo of you."

"Eyes on the road," I practically yelled.

He did as he was told. Nonetheless, the phone stayed in his hand. "Can I have a picture of you?"

"No," I replied. There was no way I would let this perv have a picture of me on his phone.

"Just one, to remember you by." It was obvious he considered that the greatest compliment.

I was disgusted. "No."

"I've photographed all the celebrities riding in my car," he said, raising his chin ever so slightly, as though to show me that I should feel special considering I wasn't a celebrity after all.

I wasn't impressed or amused.

If I could, I would have slapped him. Since he was driving, and I didn't want to cause an accident, I had to settle for doing nothing, which I hated.

"I said no." I remained adamant.

Thoroughly pissed off, I stuffed my work papers back into the briefcase. There was no point trying to do anything, especially in this mood.

While I did that, I saw from the corner of my eyes he was still trying to take a picture of me.

That crazy son of a bitch. I'd really had enough of him.

I raised my hand. "Stop this now," I said firmly. I glanced through the window to determine where I was, calculating if I should go the rest of the way on foot. Like always, the problem was my high heels.

"Please, just one," he continued to insist.

Tired of this situation, I grabbed hold of his phone and yanked it from his hand.

"Hey, give it back," he rebelled.

"No, and you should feel fortunate I haven't thrown it through a window."

"That's destroying personal property."

I gritted my teeth. "And you trying to take my photo against my protests is called harassment. And if you don't stop behaving in such a manner, right this instant, I will make a living hell out of your life."

"Calm down. It is just one photo. I really don't understand why you're making such a big deal out of it," he had the audacity to say, all the while sounding as though he were the wronged party, like I was the unreasonable one. That was one of the weapons weak men used to try to control women.

"The big deal is that you are using this situation, with me trapped in your car as you are providing a service, to harass me. What you are doing is highly inappropriate, not to mention creepy."

"Well, that's your opinion, lady."

I hated when someone called me lady using that tone of voice. It practically meant fuck off.

"Actually, it would be any judge's opinion in the state of California."

He snorted. "What are you, a lawyer?" he said, still not grasping the gravity of the situation.

"As a matter of fact, I am. And as a lawyer, I deal with a lot of creepy inappropriate people, not to mention real criminals. It really wouldn't take me that much, one phone call, actually, to get all your personal information and have you arrested for harassment. And while doing that, I would definitely reach out to other clients of yours to see what they had to say about you and your behavior. Then it wouldn't be just my opinion, would it?"

His eyes went wide. "Please don't do that. I wasn't thinking," he tried to defend.

It was my time to smirk. "You clearly weren't thinking you would come across someone like me, who wouldn't just tolerate your behavior. You are a bully, and a creepy one at that, and someone needs to stop you," I countered, getting all high and mighty. Feeling ready to start a war.

"Please don't report me. This is all that I have. I didn't mean it."

"The problem is you did mean it, and you thought you would get away with it." Too many men operated in such a fashion, especially if they were of lower education, being taught gender superiority. And too many women, on the other hand, were thought to keep silent and suffer, which enabled such behavior. Well, not me. I was having none of it. And if it took me to show him the error of his ways, then so be it.

"I am really sorry. I will never do it again," he promised.

"That is not good enough." I was adamant. "Especially since I don't believe you actually mean that."

"I do, I do mean it," he insisted frantically.

"You were pretty cocky just moments ago, thinking you could do whatever you please."

"I made a mistake, but it won't happen again. Please, please do not ruin my life. Please, I will do whatever you want me to do," he begged. He was practically in tears as he stopped in front of my law firm.

That's more like it, I thought, looking at his sniveling face. *Now I am one of his satisfied customers,* I joked. I threw his phone back to him before leaning forward. There was one last thing I had to say to him before departing.

"I am watching you, Randy, so you'd better behave from now on, because if you don't, I will know, and I will take you down," I threatened without batting an eye, and meaning every word.

I hated creeps like him, and I loved putting them back in their place. Besides, I was doing community service. Some other poor girl wouldn't get harassed by this creep thanks to what I'd done to him today.

And I felt zero remorse that he looked ready to shit his pants as I spoke. His head went up and down like a bobble-head.

Nodding at that, pretty satisfied with myself, I exited the car.

I hoped that would keep him straight. All the same, I wondered if I should contact Uber customer service and report him. Someone certainly needed to keep an eye on him.

Then again, he looked pretty scared of me. And he sped away the instant I shut the car door as though in fear I would say anything else or, God forbid, get back inside.

That kind of made me smile. *I haven't lost my touch.*

All the same, I'd let him off the hook too easily. A few

years back, I would definitely have filed a report against him and made sure he lost his job, because men like him should be punished not rewarded for such behavior, but now I didn't want to bother. I had more important things to deal with, bigger fish to fry, as the proverb went.

As I pondered that Uber driver's future, someone approached me, a blurry tall figure, since I wasn't paying attention, and snatched the phone right out of my hand, then dashed away.

"Hey," I yelled as he ran away, as any normal thief would in such a situation.

I ran after him, and then it dawned on me. That phone thief looked very familiar to me. He was wearing that same gray hoodie and baggy pants as the punk who'd trashed my car.

If there wasn't a store in this city called Thieves R Us, there was a chance it was the same guy.

"Stop that thief," I yelled, pointing, feeling extra motivated to catch him.

Unfortunately, nobody was paying any attention. Most had headphones; others didn't want to get involved. All were minding their own business.

And in that moment, it was hard not to lose hope in humanity. An asteroid should wipe us all out, and nature should start anew. Perhaps the next version of people would be better.

And that was when my heel broke, and I lost him in the crowd.

10

PUZZLE PIECES

"D id you try using—Where's My Phone—app?" the operator asked in her monotone voice. "Of course I have. It's just that I never turned it on," I confessed reluctantly.

Since I'd stepped into my office, I'd been forced to deal with the fact my phone had been stolen in broad daylight in the middle of the street, surrounded by witnesses. *And nobody did anything to help,* I still fumed.

Instead of working, I was making sure whoever stole my phone couldn't steal all my data as well. That was my biggest fear.

I could get a new phone; that wasn't a problem, an inconvenience at best. The information I had stored on that phone was priceless to me, though. And I was sure the right people could take advantage of it as well.

"When was the last time you used your phone?"

Is she serious? "Right before it was snatched from my hand." I tried hard not to start yelling. Although I was on the verge, I knew I couldn't do that; it would make matters worse, not better.

"Have you reported the incident to the police?"

Another brilliant question. "Yes, I have."

"Then I don't have to tell you most stolen phones are never returned to their owners."

"Yes, I am aware of that." I stressed the words. "I just need you to tell me how to prevent the thief from getting all my information."

"I am afraid I can't do that."

"Excuse me?"

"If you have sensitive information, I suggest you contact your bank, then change all your passwords."

"That's it?" I asked incredulously.

"At the moment, all I can offer is a replacement SIM card with the same number."

This was ridiculous. I couldn't believe that for all the money I was giving my phone service company, that was the best they could do for me.

"Thank you very much," I said snidely, *for nothing*, before hanging up. Afterward, not seeing any other way, I contacted my bank. Google Pay had my credit card number, so I needed to cancel it.

I groaned. *Why is all of this happening to me?*

Speaking to my bank took forever, and they asked questions that, at times, left me speechless, which was a rare occurrence.

It didn't take long to fully lose my patience. I was tired of dealing with calls about lost or damaged items. I'd lost too many precious hours dealing with idiots and answering all of their idiotic questions.

It wasn't fair I'd lost both my car and my phone in just

one week. *What the hell?* Although lost was definitely the wrong choice of words. I hadn't lost anything. My car had been vandalized. God only knew what could have happened to it if I hadn't stumbled upon that punk, completely by chance. And my phone had been stolen.

If my memory served me well, and it did, both perpetrators wore the same type of clothes, down to the gray hoodie that covered their face.

Once again, I started to wonder if that was purely a coincidence. Was it possible that the criminal enterprise in this city was uninformed? Or was it possible it was the same guy? That thought made me feel wary. I didn't like thinking there was someone who was intentionally targeting me over and over.

And then I reminded myself it wasn't my job to think about that. That was a job for the police. *Not that they will do anything to help me*, I thought glumly.

These were too small crimes for the police to bother with. *They will never find the guy who trashed my car and stole my phone.* I was aware of that. This was my world, after all. I dealt with the police all the time. I knew how they operated and how they thought.

To them, I was merely a lawyer who could afford to repair her car and get a new phone, which wasn't the point.

I had been violated twice now, and they had to protect me. I had been wronged, and I deserved justice. I deserved the satisfaction of knowing those criminals were punished for what they did. Sadly, it didn't look like that would happen any time soon.

And that wasn't fair. Yet we didn't live in a fair world. I knew that better than most. *If you wanted something done, you had to do it yourself or cheat the system.*

I stopped my rant there, realizing that, by getting riled up, I would solve nothing.

"Bonnie," I yelled for my assistant. She took her sweet time coming.

"Yes?"

"When I call for you, please come immediately. It's important."

"Ok," she replied, somewhat confused, which I didn't understand. "Is that all?"

It was my turn to stare at her. "No. I called you because I need you to go to my mobile phone provider and get my SIM card. Oh, and when you're there, buy a new phone as well."

"Is there something wrong with your old phone?"

"Yes, it got stolen."

"Did you call the police?"

"I did. And I spoke with the phone company as well."

"When should I go?"

"Now. And restore all the information from the stolen one to the new one," I added as an afterthought.

"Um, I don't think that is possible. You need the old phone to transfer data."

I frowned. "I am not interested in hearing excuses. Speak with them and make it happen," I commanded. I knew they stored all our information, so it would be fair to expect they would provide that information when needed.

Still, she hesitated.

"Yes?" I stressed the word.

"Miss Dennis, I haven't managed to finish the letter you gave me to type," she confessed.

"Just go," I snapped. "You can do that later."

I was already having a super bad day, and I didn't need her piling on that with her incompetence. I really needed a new assistant. Unfortunately, it didn't look like I would have enough time in the near future to deal with such a huge task.

Regrettably, the universe wasn't done with me yet. There was still much more I needed to endure that day, as it turned out.

Phoebe was passing by my office while I was speaking to Bonnie. And by the look on her face, she wasn't pleased with how I treated my assistant. Which wasn't that bad, to be perfectly honest. I expected a certain level of skill and competence. That wasn't too much to ask considering she was paid for that.

All the same, Phoebe felt the need to interject. "Is something the matter?" she inquired.

I had to work hard not to show how displeased I was by this turn of events. I hated when she felt the need to stroll into my office and have a "talk" with me. She never missed an opportunity to show me she was still my boss.

Not for long.

"My phone got stolen right in front of the building," I replied.

"Did you report it?"

"Of course."

"Was there any sensitive information on the device?"

I instantly understood what she was aiming at. She was asking if there was something on my phone that could be used against one of my clients. That could be harmful to the firm. And the short answer to that was yes.

"It has all been taken care of. And Bonnie will go to get my new phone while I try to catch up with my work. Don't worry. I'll work overtime to finish everything."

Phoebe nodded. "I have no doubt about that."

I remained silent, waiting for her to make her move because this wasn't it.

On her way out, she paused by the door and glanced from me to Bonnie, who was grabbing her things from her desk, and then back to me again.

Here it comes...

"Oh, a word of advice?"

"Certainly," I said with a fake smile.

"Just because you are having a bad day doesn't give you the right to take it out on your assistant."

"I wasn't doing that. I was merely giving her instructions; however, I will accept that advice for the future."

"Your tone suggested otherwise," she insisted.

"True. I admit I lost my temper, but that has nothing to do with me having a bad day. It is not my fault she's too incompetent to follow the simplest of instructions." I didn't care if Bonnie overheard me now.

"I am sure that's not true. We are pretty selective in who we hire."

"Not selective enough," I replied as I stared at Bonnie's back, watching her walk away. I was sure she heard me by the way her shoulders hunched.

"Then you should definitely fire her. Then again, that would be your fifth assistant this year alone. Perhaps it's not the assistant's fault," she jibed not so subtly.

"I assure you it is. HR is constantly sending me incompetent people." I dug my heels in. And what I said was true because Millie from HR hated me, always had, and that was why she'd been trying to sabotage me for years by sending me the worst legal secretaries possible.

I always tried to make it work, but sadly I couldn't allow my job to suffer. That was why I'd had to fire my previous assistants, because they were not good enough. Naturally, that wasn't something Phoebe cared about. She only wanted to humiliate me.

"Speaking of incompetence," Phoebe countered with a humorless smile, "I should tell you I was against you becoming a junior partner. I never believed you were mature enough to handle such responsibilities."

Not mature enough? I couldn't believe my ears. *What a stupid thing to say.* This only showed how envious she was.

I already knew she'd been against me. She'd even tried to convince others not to vote for me, but Grant had had the last say. Much to her chagrin.

I wanted to lash out at her, defend myself, and knew I couldn't. She was baiting me intentionally. She wanted me to throw a tantrum so she could go to Grant and rub his nose in it. I wasn't going to allow that to happen.

I will show her I am right where I am supposed to be. I will show her I am better than her once I assume her job. She might have more power for now, but that would change, and I would definitely have the last laugh.

"Well, I am glad you changed your mind in the end and voted for me," I replied calmly, trying to end this.

Unfortunately, she was having none of it. "Not really. Grant made me. Sadly, my doubts about you still remain."

"I am really sorry to hear that. I hope in time I will manage to change your opinion of me," I replied gracefully.

"Seeing how you treat your coworkers really does not work in your favor. I hope you will change that, for your sake. At GBD, we only want team players." And with that, she left.

I grabbed a stapler. It took everything in me, every ounce of willpower, not to throw it. *What a jealous hag.*

This had nothing to do with how I treated Bonnie. I was aware of that. Phoebe obviously had to come and humiliate me, put me back in my place no matter what. She would find an excuse to do so regardless, because she hated me, couldn't stand I was the junior partner, not her protégé Patricia Miller, and wanted me gone.

Although, it was foolish of me to hand her an excuse on a silver platter.

This little visit from her did nothing to improve my already bad mood. And the fact she'd chastised me in front of Bonnie made matters even worse.

I definitely couldn't fire her now. Not when Phoebe had acted as her protector.

This is the worst day ever.

Sadly, I spoke too early, as it turned out, and pretty soon discovered this could get much worse, still.

Since I didn't have my phone, didn't have all my contacts with me, I was forced to communicate as though in the Stone Age, via email. And that was how I discovered two more threatening emails.

In retrospect, I should have deleted them, but since it was that kind of day, I decided to read them.

Why won't they leave me alone? Haven't I suffered enough?

Apparently not, I seethed, needing to channel the day's cumulative anger into something, and this was the perfect opportunity.

I opened the first email. It was the typical rambling of a madman, clearly written on the spur of the moment and under the influence of heavy liquor.

Unfortunately, the second one was an entirely different story.

Is it hard to ruin other people's lives without your phone?

I could actually hear the mocking tone as I read it.
What? How does this person know about my phone? I had to
wonder.

*I feel so sorry I wasn't there when that device of evil was
snatched from your hands. Because what is a devil
without its instruments of torture? I feel so sorry for
you. Not.*

Reading that, a chill went down my spine. All of this
could not be a coincidence. I didn't have to be a genius to
realize there was nothing random about what was
happening to me. It was beyond obvious how it was all
connected. The threatening emails and my phone being
stolen were obviously the work of the same person. And who
knew, perhaps the vandalization of my Tesla was part of all
of that as well. I wouldn't rule that out.

The perpetrator couldn't resist taunting me with this
email because they clearly wanted me to know what they'd
done.

Someone truly has it in for me, I thought, feeling quite
uneasy about the whole situation. I had been stalked and
harassed online and offline, and I didn't like that one bit.
The problem was I had no idea why this person was doing
all these things to me.

Nonetheless, I was going to find out.

11

THE POLICE BUSINESS

The day I'd had, receiving those emails, especially the second one, had certainly pushed me over the edge. I wasn't going to tolerate someone doing this to me. I wasn't some weak, unimportant woman who would cower in fear just because some deranged lunatic had it in for them.

Whoever was doing this had made a huge mistake thinking I was an easy target. I wasn't going to stand for someone playing with me. Or trying to play with me, as it turned out, because I'd managed to piece everything together.

Without wasting time, because I truly hated that, I gathered all the evidence. Unfortunately it wasn't much, several threatening emails I wasn't sure were all from the same person, and two police reports, one for the car and the other for the phone, and sent them all together to our legal department, which handled such things.

Naturally, at this point, there wasn't much they could do. I frankly wanted them informed of what was happening.

Once I took care of that, I took the afternoon off so I could go to the police and report yet another crime.

Is it possible there is a bigger spike in crime in this city than I thought, or have the police simply stopped doing their job? I wondered while riding in an Uber. Luckily, this driver left me alone. It was heaven.

The police station looked busy. Since I wasn't there for a high-priority crime, everyone seemed reluctant to speak with me. Nonetheless, I insisted someone should take my statement and write a report. Eventually I managed to speak with Desk Sergeant Cooper.

Very calmly, using only simple sentences, I explained what had been happening to me. I mentioned the emails, showed the report and the pictures of the car, then added the incident with my phone, which was the freshest.

"I suspect it's work related, yet at this point, I can't say for sure," I concluded.

The police officer took his time replying as he looked at the file I'd brought with me. "Mrs. Dennis—" he started.

"It's Miss Dennis," I corrected instantly.

"Miss Dennis, this is all pretty circumstantial at best." He looked dubiously at my evidence, toying with the edge of the file.

It irked me when someone did that. Damaged paper documents were the worst. It always distracted me from reading when I spotted crooked edges. I shuddered inwardly.

"There are no leads we could follow. You have no witnesses and no CCTV footage. All that you have are a few angry emails."

"And my statements about the person who stole my phone and vandalized my car," I reminded him.

"Could you pick that person from a lineup?"

"No, I do not think I could," I admitted reluctantly.

He shook his head. "Then as I said, this is all circumstantial."

In other words, everything I had was not good enough.

What am I supposed to do? Let this stalker kill me, then spell his name in my own blood for the police to find so they could do their job and actually arrest the culprit? I ranted.

Sadly, the desk sergeant wasn't the only one looking suspiciously at me in the precinct. I was sure that at least a couple of officers recognized me. Their displeasure was almost palpable. I paid them no mind. It wasn't my fault they were not as good at their jobs as I was at mine. Nonetheless, they held grudges, which was ridiculous. Besides, if they spent half the time actually doing their job, solving crimes, rather than hating me, this would be a far more peaceful city.

Perhaps I made a mistake coming to the police. I had a moment of doubt. On the one hand, I genuinely believed this needed to be reported. On the other, I realized how difficult it was to find someone sympathetic toward me and my case. Someone who would listen to what had been happening with an open mind.

Of course, none of them acted as though they didn't believe this had actually happened. It was just that they all thought I deserved it, and that was unacceptable; it was highly unprofessional.

All the same, I kept my mouth shut. I didn't want to make a bad situation even worse.

So I said, "I understand all that, Desk Sergeant Cooper."

"Then why are you here, Miss Dennis?" he asked blatantly.

I pushed through my anger to form a reply. *In the unfortu-*

nate event I end up dead tomorrow, I want all of you to know where to look for the culprit and why. "I'm here because I would like to file a report."

"Miss Dennis likes to file reports," someone said behind my back. When I turned, there were a few police officers standing about, and I couldn't determine who'd mocked me. *All of you are cowards,* my icy glare was telling them.

"If you really think that's necessary," the desk sergeant replied reluctantly.

"I really do. I want this on record if things escalate," I explained, since clearly, I had to. It was frustrating I had to do their job for them as well.

"Do you expect it to escalate?" he asked, looking interested in me for the first time since I'd come in to speak with him.

I shrugged. "That is something I cannot predict." *It is your job to investigate, not mine.* "However, I see nothing wrong in taking necessary precautions to avoid tragedies."

"Do you feel the same about creating tragedies?" someone interjected.

I turned again. "Who said that?"

They all ignored me and pretended to be busy when I knew they weren't. They were all eavesdropping so they could gossip later.

Pathetic.

"I think that's a good call," an officer at the nearest table commented, making me focus on him.

"Thank you," I said politely. Finally, someone with common sense worked here.

"I mean, if anyone knows how many scumbags are walking the streets, it's you, right?" he finished his thought, making me frown as all his colleagues started to snicker.

I gritted my teeth, deciding not to fall for that obvious taunt. He wasn't worth losing my temper over. He clearly held a grudge over something, which told me everything I needed to know. He was a boy with a badge, who was obviously bad at his job. End of story.

I put on my most dazzling smile. "Same as you, Officer," I replied politely. I wanted him to see he couldn't get to me, no matter what he said.

As he said, I knew many scumbags, I dealt with them on a daily basis, and this officer, compared to them, was an amateur.

As though my words had provoked him, he got up and walked toward me, then leaned against the table I was sitting at, turning his back to the desk sergeant, giving me his full attention. "Tell me, how many scumbags have you set loose on the public this year alone?" he practically accused.

"I was simply doing my job, Officer."

"Well, your job is despicable," he said, pointing a finger at me.

"I didn't come here for a lecture on false morality. I came here for help," I pointed out. It was pathetic to see someone incapable of separating personal from professional.

"That's exactly my point," he said with a smirk. "Now you have the audacity to ask for help after all you did. If you ask me, you are as bad as the criminals you defend. Why don't you ask one of them for help?"

"Because that would be against the law. And despite what you think, Officer Malone," I read his name tag, "I very much abide by the law."

He shook his head. "You are so full of it."

I'd had enough of him. "I see you are one of those men who want to ignore due process so you can do whatever you want, arrest whoever you want, without any culpability," I snapped in return.

He straightened up and started to loom over me. "Listen, lady, you are everything that is wrong in this city," he yelled.

Many of his colleagues moved closer. To watch the spectacle or prevent him from doing anything stupid, I couldn't tell. I was sure I was about to find out anyway.

"Just in this city?" I countered, with a fake smile. "Are you sure I am not responsible for global warming or world hunger as well?"

"That's all you can do, mock."

"And what is it that you do around here other than harassing me? Did you shoot any innocent persons lately?"

That triggered him, and he looked as though he was ready to grab me and pull me up out of my chair.

"Malone, that's enough," the desk sergeant yelled, finally deciding to step in.

And he wasn't the only one. Another colleague approached to pull Officer Malone away.

Malone looked like he wanted to argue some more. Luckily for him, the sane part of his brain, no matter how small it was, prevailed, and he allowed himself to be pulled away from the desk before our argument escalated further and turned into something ugly.

This definitely wasn't the first time someone had come at me, which was precisely why I was able to remain calm and levelheaded. I could see it in his eyes, he'd actually wanted to hit me.

What a bully. Neanderthals like him thought everything could be solved with violence. He was probably a wife-beater as well.

All of them were the same, no better than the criminals

they were paid to catch. The only difference was that they had badges. And he dared to say I was the bad guy. *What a joke.*

I could see him exchanging a few words with his colleagues, but I was too far away to hear what had been said. Probably the usual, how he needed to think about the consequences of his actions. I was a shark lawyer, after all.

Part of me was saddened he didn't try anything. It would have been fun to take him down. Not to mention that it would be great PR for our firm. Grant would be thrilled.

I could already see the headlines. *Maniacal cop savagely beat down a woman lawyer right in the precinct, in front of all his colleagues, who did nothing!* The headline practically wrote itself.

It would be the scandal of the year and something I could really use to my advantage. I could lead a crusade against all cops who didn't abide by the law. After something like that, switching to politics and becoming governor would be a sure thing.

All the same, that wasn't something that interested me. I never cared to become a politician.

Shaking his head, Officer Malone furiously stormed away. Men like him should not be allowed to work for the police. They were a disgrace, and he'd just proved that.

The police officers who'd gathered around dispersed as well, probably realizing they actually had a job to do.

I turned to look at the desk sergeant, as though none of what had happened mattered. He didn't offer an apology for his colleague's behavior, probably because he thought the same way but was too much of a coward to voice it, so I moved forward.

"Despite what you all think of me, I am not a bad guy,

and to prove that, I won't file a report against your colleague."

It was clear he had something to say to that, but I wouldn't let him. "Nonetheless, I would appreciate it if you would take care of this other report from me, against the anonymous vandal."

I really didn't give him any other choice than to comply, because although subtle, my threat was real.

"Of course, Miss Dennis," he replied eventually.

I had to admit I was proud of myself and how I'd handled this situation. Officer Malone had actually done me a favor with his tantrum.

The desk sergeant had been ready to blow me off before Malone had come and started a fight. So thanks to him, I got exactly what I wanted. And that felt good.

Of course, I was irked it had had to come to that. The whole experience was rather dissatisfying from the perspective of a civilian coming to the police station to ask for help, only to get yelled at. The problem was I wasn't merely a civilian. As it turned out, there was a lot of bad blood between me and the men in blue, something I hadn't been particularly aware of beforehand.

I certainly was aware of it now. And it made me think.

What if my perp is actually a cop who is salty over the fact I am a better defense lawyer than he is at making solid arrests that would stick?

A police officer would definitely know whom to turn to in order to vandalize a car or steal a phone. And that Malone guy and his colleagues were definitely at the top of my list.

Perhaps this visit wasn't a complete waste of my time...

12

EMPTY THREATS

Going to the police had accomplished absolutely nothing. Although I'd reported a crime, apparently the officers had no interest in investigating it. It was as though they were all waiting for something really bad to happen to me to actually do their job. Or at least pretend to do so, for the public.

I banished all those glum thoughts because thinking like that would solve nothing. And I needed this resolved. I had more important things to focus on but couldn't because of the threats.

Speaking of threats, they kept coming. And in vast numbers at that, as though whoever was sending them was becoming bolder, knowing there was nothing I could do to stop them.

I had to admit they were pretty creative in their emails as well. Sure, they promised me complete ruination, suffering, humiliation, but it was done in such a manner I didn't believe that someone of a lower breeding wrote them anymore.

Someone pretty well versed was just trying to sound ignorant. Nonetheless, there were clues to the contrary, like the usage of certain words, perfect grammar, and so on.

I spent a great deal of time studying those emails, and for the life of me, I couldn't understand why this person hated me so much. I hadn't managed to find a cause for such outbursts of hatred in any of them, and I had really looked for it.

I spent many sleepless nights thinking about the person who'd vowed to destroy me, my whole life. The problem was I still couldn't tell for sure whether all the emails were from the same person.

After that one email in which they taunted me about my phone, the rest of the emails were pretty general. So it was hard to keep track of whether one person wrote them, especially since they all came from different throwaway email accounts, which was maddening.

I kept copies of all the threats I had received since my car was vandalized in a special folder marked Maniac on my laptop. Although the police were pretty dormant about the whole thing, I still felt compelled to gather everything. That was the lawyer in me, always prepared for the worst while expecting the best.

To say I was frustrated by this whole situation would be a vast understatement. Just when everything was going my way, just when my life was finally at the place I wished it to be, this menace had appeared to ruin everything.

Well, I found that unacceptable.

Still, there wasn't much I could do about it. Until they revealed themself or made a mistake, my hands were tied, and I hated that.

And living as though this wasn't happening wasn't an

option because I wasn't only receiving threats online. This person had been very disruptive to my life, stealing my phone and destroying my property, and that was making me angry.

I wanted to find this lunatic and turn it around. I wanted to torment them for a change. I wanted them to know what it felt like when I put all my time, resources, and energy into ruining his life.

See how he'll like that.

Pissed off on too many levels to count, since it had been a rough couple of days, not to mention I was quite tipsy, I tried to form a plan and determine my next course of action. Which wasn't an easy thing to do in my state. Everything I came up with involved physical pain, involved violence, and I wasn't that kind of person.

I liked a more subtle approach in life, in all things, especially in business, in revenge. I blamed the brandy for my bloodthirsty thoughts. It was an excellent brand, and the liquor slid down my throat easily, numbing my senses.

That expensive bottle of alcohol was actually a gift from Kelly for my promotion. I'd opened it, although I had been planning on saving it for a special occasion, because I was angry and feeling just a tad sorry for myself.

I couldn't decide what stung more. The way the police had treated me, like I was some common criminal; the way this stalker wasn't leaving me alone, disrupting my everyday life; or the way Phoebe had dared to speak to me, and in front of my secretary.

Damn them all, I grumbled. *None of them mattered. They are dirt underneath my high-heel shoes, and I will treat them all as such.*

I poured myself another glass as I twirled in my chair. I'd

stayed in the office, although it was quite late. Firstly, because it took me forever to finish my work; thanks to all the distractions I was quite behind. And secondly, because I didn't feel like ordering myself an Uber.

I miss my car, I whined again. I couldn't believe it was taking so long to fix. It seemed they'd found more wrong with it than they'd first realized, which was extremely irritating.

The twirling made my stomach uneasy, so I stopped. As I did that, my eyes landed on the monitor. While I tried to drink my sorrows away, I received another email.

"That son of a bitch," I cursed. It didn't matter I didn't know whom I was cursing. It felt good to do so, nevertheless.

I instantly opened it up. For some reason, I needed to see what that lunatic had to say.

How do you like your new reality? Is it stressful? It's not fun when someone is ruining your life for a change. And be warned, this is just the beginning. I will not stop until I completely ruin you, your whole fake world, you greedy, heartless whore.

"I will end you for this," I screamed at my monitor, feeling absolutely unhinged. I prided myself in always being in control, in always being able to predict the moves of others, putting me ten steps ahead of everybody else; however, this stalker was managing to do things no one else could. They'd managed to push all my buttons, and it didn't matter that was precisely what they wanted, it couldn't be helped.

That was why I decided to reply. Intoxicated and thoroughly riled up was a potent combination, as it turned out, and it was no surprise I decided to do something out of character.

At this point, I didn't even care if this maniac received the reply or not. I had to write it all the same. For my sake. For the sake of my shredded sanity.

"I really liked your latest email," I started to type, speaking out loud as though having a conversation with this lunatic. "It is very brave of you to write anonymous emails and empty threats while hiding behind a screen. Do you think that's what it looks like to ruin somebody? Oh, poor you. Word of advice, if you want to play with the adults, you have to abandon such childish tactics because they will accomplish nothing.

"You are a coward, nothing else, if you weren't, you'd tell me who you are, and why you are doing this. If you weren't such a pitiful coward, you would come and battle me face-to-face, not hide online and organize sneaky attacks.

"Sadly, I know you can't face me; you lack all the characteristics of a true fighter. You will never be my match. This is the peak of your potential. You are nothing but a sad, despicable human being whose highlight of the day entails writing laughable emails.

"You are nothing. You will remain nothing until the day you die.

"And you'd better stop with this nonsense before pissing me off, because then I will be forced to show you what it actually looks like when someone like me decides to completely destroy someone like you."

Typing all that, I pressed send.

"Now that's how you write a threatening email," I told no one in particular.

I had to say I felt much better after getting that off my

chest. Writing that email was precisely what I needed, and I instantly felt like myself again. I was still drunk, but all other thoughts and negative feelings had vanished. I made a toast to myself, taking another sip of my drink, ready to call it a night.

Purely legally speaking, that wasn't the smartest of moves. As an attorney, I would advise my clients and try to discourage them from engaging in such behaviors.

Unfortunately, lawyers were the worst clients. I was glad I'd done it. I was the wronged party here, and it felt good to strike back and not simply do what was right. I kind of hoped that email would make them leave me alone.

All the same, after a few minutes, my victory started to look pretty hollow because ranting like some lunatic, similarly to my stalker, would accomplish nothing. The only thing I did accomplish was to stoop to their level, which was unacceptable. I also realized that all the feelings, all the thoughts I'd had beforehand had returned, and with a vengeance.

Not wanting to end up like some alcoholic, finishing the whole bottle of brandy in one night, I decided it was time to leave the office.

I tried to ignore how tense I felt on my way home. But the sentiment was still present. It couldn't be helped.

After all that had happened to me lately, I didn't feel safe anymore. And I really resented that anonymous person, that crazy stalker, for managing to mess with my head and take my peace of mind.

Nothing that is not offered can really be taken, I reminded myself.

I scowled, banishing that thought because I was in no mood to listen to myself. I was in no mood, period.

David had kept calling me throughout the day, but I'd turned my phone off. I couldn't deal with him and his clinginess. Then again, perhaps some sex could take my mind off the train wreck that was my life.

Although that might be the case, I couldn't be bothered. *It is better to be alone than in bad company.* I scowled. That brandy was really showing another side of me. I was full of rich anger and folklore wisdom. *Who knew...*

Reaching my building, leaving an adequate review for my latest driver, I went straight up to my apartment. I was in no mood to interact with other people.

Unfortunately, being inside my home and locking myself in didn't make me feel better.

No matter what I tried to tell myself, I was worried about this stalker. Worried about what they might do next. *Where will it come from, the attack?* I pondered, looking through the window at the panoramic views of the city.

In what form will the threat come? Unfortunately, I was sure they wouldn't stop at threats alone.

And my angry email was of no help at all, I thought, glumly walking away from the window and sitting on the couch.

I couldn't think about all of that. I would drive myself crazy. No matter what that maniac did, I would deal with it when the time came, and win, because there was no other option.

Needing something to take my mind off my mysterious stalker, I grabbed my phone and decided to keep myself busy by organizing it. Predictably, Bonnie had proved to be pretty useless about the whole endeavor.

Perhaps I should be grateful she bought my new phone in the first place, I thought sarcastically.

It was a relief I still had the same number and that

everyone who needed to reach me still could, but I was missing everything else.

So I downloaded all the necessary apps, logged in, using new passwords, and then started the painstaking process of adding all my contacts to my new phone. Repopulating the contact list was tedious work because I knew a lot of people in this city, and beyond, thanks to what I did for a living. All the same, it needed to be done.

And that was when it occurred to me. Perhaps I was having a hard time doing something so simple, although time-consuming, because I was drunk. However, being inebriated helped. It gave me the necessary patience to not throw my phone over the balcony before setting everything up.

Also, this time around, I made sure that its tracker was on at all times.

Fool me twice, shame on me...

But then I paused. *Can someone track me with it?* That thought wasn't all too optimistic. Yet considering my current mood, it was understandable.

It would take a pretty skilled tech person, a hacker, to do that, I presumed.

The only person I was worried about was my stalker, naturally, and I was fairly sure they didn't possess such mad skills. If they did, they certainly wouldn't send me emails from random accounts. They would do something far more creative, I was sure of that, I mused, trying to reassure myself. And it worked, I was.

Eventually, I came to terms with the fact that the risk of having the app up and running was worth taking. If the aforementioned stalker tried to steal my phone again, I would be ready to catch them.

Picturing them caught, in handcuffs, almost made me smile. No matter what, I wasn't going to lose another phone, or anything else for that matter.

I was done playing offense; it was time to switch to defense and nail this son of a bitch.

Feeling quite good about myself, which was a miracle after the day I'd had, I decided it was time for bed.

13

SOUND ADVICE

Although I hated showing any weakness or having to rely on somebody else, because I was a firm believer in dealing with my own problems, I reluctantly accepted that wouldn't be good enough this time around. I needed professional help.

Besides, that was a sign of strength as well, recognizing when you needed to step down and allow professionals to take charge to solve what needed to be solved, do what needed to be done.

And no, I wasn't speaking about the police. They were a useless bunch who would gladly leave me to rot somewhere in a ditch if that stalker decided to stop wasting time online and murder me.

Drinking all that brandy had left me hungover and in a glum mood.

I remembered how my new neighbor had told me she was some kind of techy and had an IT business or something, so I decided to go and ask her for help. I wanted to see if there was something that could be done about my stalker.

Grabbing my laptop, I started walking toward my neighbor's door. *What was her name again?* I racked my brain to remember.

Mercy, I thought victoriously.

Once there, I reconsidered. I decided to leave the laptop in my apartment. I didn't want it to appear as though the only reason I'd come knocking was because I needed her help.

It's better to come without, I thought, knocking.

While I waited for her to come to the door, I experienced second thoughts. Mercy looked like a nice enough girl, but was she smart enough to help me? Was she skillful enough to do what I needed her to do?

Then again, she must possess a certain set of skills if she has her own firm, I argued. And not only that, but she was successful enough to relocate from Kansas to California.

Was she reliable though? I didn't want her blabbing around the city about my problems. Unfortunately, that was something that could only be determined by testing a person.

As I pondered that, the door opened, and Mercy's smiling face welcomed me.

"Amber, hi, what a nice surprise," she greeted.

Once again, she was in a rather unique fashion ensemble. She wore jeans that looked too big on her, held by a rather oversized belt, probably a man's, and a cut-off T-shirt. On her feet, she had neon green crocs.

Who was I to judge? Besides, it wasn't like she had to dress for work. Nobody could see her while she conducted her business, anyway. Which was a blessing in disguise.

"Hi, Mercy," I greeted in return.

"You know, I've been meaning to call you. I was craving

some chicken spiedini, and then I thought to myself, Amber eats much nicer food than that, so I didn't call," she said all in one breath.

She was probably right since I had no idea what she was talking about. I decided to cut to the chase. "Mercy, I am really sorry to ask, but I think I need your help."

By the look on her face, I guessed I'd surprised her. "Do you need help with moving too?" she asked in return.

What? It was my turn to be surprised. "No, I need your professional advice," I explained.

That made her serious. "Oh. Do you want to come in?" she offered.

"I think that would be best," I replied, giving her a curt nod.

She moved and gestured with her hand for me to enter, and I did.

I was pleasantly surprised to see all the cardboard boxes were gone, and she actually had some furniture in this time around. I half expected she would make furniture out of the cardboard boxes, while using them for storage. I stood corrected.

The furniture was all mismatched and cheap looking. Then again, it somehow went with Mercy perfectly. The only thing that stood out was the massive L-shaped desk in the far corner, which held all of Mercy's computers and monitors.

It was somewhat reassuring to know that she took that part of her life seriously at least. Or that was the hope.

I sat on a red chair, and she offered me a steaming cup of tea without asking, before settling on a green couch herself.

"So what is the matter?" she asked with a frown, which looked strange on that innocent face of hers.

I decided to share everything with her, about what had

been happening to me, and hoped for the best. Taking a deep breath, I opened my mouth. "I don't know if you remember that I work as a defense lawyer."

"Sure, I remember. You are one of those fancy lawyers who work at a big firm and defend all the celebrities, right?" she chatted, brightening up, which I took as a bad sign.

This wasn't a social visit, and I definitely didn't want to, nor could I, speak about my high-profile clients. And Mercy looked like she was preparing herself to hear some juicy gossip.

"Something like that," I replied vaguely.

"I knew it. I watched *Legally Blonde*."

My skin actually crawled at the mention of that movie. That motion picture had ruined my life because I was blonde and good-looking, and because of that film, many assumed I was bubbly as well. I hated it. It took me years to discourage people from calling me Legally Blonde.

"Well, as a defense lawyer, my job is to defend people whether they are innocent or guilty," I explained, using simple words, feeling it was necessary. This was definitely not going the way I imagined, which was disappointing.

"Right, right," she commented, nodding.

I pushed forward. "I am used to people having problems with me, but something happened recently that has me worried."

"What do you mean?" She cocked her head while asking.

"I think I have a stalker; actually, I know I have a stalker," I corrected. "And I believe they're pretty dangerous."

Her eyes instantly grew big. "Oh my God," she exclaimed.

"Exactly," I agreed. "It first started with a bunch of crazy emails that looked harmless enough; sadly, it escalated."

"What do you mean?" she asked, leaning forward.

"Remember when someone trashed my car?"

"Yes, you said it was some punk."

"I'm not so sure about that anymore."

"What makes you say that?"

"Because my phone got stolen as well, and then I received a taunting email about it."

"Oh my God," she repeated, placing a hand over her mouth.

For a girl from Kansas, all of this must have seemed like a movie plot. Then again, it seemed that way to me too. And I should know, I was born and raised in LA.

"That is terrible, Amber. And I agree, it really sounds like someone is targeting you," she said.

"I am worried things could escalate further," I forced myself to confess.

"Did you call the police?" she asked.

"I filed reports," I said, making a face.

"But?" she prompted.

"There's only so much they can do at this point..." Or even less, considering they hated me.

"I'm sorry all of this is happening to you," she replied, looking genuinely distraught.

I appreciated it, although I was hoping for a little bit more than sympathy.

"I will definitely keep an eye out. And you should speak with Alex. He can let you know if someone suspicious is sneaking about," she offered.

Yeah, because Alex was of much help so far. "I was hoping there's more you can do," I replied honestly.

Once again, she gave me one of those blank stares. "What do you mean?"

This is a bad idea; she can't help me, passed through my head.

"I was wondering if there's any way to track this stalker using their random email accounts?" I asked what interested me the most.

Mercy made a face as though it really pained her to say what was on her mind, as though not wanting to pile on more misery. "There isn't, unfortunately."

"You mean it's not possible legally," I prompted.

"No," she exclaimed, like I'd just insulted her or something by even suggesting that.

"You can't track something that doesn't stay on servers. I'm sorry," she added as though it was somehow her fault it couldn't be done.

"But I thought digital data is eternal," I argued.

"Yes and no. Data remains, but paths to them get erased or corrupted or whatever, making it junk, like debris in space. It's out there, but nobody can reach it."

I didn't think that was a good analogy, but I think I understood what she meant. "I see, well, thank you for clearing that up for me," I said glumly.

Perhaps it was foolish of me to hope all my problems would be solved with a few clicks on a keyboard. Although it would have been nice.

Despite what Mercy said, I started to wonder. I bet the CIA or NSA could find the person who was bothering me, because they had those supercomputers that monitored everything, I mused.

Unfortunately, I didn't know anyone working for the government. At least I didn't think so. *Who knows, perhaps someday, someone might approach me to do service for this country, and then I can ask for a quick quid pro quo,* I joked.

I couldn't wait for that to happen though. I needed this solved as soon as possible, today, because I couldn't live with this threat hanging over my head.

"No problem, Amber, I wish there were more I could do," she replied, snapping me from my thoughts. "However—"

"However?" I repeated, sitting on the edge of my seat. Perhaps there was something that could be done. Something I hadn't thought of.

"There are ways you can protect yourself, virtually speaking."

"What do you mean?"

"You can make your system and your passwords more secure."

"I already changed my passwords. What more can I do?" I asked.

"You can make them pretty difficult, random, harder to crack," she explained.

"You really think that would work against this stalker?" I asked, my doubt plain to see on my face.

"If the person doing all of this is an amateur, then it should," Mercy replied confidently.

"Great," I replied, feeling quite reassured. Suddenly I felt like a great weight had fallen off my shoulders because I now had a clear course of action, a solid plan. "Then that's exactly what I'll do."

And then I had a moment of doubt. My stalker didn't just send threatening emails, they were harassing me in the real world as well.

What to do about those attacks that did not happen in the virtual world? There wasn't an easy fix for those because I didn't know what they would do next.

Realizing what I was doing, ruining my first good news in a while, I banished all those thoughts.

I should start looking at things more positively. Doing what Mercy advised was the first step in the right direction, in dealing with this menace.

Wasn't the first step going to the police? part of me challenged.

"Thank you, Mercy. I truly needed someone to talk to about this," I said, realizing that was actually true.

She was the first person I'd told apart from the police. I hadn't even told Kelly, not wanting to concern her. And I hadn't told my mother because that would be beyond useless. There was nothing she could do to help anyway.

"You are most welcome," Mercy replied, offering a reassuring smile.

Checking the time, I said, "I should probably go. There's a lot I have to do before bedtime."

"The glamorous work of a lawyer never stops."

"Something like that."

"Well, drop by any time you want, and please keep me posted about this stalker business." She practically whispered the last part as though it was a big secret between us.

I nodded in return, but then I decided to say, "Next time I'll bring a bottle of wine."

"As long as it's white, I have no complaints," she said immediately.

"Deal," I replied as I left.

Mercy was just as friendly as I'd thought her to be. She was also more reliable than expected, and I was glad I'd made a mistake about that. She looked kind of strange and goofy, with a terrible sense of fashion, but she was a true professional and actually knew what she was talking about.

She had helped me that evening, and I appreciated that. I left her apartment with sound advice and with peace of mind as well.

Returning home, I felt like our visit hadn't been such a huge waste of my time as I originally believed, and I decided to implement all the things she said as soon as possible. It was fortunate she'd moved in right across the hall from me and had managed to help me when the police couldn't.

For that I will bring her a nice bottle of wine, a really expensive one, I mused.

14

HOT ENCOUNTER

Two days passed, after my talk with Mercy, without any incidents. I received no threats, and nothing had happened outside my apartment or at my workplace.

I was careful, mindful, always on high alert, waiting for something to happen to ruin my day, but nothing did. I constantly checked my inbox, but the threats were absent. The new measures enforced were working. I was pleased that Mercy's advice had helped.

Still, I didn't allow myself to hope that was the end of it. I was still living in fear.

I realized I was succumbing to fear, allowing that crazy man who vandalized my car and stole my phone to get to me, doing precisely what he wanted. I was stressing over him, fearing him, instead of living my life to the fullest. I forced myself to stop thinking about that insignificant person and refocus on what was really important to me, my next promotion.

All the same, that didn't mean I was about to ignore any warning signs. I planned on remaining mindful, within healthy limits, and if something did happen again, then I would act accordingly and solve the problem. The point was not to stress without reason because it was a waste of time and energy.

That lunatic wasn't stronger than me, and I wouldn't let them win. My time, my energy, each piece of me belonged to me, and they couldn't have any of it. *Period.*

Having that epiphany, I called David to come over. I felt like celebrating. At first, he was angry because I'd stood him up the other day. He pouted because he'd waited for me for hours before realizing I wasn't coming.

Once I explained what had happened and how I'd had to deal with car troubles of my own, he was more than happy to come over and comfort me.

Men were so easy to handle, I couldn't fathom why women complained about them. Or even worse, allowed themselves to get bullied and harassed by them.

As was customary, I waited for David by the door. This time I was fully clothed, wanting him to peel each and every item off me slowly before revealing what was underneath.

The big reveal was there was nothing underneath. I was wearing no panties and no bra, and my breasts were really perky in anticipation of what was to come. He instantly kissed me as though he was a starving man and I was his favorite meal.

"I really missed you," I moaned between the kisses as he touched my body all over.

I tried to take his clothes off the instant he stepped inside my apartment. I was constantly mindful that Alex was on watch and made sure we were properly locked in and hidden inside my place before starting anything too graphic.

"I missed you too," he breathed against my lips, and I shivered.

After all the stress I'd endured, this was exactly what I needed. It was such a shame David couldn't handle us being only sex buddies because having him more frequently in my bed would have advantages. As it was, I had to pace myself and him.

And then he started to speak again, breaking my trail of thoughts. "You know, while I waited for you that night beside my car—"

"I said I was sorry," I countered defensively. I couldn't understand why he felt the need to bring that up again during such a passionate moment. I'd already explained what had happened and apologized. What more could he want? "Let me make it up to you," I said to him seductively. Though when I went for a kiss, he wouldn't let me kiss him.

"Oh, I know," he was quick to reassure me. He grabbed me by the hands and walked me toward the couch so we could sit down.

What the hell?

"It's just that while I was there, I spotted this nice family restaurant that looked kind of cool."

"That's great," I mumbled in return, not seeing the point of this conversation. *Why are we not naked by now?* I reached for him.

"I would like us to go."

I recoiled. "Where?" I asked, a bit confused. Was he still droning on about that restaurant? *Why? Why is he doing this to me, and now?* I wanted him to fuck me not bore me to death with his nonsense.

"To that restaurant, on a proper date," he replied, wearing a pretty sheepish smile.

"We can't go out on a date, you know that," I countered adamantly.

"Why not?" David rebelled, crossing his arms over his chest.

At times like this, I wondered if he was worth it. If sex with him was worth all the drama, no matter how young and hot he was.

"Because someone could see us." *And tell your father* was heavily implied.

"I don't care about that," he rebelled like a petulant child.

I knew he didn't actually mean it. He was terrified of his father, and I only had to remind him of that. However, I couldn't do that because he would rebel. So I changed my tactics.

"I can't have rumors spread about me. Not when I just started my new job," I said, making a sad face.

"We'll be careful," he tried to reassure me. "This place is super remote and private."

There was so much hope in his voice, which was irritating. *Why won't he let this go?* I silently screamed.

"I can't take that chance. I've worked hard to earn my place and build a certain reputation. And one wrong rumor could ruin all that, David," I replied. It was the absolute truth too.

I didn't want people to think I got the job merely because I was sleeping with Grant's son. I was sure that was exactly what people would believe because they were envious and spiteful.

Although I knew Grant wouldn't say anything if he found out, I would lose his patronage to a degree, and that was something I couldn't let happen. No amount of sex with David was worth that.

David's face darkened. He stood up from the couch, shaking his head. He turned his back to me, but I could see there was something going on inside his head. He was thinking way too much.

"David, please understand how that would be impossible. We could have a date here, though," I offered, although I didn't know why I bothered.

That made him turn to look at me. "You know what?"

"What?" I asked although I knew he'd said it rhetorically.

That threw him off a little, as I intended, but he recovered quickly, continuing, "I've been trying to convince myself all this time that I was crazy, that you really do care about me, but now I see you don't really care about me at all. I'm nothing but a booty call for you, a piece of meat you can play with and then discard."

While he was having his hissy fit, all I could think about was how our roles were reversed. He was acting like a wronged woman, and I was the sleazy man. Of course, nothing could be further from the truth.

He had been fine with all the sex at first. The problem was, his ego was now because I wasn't expecting anything else from him, and that stung. It wasn't that he wanted me that badly. It was that I didn't want him enough. And that was sad.

He should get over himself. He wasn't that young, to still be plagued by such childish things. Then again, I knew some men in their prime, even older than that, who still behaved similarly. So perhaps it was a man thing, not a David thing altogether.

All the same, I wasn't in the mood for this kind of behavior, not now, not ever. Then again, if that was how he wanted to spend the evening rather than having an amazing time in bed with me, then so be it. He would definitely lose the argument because I was born to argue, in and out of the courtroom alike.

I leaned against the back of the couch, mimicking his posture by folding my arms across my chest. "If that were true, if I simply wanted a boy toy and nothing else, I would pick someone else." I could see him recoil.

He definitely didn't expect to hear that. I didn't stop there, though. There was more that he needed to hear because David had to be put back in his place, and fast, so things like this wouldn't happen again.

"I definitely wouldn't be risking my new job and my flawless reputation to sleep with you specifically," I snapped in return, irked it had to come to this. Annoyed he'd ruined a perfectly good night for us with his petty feelings. And I wasn't sorry I was trying to make him feel bad. He tried to make me feel guilty first, so he needed to see I could play that game too.

"You are just saying that to win this argument," he huffed in return.

He'd clearly picked up on some things being constantly surrounded by lawyers, I noted.

"When two people argue, they are both trying to win in a way, yet that doesn't mean you're right. I was saying that because it's the truth."

And it was to a degree. It was just not the whole truth. I was with David because he'd offered himself on a silver platter. I thought it would be fun. And then I discovered how thrilling it was to have Grant's son in my bed. All the sneaking around was exciting.

Then again, arguing about dates and things like that was anything but fun.

"I'm with you because I want to be, despite my better judgment," I added, being honest again.

"What do you mean by that?"

"What I've been saying the entire evening. It could be very harmful to me, and for you too, if somebody discovered we were in any kind of relationship together. Yet here I am."

His eyes narrowed. "If that were true, if you really cared, then you would prove it."

"I don't appreciate being blackmailed," I said in return, with such finality that I hoped he would pick up on the fact he was on thin ice.

"This is not me blackmailing you. This is me asking you to put money where your mouth is."

"What?"

"Go out on a date with me."

I groaned inwardly. I couldn't believe how stubborn he was being about this. And why was he digging his heels in tonight?

I realized I couldn't accomplish anything with reason, so I decided to change tactics. "Why am I not enough for you? I feel like you're doing this because you have this need to show me around, secretly hoping your dad will catch us together. Well, I'm not going to be used like some pawn in your game against your father. That's not only childish, but it's also irresponsible, not to mention harmful to me."

"That is insane. I want to spend some time alone with my girlfriend outside of this..."

A loud bang, which ended with a crash, made us pause. The noise came from my front door. Something was clearly thrown against it. And then a strange, potent odor reached our noses.

It's him again, passed through my head.

"Stay behind me," David ordered as he reached the door.

With one swift movement, he opened the door, and I screamed.

My front door and the hallway beyond were on fire.

15

FIRE AND SMOKE

Someone had broken a bottle of something highly flammable because my front door and the hallway beyond were ablaze. I just stared at it, motionless, as though spellbound, while the fire advanced.

I couldn't believe this was happening. I couldn't believe someone had tried to burn down my apartment. This couldn't be a coincidence. I was on the twenty-fifth floor, for crying out loud.

I wanted to rub my eyes because I couldn't believe what I was seeing. I realized the smoke was starting to irritate my eyes; the compulsion came from that, not my emotional state. Although there was a chance it was a little bit of both.

Luckily, David recovered quickly. "Where is the fire extinguisher?" he asked, moving away from the door.

"I don't know," I managed to stammer.

How are we going to get out? That door was the only way out. We were trapped. I was going to die, suffocate, burn alive. *Someone is trying to burn me alive.* My mind started to spiral.

"Amber, are you listening to me?" David started shaking me.

"What?"

"Do you think there's one in the hallway?"

"I don't know, maybe."

"Ok, let's go," he said, moving toward the fire.

"What are you doing?" I asked, in panic, stopping him. "We can't go through that; it's on fire."

"It's our only way out," he argued. "Or do you want to jump off the balcony?"

Falling from the twenty-fifth floor wouldn't be pretty. *Is it better than being burned alive?* I shook my head. I couldn't die. I didn't want to die.

"No. But we can't walk through fire. We'll get burned," I argued, not really sure why. David was trying to save us. But my panic was stronger than my reason at that moment.

"We have to do something. We can't stay here."

While I was looking around, trying to remember if I had something big enough to collect water in, David grabbed a blanket from my couch and went to the guest bathroom.

"What are you doing?" I chased after him.

"I'm going to soak this so we can walk through the door."

"Please hurry; it's getting worse," I urged, looking behind me, at the door, as though expecting the fire to sneak up on me, catch me, trap me, burn me.

Stop it, I screamed at myself as my heart beat like crazy.

I was scared out of my mind. Nothing I'd ever experienced in my life so far could have prepared me for this moment, and I couldn't prevent how I was feeling: helpless, desperate, terrified, and small. I couldn't wrap my head around the fact someone was actually trying to kill me.

This was no coincidence. This didn't simply happen. Someone had thrown that bottle against my door, hoping to trap me inside. And the worst part? It was late enough for that person to think I was asleep.

"Let's go." David threw the soaked blanket over the flames in the doorway for us to walk over.

The place was filled with smoke, and I couldn't stop coughing. And then the sprinklers finally came on, and the smoke doubled, making it impossible for us to breathe, let alone see anything.

"Cover your mouth," he ordered, and then took his shirt off to create masks for us. He used his free hand to grab mine and started dragging me out the door.

Every part of my body screamed I should move away from this danger. Despite my fear, I allowed David to lead the way.

As the sprinklers did their thing, dousing everything with water, we dashed out of the apartment. Only then did I realize that the fire alarm was blasting, and other people had started to leave their residences as well.

Not wanting to risk taking the elevator, we started the descent down the stairs. It took us a while. Luckily, I was in my house slippers instead of heels, and we managed to reach the hall.

Alex looked at us with a bewildered expression on his face. A phone was plastered against his ear. I hoped that meant he was on the phone with the fire department.

We watched from across the street as black smoke gushed through my windows. I felt like crying. In one moment, my perfect apartment had been ruined by the fire, the smoke and water.

The firefighters came in record time, rushing inside the building and taking care of the remains of the fire. But it was too little, too late. I was sure everything was ruined by now. *I just lost everything*, I thought in despair.

Where was I going to live? I didn't want to move. Then again, I had much greater concerns to deal with right now. Still, it was easier to deal with the easier problems than face the hardest ones.

I can't believe someone did this to me. Someone tried to kill me! Tried to burn me alive.

David embraced me, holding me tight in his arms, and only then did I realize I'd said all that out loud.

"Don't worry, everything will be all right," he tried to comfort me. "You're all right, here, with me. I won't let anything happen to you."

The way he said that, although I was sure it was for the purest of reasons, as though I was his beloved, the most precious thing in his world, freaked me out. And the fact I was crying without realizing it only added to that. I moved away from him somewhat awkwardly.

Trying to move past this moment, I returned my gaze to the apartment above.

I will return fire for fire. I will burn the person who did this to me, I thought, starting to get angry. It was much easier and more productive to be enraged than scared. I never wanted to feel this scared ever again in my life.

"Who would do this to you?" David asked. "I mean, this can't be an accident. Someone aimed for your door specifically."

Wow, that is very smart of you, I wanted to snap at him, since he was being Captain Obvious, but held my tongue. Lashing out at him would accomplish nothing. It would definitely not make me feel better after witnessing my apartment go up in flames.

Naturally, I was exaggerating.

The only thing that could make me feel better at the moment was justice with a large scoop of revenge. I wanted whoever did this to suffer the way I was suffering as I witnessed this scene, experience the feeling of knowing someone hated them enough to want them dead.

I would only feel better once they'd experienced and felt what I wanted them to feel, which would be so much more, so much worse, because they definitely deserved it.

"Please, Amber, talk to me," David begged.

Probably because I was so rattled and distraught, I decided to tell him everything. "I have a stalker."

"A stalker?" he repeated, eyes wide. "Since when?"

"Since I got promoted."

"That long, and you didn't tell me about it?"

Why are you making it about you? I wanted to say but held my tongue.

"Do you have any idea who this stalker is?"

If I did, I would be knocking on their door with a baseball bat, or hiring a hitman. "No."

"Are you sure?"

I gritted my teeth. "Of course I'm sure. Sadly, the list is too long, considering what I do for a living," I replied, getting angry, but David didn't seem to take offense. Not that I cared.

"Has he tried anything like this before?"

"No, not like this." This was definitely an escalation. I knew this or something similar would happen. And I was right. And the worst part, the most infuriating part was that I'd warned the police it would come to this, and they didn't believe me. Somehow all that didn't make me feel any better.

"So what happened before?"

"I received a bunch of angry, crazy emails, my car got trashed, and my phone was stolen. That's it so far."

That's it? That sounded silly to me, as though what had happened wasn't anything important at all, yet here I was.

"Did you tell the police?"

"Yes, I have spoken to them. They said there wasn't enough evidence, so there's nothing they can do."

"Did you ask my father for help?"

"No, I didn't want to trouble anyone."

Perhaps that was my mistake. Trying to deal with a crazy person on my own. Then again, I didn't do that by choice. I was forced to deal with a crazy person on my own because the police wouldn't help me. The fact I'd almost got killed was on them.

"And you think this fire tonight is the work of the same person?" David asked next.

It would be too horrific to think I had two crazy people after me. "Yes," I replied.

His grip around me tightened. "I can't believe someone tried to set fire to your apartment."

With me in it. I couldn't think about that, because if I did, I would start to spiral again, and I couldn't afford that. I needed a cool head to plan my next course of action.

"I'm so glad I was here with you tonight."

Surprisingly, me too. If David weren't there, I would have—

"Thank God for sprinklers."

A far worse tragedy would have occurred if I lived in a building that wasn't as secure as this one. Then again, I was really starting to doubt the building's security, if this maniac had managed to reach the twenty-fifth floor and set my apartment on fire.

"Maybe you should move someplace more secure, or hire a bodyguard," David offered as solutions.

I frowned while every part of my being rebelled against those ideas. I didn't want to move from my apartment. I'd worked really hard to acquire it. And I definitely didn't want some man following me around, "guarding" my every move. That wasn't living. That was a prison sentence. And I wasn't the one who belonged in a jail cell. This maniac who tried to kill me did.

Besides, why even think about relocating before inspecting the damage to the apartment? Perhaps it wasn't that bad. Perhaps everything could be fixed quickly.

Then again, even if I was lucky and the fire damage wasn't extensive, I still had to think about the water damage and the fact the whole place would stink of smoke, probably forever.

Not even that convinced me moving was the best idea. The most stubborn part of me woke up, refusing to see reason in such an action. I wouldn't move. I wouldn't give that lunatic the satisfaction of knowing they'd managed to force me out of my home.

I was staying. *Period.*

"Amber, did you hear what I said?" David prompted.

"I don't want to move," I replied adamantly.

"It doesn't have to be permanent," David tried to reassure me. "Only until this maniac is caught."

"I won't run away just because they're trying to intimidate me," I argued, breaking my embrace with David.

"They've tried more than that, Amber. They tried to set

your apartment on fire. Not caring the entire building could have gone up in flames, as well," he said blatantly.

I shook my head. "I've made up my mind."

I could see the firefighters finally leaving the building. I took that as a good sign, that they'd managed to deal with the fire, which was a relief.

"Then I'm staying with you," David said, taking me by surprise. "I'm not leaving you alone to deal with this."

I raised my hand, as though to stop him. "I can't talk about this right now," I replied and turned to cross the street. I knew the police and the fire department had to be desperate to speak with me, seeing as the fire had been intended for my apartment and me.

I gave my statement and was proud of myself for how calm I sounded considering what had just occurred. I told them what had happened, how David and I had heard a noise right before my door caught fire.

The fire chief corroborated my story, offering a piece of charred glass that he believed contained gasoline, which had been used to start the fire.

Someone made a Molotov cocktail and threw it against my door, hoping it would be enough to kill me.

Once the emergency services left, I knew I'd have to deal with my insurance company once again. I decided to leave all that for tomorrow. I was thoroughly spent tonight.

Although it pained me, I forced myself to wait for the elevator, ignoring the stares from the other residents around me, and ride to the twenty-fifth floor.

The front door was pretty much ruined, but it did close, thankfully. The carpeting inside was charred and soggy from the water. The whole place reeked.

Without uttering a word, I left all the windows open and

went to my bedroom. Still fully clothed and dirty, I curled in my bed. A few moments later I felt David wrapping his arms around me.

David stayed by my side the whole night, offering moral support. And despite my complaints, I had to admit, if only to myself, it felt kind of nice having him around.

I fell asleep.

16

THE LIST

The day after the fire was pure chaos. Being confronted with all the damage in daylight was beyond heartbreaking. But it wasn't as bad as it could have been. I would definitely have to replace a couple of things, the front door included. However, the wooden floor beneath the rugs bore no real damage from the water, which was a huge relief.

The whole place reeked beyond imagination, though I had faith it would all air out with time. If not, I would buy incense in bulk.

Unfortunately, my misfortunes didn't stop there. Once I'd dealt with the insurance company, I had to deal with a lot of whiny neighbors who acted as though their apartments had suffered fire damages, not mine.

Also, Mercy came at some point and looked beyond freaked out that this had happened to me. She hadn't been home when all of it went down, I learned. She had been out with a new friend for the evening.

"I'm so sorry I wasn't home. If I had been, then maybe I

would have seen who did this to you," she said, sounding sincere.

"It's not your fault. Besides, I should be the one who's sorry. This maniac could have burned down your apartment as well."

It was a miracle her door hadn't been damaged. More to the point, it wasn't even singed. That was a huge relief considering she lived right across from me, and the fire had been pretty substantial. The last thing I wanted was to have to pay for her repairs as well.

"Did the security cameras see anything?"

"No, it was blacked out." I huffed, annoyed that I didn't even have that to rely on to catch this person.

"So they knew what they were doing; that's terrifying." She shivered.

If there was a silver lining in this tragedy, it was that the police had finally decided to do something about my case.

Apparently, someone trying to burn me alive was a clear sign to them they were wrong in thinking I was making a big deal out of nothing. It made them believe I had a maniac harassing me. It was obvious they wouldn't stop until they were caught, which forced the cops to do their job for a change.

Although I wanted to take a day off, I decided to go to work anyway. There was nothing I could do while the apartment aired and dried itself, so it was better not to be home and brood, and instead actually accomplish something at work.

Besides, David had helped me throw the damaged carpet away, which was all that needed to be done right then.

Naturally, I told Grant about what had happened, and he

gracefully offered me one of his townhouse apartments to stay at while I dealt with my own.

To be perfectly honest, I was tempted for a moment to say yes. It would be better to stay at his place, where I could be anonymous, rather than check into a hotel. But knowing such a generous offer would come with strings attached, like night visits from Grant, I declined.

I tried really hard to keep myself busy because if I stopped to think about what had happened, I would go mad. Fear and anger combined. Intertwined, it would consume me, and that was something I couldn't allow.

While I was immersed in a case, once again having to bail my client from some shady business, I got a call from the assigned detective, who asked when he could come to speak with me. Apparently, the statement I gave to the officer on the scene last night wasn't enough. Detective Ronnie Sheldon had to personally speak with me because he had questions.

I invited the detective to my new office. I knew it would be better to do this interview at my apartment so I could walk him through everything that had happened, so he could see all the damages, but I couldn't stand being there while the place reeked of smoke and burned wood.

That was precisely why I'd decided to spend a few nights in a hotel. Last night I had been absolutely exhausted and could have slept anywhere, but from tonight on I would choose better accommodations until everything was fixed.

Naturally, David offered to let me sleep at his place, but I declined. The last thing I needed was for Grant to discover I was sleeping with his son. Not to mention David would get the wrong idea and think that sleeping at his place meant we were in a real relationship.

David kept calling, but I ignored him.

When did my life turn into such a soap opera? I had no idea.

Soon Detective Sheldon arrived. He looked at least ten years older than me, really tall and lean, wearing a plain black T-shirt, and jeans paired with a leather jacket. His skin was really dark, his eyes dark brown, and his hair cropped short. There was a perpetual frown on his face.

Overall, it was obvious his job was taking a serious toll on him; then again, *the same could be said about all of us.* I didn't know why, but he was the first police officer I'd met who actually looked competent.

I believed he could help me, which was why I decided to fully cooperate and do everything I could to help him catch the guy because it was in my best interest, after all.

After Detective Sheldon settled in a chair opposed to mine, he went straight to business. "Miss Dennis, could you walk me through last night's events?"

"I was home, with my"—I had no idea how to define my relationship with David, I realized in a split second—"boyfriend," I settled on, although it pained me to give him such a title, "when it happened. We heard a loud thud, like something hitting the door. Then there was a crash, and when David opened the door, we could see everything was on fire. We barely managed to escape before the sprinklers came on, and the fire department arrived."

He was making notes, although I was sure he already knew all of this from the report I'd given last night to the officer on the scene.

"Has this happened before?"

"Did someone try to burn me alive? No," I replied a bit defensively.

"Has anyone threatened you recently?" he corrected.

"Actually, yes."

I told him everything about my stalker. "It started with threatening emails; however, it escalated from there. My car got trashed, and my phone was stolen right out of my hand."

"How do you know it's all connected?"

"Because the stalker mocked my loss of the phone. It was obvious they organized it to torment me," I replied. "Naturally, I went to the police to report those crimes," I made sure to mention, offering him all the documentation I possessed.

Detective Sheldon sifted through all the reports and the copies of the threatening emails. "Do you mind if I keep these?"

"Not at all." I had another set of copies anyway.

"Do you have any idea who would want to hurt you in such a way?" He asked one of the most obvious questions.

It always astounded me that the police expected me to do their job. Perhaps I was wrong in believing him to be a competent detective.

"I don't know, Detective."

"What about love interests, past and present alike?"

I leaned back in my chair. "If you are about to insinuate this was the deed of someone I was romantically involved with, then I would have to say you are seriously mistaken."

"Women are most often stalked by either unsuccessful would-be lovers or exes," he insisted.

There were a lot of people in my life who fit that bill. Most obvious was Grant, but that was beyond ridiculous. Grant would never threaten me just to get me into bed.

He did offer his apartment. I stopped myself there. I wouldn't allow this detective to fill my head with nonsense. Still, he was a detective, so I was sure he knew what he was talking about. Perhaps there was someone in my life I was overlooking.

Still, I shook my head. "Unfortunately, no one comes to mind. And all my split-ups were pretty amicable." Not to mention I was not the dating type, so it was a pretty short list.

"Have you noticed someone at work? Is someone acting differently around you? Out of the ordinary?" he asked next.

"No, not really." I didn't even have to think about that. All my colleagues were just that. I had adequate working relationships with most of them. The rest I avoided because they were incompetent fools, and I hated working with dead weight. It was easier and better to work alone than have to deal with people with such attributes.

"Tell me about the man you were with last night, then."

I knew it would come to that; however, I still resented the question. I didn't want to speak about David because I was paranoid enough to think it could reach Grant.

"He saved me. If he weren't there, I don't know if I would have been able to get out of the apartment," I said and offered nothing else.

Detective Sheldon tried one more time to engage me in conversation about David. Get more information about him, but I refused. The less he knew, the better. Better for me, naturally.

"You're aware that the more information I gather, it will help me do my job and catch this perpetrator," the detective said.

"There isn't much to be said about David. He is not someone you should focus on."

"Shouldn't you let me be the judge of that?"

"In this case, no."

"Are you hiding something, Miss Dennis?"

"Plenty, since that is part of my job, to keep my clients' secrets. Nonetheless, in this case, no. I want this monster caught. Never doubt that."

"This was done by someone who knows you. Has a close watch on you," he said.

I couldn't decide if he'd said that because he wanted to scare me into sharing more information about David, or because he was an asshole who wanted to scare me. Either way, I wasn't falling for it.

"Now that you've mentioned it, I can think of a few clients who might hold grudges against me."

"Why do you think one of those individuals could be targeting you?"

"To put it bluntly, either for not getting them off the hook for what they did, or for failed romantic advances."

"Do you have their names?"

I hesitated. The only reason I'd mentioned them was to move this conversation past David. I didn't want any one of my former clients to get in trouble, especially since I didn't really believe any one of them was doing this to me. Then again, this detective wouldn't stop until I gave him something.

"Yes, of course." Seeing no other way, I wrote four names on a piece of paper:

Tom O'Brien, Nihal Johnson, Jeremy Selke, and Georgina Pyke.

They were already lost clients, so it was no great sacrifice if the detective visited them and accused them of harassing me.

"I will definitely speak with them," he said, going through it.

"I wouldn't dare tell you how to do your job, Detective, all the same, I really think you're on the wrong track there. These clients are a long shot at best."

"It's better to check all the leads, just in case." He remained adamant.

If he wanted to waste time, that was his right, his problem. But while he did that, this lunatic could target me again, and that was something I wasn't all right with.

"Of course, Detective," I replied, but it was obvious I thought of it as a huge waste of time.

"Now tell me, Miss Dennis, what about your coworkers? Is there someone who harbors a grudge against you?"

Instantly Phoebe came to mind. That woman absolutely detested me. And then Caleb, Patricia, and Mina because I beat them in the race for promotion.

I shook my head. "Sadly, nobody comes to mind," I replied eventually.

Even if it was one of them, I was sure Grant would want this kind of thing dealt with internally. If it wasn't one of them and I sent a detective after them, that would cause a major scandal in the firm. Everyone would turn against me, and that was something I couldn't afford.

"Miss Dennis, whoever did this clearly harbors a personal grudge against you of some kind. If you want me to catch this person, you should be one hundred percent honest with me," he said, calling me out on my bullshit.

"I understand that, Detective. And I am sorry I can't be of more help."

It was obvious he wasn't pleased with my reply and decided not to press. "If you think of someone, or if anything else happens, please call me personally," he said, offering his business card.

"Of course," I promised.

"Oh, and where are you staying?" he asked as an afterthought.

"I'll be sleeping at a hotel tonight, and I plan on returning to my apartment as soon as I can."

"Perhaps it would be better if you stayed in a hotel until the perpetrator is caught," he suggested.

I was really sick and tired of hearing that. "I refuse to cower from this person. I will return to my apartment as soon as possible because that's my home." And I paid way too much for it to simply abandon it.

He was about to say something else, clearly wanting to instill some last-minute wisdom, when Grant barged inside my office. Without knocking of course.

"I just wanted to see if everything was all right in here," he said gruffly, eyeing the detective.

"Yes, it is. The detective and I are finished. Detective, this is my boss, Michael Grant. Detective Ronnie Sheldon." I made the introductions.

The two men nodded at one another.

"You'd better find this man, Detective. I can't have my star lawyer in danger," Grant said.

"I'll do my best," the detective replied, looking at me.

And for some reason, I believed him.

17

THE REPAIRS

Two days later, in the midst of all my pain and frustrations over my apartment, not to mention the knowledge someone had tried to kill me and the stress of worrying about what was happening, why it was happening, and what my life had turned into, there was a knock on my door that changed everything.

I opened the door timidly, wondering if David had come to surprise me, only to find a stranger on the other side. He was tall, muscular, with a deep tan. His hair was blond, streaked with brown, and he had hazel eyes.

What if this is my stalker? Fear rushed through my body. I took a step back, ready to slam the door. And then I noticed the tool belt.

"My name is Allan Whatley. I've been sent by the building's manager, Hughes, to assess and repair the fire-related damage."

"It's about time," I replied, although this was a very nice surprise. I knew everything would be taken care of, but I had started to lose hope as too many days had passed.

"Sorry," he replied a bit sheepishly, scratching the back of his head. "I had to finish the last job before taking on another."

A man with integrity. I could understand that.

"Well, these are the damages," I said, pointing to the area we were standing in. "The front door sustained the most damage, and then there's the carpet."

The hallway carpet. The one inside my apartment was already gone. David and I had thrown it out. I decided I kind of liked not having it. The wooden floor was nice, and I wanted to show it off a little. The walls were slightly singed on both sides too.

"Mr. Hughes informed me as much." He crouched to inspect the carpet more closely. "Something really nasty happened here," he commented, standing up again.

Someone tried to burn me alive. "I have a psycho stalker harassing me." Somehow saying that out loud didn't sound any better.

Allan gave me a strange look, as though he wasn't sure if I was joking or not. His next words confirmed as much. "You're kidding, right?"

"Unfortunately, I'm not."

"That's terrible," he said.

I nodded.

He scratched the back of his head again, and I wondered if that was a nervous tic of his. "And here I was thinking this was a drunken party gone wrong."

"I wish," I replied honestly.

"I'm glad nothing happened to you," he offered next, clearly uncomfortable that this conversation had taken such an unexpected turn.

Nothing happened to me this time.

"That makes two of us," I said, trying to brighten the mood. I wasn't successful, and an awkward silence ensued.

Allan was the first to recover. "I took the liberty of ordering you a new door," he offered, pointing at the wall to the left. And true enough, there was a new door waiting there. Identical to the one ruined in the fire.

I made a face. "Actually, I was thinking of getting a metal one this time around." I didn't want to take any chances; I needed something that wouldn't burn down.

"Metal?" he repeated. "I don't know if that's up to the building's code."

I waved that away. "Let me deal with Mr. Hughes. I want a metal door."

Let's see that man stop me from feeling secure in my own place. He was lucky I hadn't sued him and the rest of the building for almost burning alive right under their security noses.

Allan looked unclear about his next course of action. "How about I install this one for now so you have a new door that doesn't stink up the place, and then we can order you a metal one," he offered, clearly trying to find a way to still do some work today and not waste time while billing more hours.

"All right," I agreed.

"As for the hallway carpet, I will need several days since it's custom made," he offered next.

I just stared at him while he spoke. He was really beyond hot, in that rugged handyman kind of way. He wasn't someone you wanted to introduce to your friend circle, but he was definitely someone you'd want in your bed. At least for a little while.

"How about the walls?" I asked, merely to stop myself

from thinking about him in such a way. I had David if I needed to scratch that itch anyway. Not that I had seen him since the fire, though he did text and check on me.

He'd insisted on staying with me, since his primal protective instincts were running wild, but I'd nipped that in the bud and kicked him out. I couldn't tolerate such behavior while in the midst of a crisis. Especially in the middle of a crisis.

Allan leaned forward to inspect my walls. "It's the same color. I can paint all the walls the day after tomorrow."

"Excellent." The sooner I was done with this hassle, the better. "Do you need anything from me?" I asked, trying to be helpful.

"At the moment, only access to your door."

Was that him flirting or merely being professional? Either way, I nodded. "All right, access granted. Do your thing."

"Thank you," he said, moving his tools forward as he started to inspect my door, to determine how to take it off before installing the new one. "I will try to keep it down," he added as an afterthought, pointing at all the papers and my laptop on the table next to a couch.

"I would appreciate that."

I did have some work to do that morning before going to the firm. And I didn't want to retreat to the home office, partly because I wanted to keep an eye on him, make sure he was doing everything correctly and only what we'd agreed upon since he was a stranger, after all. And partly because I wanted to watch him while he worked.

I sat on the sofa, making sure I had the perfect view of him while I went over my documents. I was happy to see Allan didn't disappoint. All the bending over, heavy lifting, and moving the old door away to install the new one made his muscles bulge over and over. It was a true delight to ogle him while I pretended to work.

Realizing I actually needed to work, because I was meeting an important man that afternoon whom I needed to impress, I forced myself to concentrate on the papers in front of me and not on Allan.

"I'm sorry if the noise keeps distracting you from work," he said, clearly noticing I'd been looking at him.

Busted.

"It's fine," I reassured him instantly. "I just needed to review something before work," I explained with a smile.

"What do you do for a living?" he asked, looking genuinely interested.

"I'm a lawyer."

"It figures," Allan commented.

"Why do you say that?" I asked, offering a smile. I was genuinely curious, not only trying to keep up a conversation. I had never before been characterized as a typical lawyer. Usually, people told me I was too beautiful to be a lawyer, which I found insulting.

I hated when people tried to compliment me, saying I should be an actress or a model. Even one of my professors had tried to give me advice, saying how I didn't have to work so hard in life considering I already possessed the looks.

If my motivation were that low, perhaps I would have listened. As it was, I aimed much higher, and meager wealth and some fame held no appeal to me.

"You look really smart, and you dress like a lawyer."

I was wearing one of my favorite skirts and a matching jacket combination. "Are you trying to tell me I dress dull?" I countered, trying to tease him.

"Not at all. You dress like a successful businesswoman who has style."

That was a good answer. I wondered if he had sisters, a girlfriend, or a wife. Not that it mattered. "And you look like you need something to drink."

He chuckled. "Nice save," implying I had nothing good to say about him.

"Oh, no, you look very competent in what you do," I tried to compliment.

"Thanks, and you're right. I could use a glass of water. This door was heavy."

Yet it had looked featherlight when he'd handled it. "Just a glass of water? Are you sure you don't want anything else? I can make you some freshly squeezed lemonade," I offered.

"Water is fine, thank you," he reassured me.

Less than a minute later I watched him drink a whole bottle of water. Watching that mouth work gave me a lot of ideas.

Should I make a move? I started to wonder. He was friendly enough the whole time, but I wasn't sure if he was flirty or not.

At times it was hard to distinguish good manners from flirtiness. Then again, I saw nothing wrong in trying. I wouldn't be too torn about it if he refused me. But if he said yes, *Oh, the fun we would have...*

Naturally, I would make him an offer he couldn't refuse after he was done with all the work. I didn't want to make it awkward. Or for him to think he could slack off at work just because I'd allowed him to fuck me as well.

That was why it was important to let him do his job first. Men had one-track minds and were unable to multitask. Better not confuse the poor man and force him to make mistakes, especially since I didn't have a lot of patience and wanted the damage sorted as soon as possible. I couldn't stand having all the reminders that some lunatic was stalking me and had tried to kill me.

"Thanks for the water. I really needed it."

"No problem."

"Fifteen minutes more and then I'll be out of your hair," he reassured me.

I checked the time. That worked for me as well. I needed to leave soon, and there was no chance in hell I would leave this man alone inside my apartment. I would much rather miss work, which was saying a lot.

It was strange I had problems with that and not with letting him in my bed. But what could I say? I was a complicated woman.

"That's fine," I said in return.

Feeling like I'd wasted too much time on this handyman, I finally concentrated on work. In the next instant, I heard Allan clearing his throat.

"I'm done," he declared.

The way he said it, it was as though he expected an attaboy or a cookie, a golden star for a job well done.

"All your locks are the same," he added.

It looked good. I said as much. "But this is only temporary, right? I still want a metal one."

"I will bring you a catalog you can choose from," he reassured me. "Ok, see you the day after tomorrow."

Is that a promise? "See you."

"Around the same time. Does that work for you?"

Was he stalling on purpose? "Let me check my calendar." I looked through my phone quickly. "I don't have to be at the office until noon."

He nodded. "I'll be done before that."

Not if I require some additional work from you. "Thank you for the door, Allan, and see you soon," I said before seeing him off.

I caught a whiff of his cologne. It smelled divine. I wondered what it was. *Perhaps I could buy a bottle for David.*

Speaking of David, I couldn't help comparing the two. Allan was definitely a man. *I wonder if he's better than David in bed.*

THAT AFTERNOON my meeting with a potential client went great, which meant I was now representing the vice president of a major marketing company. Grant would be very pleased with me.

Returning home, I had a smile on my face when I checked out my new door. Although it looked exactly like the old one. I wasn't necessarily thinking about the door, but the handyman who'd installed it.

My good mood was short-lived because my phone started ringing. It was my mother, which was a surprise.

My first thought was that something had happened. Or she'd come up with something new to whine about why her life was so difficult, and wanted to share it with me.

"I wanted to check up on you and see how the new job is going."

"It's going great. I had no troubles adjusting."

"Did something else happen in the meantime?" she added after a short pause when it became clear I wasn't about to say anything else.

I don't know what exactly possessed me, but I opened my mouth, and all the wrong things came out. "A lot, actually, and nothing good. I have a stalker, and they're really making a mess of my life, sending threats, destroying my car, setting fires."

"Setting fires?" she repeated, clearly horrified. "Amber, that sounds scary."

The tone of her voice reminded me with whom I was speaking. That was why I said, "I know it sounds scary, but the police are handling it." I wasn't sure if I was trying to reassure her or myself. Probably both.

"Amber, are you going to be all right?" she asked. It was obvious she was worried, which, to be honest, took me by surprise.

"Don't worry, everything will be fine. Besides, I'm tougher than some person with an inferiority complex," I said and meant every word.

There was no way in hell I was going to let some lowlife ruin my life, especially not after I'd worked so hard to make everything the way I wanted it to be.

"Just be careful."

"I always am."

18

THE NIGHT OFF

Although I was super busy and dealing with a lot, I still couldn't postpone one commitment long promised, and was forced to have dinner with Kelly.

Usually, that wouldn't be an issue. I liked seeing her every once in a while. But considering my current predicament, not to mention my mood, it was no wonder I was reluctant.

Not that Kelly cared about it. She still dragged me to some new fancy restaurant we had to check out, and I complied. At times, life was easier that way, to do as Kelly wished than suffer the consequences, as in enduring her constant pestering.

The last thing I needed was for her to barge into my law firm. The last time she did that, all the men lost their heads and couldn't function for days.

Sometimes, Kelly had that effect on people. Having rich parents allowed her to have all the best beautification treatments at her disposal. Over time she'd sculpted herself into a piece of art, just the way she wanted, making herself curvy in all the right places, accentuated by always wearing the right clothes. She'd also dyed her hair platinum blonde, like me, except her eyes were brown. Every once in a while, she wore colored contacts for fun.

I hadn't told Kelly anything about my stalker problems, and I probably wouldn't either. If I did, she would panic and overthink things, and I really needed a night out, away from it all. I'd done enough panicking and overthinking on my own as it was.

As always, Kelly came to pick me up. After what had happened to her ten years ago, she didn't drive but had a car and a driver available to her at anytime, anywhere. That was a gift from her father.

The moment I entered the car, and she'd kissed me twice on my cheeks, she started to talk really fast, animated and excited about the new restaurant we were going to eat at.

"I like your hair; it's gorgeous," she said in between as though in afterthought.

"New shade," I replied.

She nodded before continuing her story about this Filipino chef who opened a restaurant on Hollywood Boulevard.

I didn't necessarily care about such things, I just wanted the food to be good, and everything around me clean, but Kelly loved to be seen at the most popular places in the city.

As always, a small army of paparazzi followed and greeted us in front of the Singing Temple restaurant. They were not there because of me, naturally. They were following Kelly around.

Years ago, it had started because she was the daughter of a very famous actress, so tabloids liked to share pictures of her, showing her doing all the mundane things. Nevertheless, as she grew, it evolved. Now they followed her because of her.

Like most children of the extremely rich and famous, Kelly did a lot of things, and nothing, really, at all. She acted, modeled, and sang. She had her clothing line and perfumes and was present on social media and was considered one of the most important influencers of our time.

She was also highly unpredictable, especially while drunk, which explained why the paparazzi loved her and always followed her around each time she left her penthouse.

Kelly posed, smiling, giving them what they wanted, and in return, they were respectful and gave us some space. I was always fascinated by how patient and controlled she was in these situations. I would probably go mad if a dozen men with flashes followed my every move, but Kelly seemed to relish it. It helped she was too good for her own good at times, if that made sense.

A few years back I'd asked her how she could do all that, endure such scrutiny; I was genuinely curious. And her answer was beyond simple. "I really don't mind."

I could see it on her face: she actually meant it. "Why do you do all those things?" I asked next. It wasn't like she needed to do that as her job.

And she shrugged. "Why not?"

For her, it was all fun and games. Besides, she craved attention in any shape and form, so I accepted that.

Kelly was my opposite in almost every regard. She was a true ray of sunshine, always in a good mood, always smiling, and always looking for a good time. And most importantly, she never allowed others to bring her down or ruin her mood.

I admired that about her. I wished I could be more like that. I couldn't. Everything bothered me, especially the incompetence of other people.

Naturally, none of that mattered while I was with Kelly. Being around her always made me feel better. It couldn't be helped. Her good mood was contagious. And although it wasn't sustainable to always look at things from her perspective, it was just what I needed every once in a while.

It took us a while to reach our table since Kelly knew everybody and had to greet a lot of people on the way. When we finally sat down, everyone left us alone and kept their distance.

"So what's new?" she asked once we were settled. "How's the big promotion?"

"Nothing new," I lied. "The new job is great although I haven't had the time to fully enjoy it." I added a dash of truth as well.

Kelly scrutinized me. "What are you not telling me?" she accused. "Spill it."

Fuck. I cursed inwardly. Kelly was far more observant than I gave her credit for at times. And it was a misfortune that this was one of those times. I had two options. Lie to her again; reassure her all was well. I could say that I was merely tired and swamped at work.

Or I could tell her the truth.

Although I knew how she would react, I opted for the second option. I didn't like keeping secrets from her. She was my closest friend, after all. Besides, as a celebrity of a sort, perhaps she had some inside knowledge on how to deal with this maniac. *Perhaps she can help.*

"There is something I haven't told you, actually," I started glumly.

"I knew it," she exclaimed. "Is it a new fuck buddy? Tell me everything," she said all in one breath just as our server arrived.

Kelly ordered a bottle of champagne, sending him away.

"It's not a new fuck buddy." Although I had one of those as well. "I have a stalker."

"What?" Kelly exclaimed again, getting all serious for the first time that evening. "A real stalker?"

I had no idea what a fake stalker was, but I nodded.

She waved her hand dismissively. "You always have a stalker."

And she wasn't wrong. I was used to receiving threatening emails, or someone trying to scare or bully me after losing a case against me. Unfortunately, this lunatic was different.

"This is different. It's not just angry emails from drunken fools. The police are involved as well."

Although their involvement was pretty nonexistent, laughable. It looked like they would be happier to deal with my murder case in the future than bother finding the person who was stalking me now.

Kelly's eyes widened. "What? What did they do to you?"

"Busted my car, stole my phone, and set my apartment door on fire."

Kelly put a hand over her mouth. "Oh my God. Are you all right?"

I found that question rather silly. My mother had asked me the very same thing. And since I was speaking with her,

I'd brushed it all off and put on a brave face, but Kelly was different. I didn't have to bullshit her.

"I honestly don't know. I try to be, but it's hard knowing someone out there really wants to hurt me."

"What did the police say?" Kelly demanded. "Do they know who it is?"

I made a face. "They're beyond incompetent and have no idea who is doing this to me."

"Well, do you suspect anyone?" Kelly asked.

I gave it some thought again. I'd already been through this with the detective.

Eventually, I shook my head. "At first, I thought it was some lunatic holding an imaginary grudge because I won a case against them or something."

"And now?"

"The detective who is assigned to my case thinks it's someone much closer to me, who has personal issues with me. Someone who truly hates me to the center of their being."

Kelly's eyes widened in fear, concern, and shock. "Do you know someone like that?"

I didn't think I did, but now it was hard not to suspect everybody. Naturally, I knew Kelly wasn't the one doing all those things to me, but everyone else was a question mark. And that was terrifying, that I couldn't trust anyone anymore.

What if it's actually David? Because I don't want him the way he wants me?

But he didn't have it in him to do that. Besides, he had been with me when my apartment caught on fire.

"The most logical assumption is that it's one of my coworkers," I replied.

Kelly nodded. "That makes sense."

"I know, I mean, Kelly, I wish you could have been there. You should have seen the faces of some of them when Grant introduced me as the new junior partner."

"Green with envy?"

"Among other things. I thought Patricia's head would explode, based on how angry she looked," I explained.

Kelly actually chuckled. Although we were speaking about serious matters, she was clearly amused at the picture I was painting for her.

"You should keep an eye on her, and the rest. And tell that detective of yours what is going on at work. I mean, it's definitely one of them trying to sabotage you, make you go insane so you lose your job."

"You really think so?" I had a moment of doubt.

"Definitely. You know, models and actors do the same shit to one another when fighting for the same job. So I say check that out," she advised.

I nodded. That sounded like a good plan. I thanked Kelly. I should have known she would be of help. She always was, in her unique way.

"And maybe you should move away for a couple of days."

"I don't want to move."

"That maniac clearly knows where you live. You'd be safer in a hotel," Kelly argued.

"The problem is I don't feel safe anywhere anymore. So I might as well stay," I replied honestly.

"I would invite you to stay at my place, but there is someone new in my life," she said, smiling widely.

That was Kelly all right. She was incapable of having a serious conversation for too long. And I didn't mind. I would much rather talk about her for a while than dwell on my gloomy circumstances.

"Kelly, are you trying to tell me you have a new boyfriend?"

"Yes, and he's just wonderful," she exclaimed.

I rolled my eyes at that, but in good nature. "You always have a new boyfriend." And they were always wonderful, right until the moment she got bored of them.

"Yes, that's true," she agreed with a laugh. "But I like this one."

I've heard that one before. "Who is he? Tell me everything about him," I urged.

"He is super-hot, from California. He's in construction or something, and he's amazing in bed," she said all in one breath.

"That's great, Kelly. I'm really happy for you. How did you guys meet?"

"That's a funny story. I was leaving my friend Net's house..."

As Kelly continued to ramble about her new boyfriend or, more accurately put, the flavor of the month, my mind unintentionally drifted back to my stalker. And the question of who it might be.

Kelly believed it was one of my coworkers, and so did Detective Sheldon. Was it possible one of them really hated me enough to ruin my life or try to kill me? That thought was too terrifying, yet I still pushed forward.

It was true I was ruthless at my job, and at times that meant creating enemies. That was an occupational hazard, and I always accepted that. Unfortunately, not everyone thought like me.

I thought of all the people who could potentially be on

the suspect list. Patricia, Mina, Phoebe, and Caleb made sense.

Then I moved past the most obvious people. What if this was the work of someone I was constantly overlooking? Someone like Bonnie.

19

THE ENEMIES WITHIN

My talk with Kelly really got me thinking. So instead of doing my regular job, earning money and trying to impress Grant, while undermining Phoebe every step of the way, I was obsessing over something else. Or more accurately, someone else.

Who is trying to ruin my life?

I went through the list of people in my life over and over, constantly stressing and worrying. That wasn't something I was particularly proud of, yet it couldn't be helped. All I could do was think about my stalker and how it was more probable than not, they were much closer than I originally believed.

During the peaks of my paranoia, I even considered Bonnie as my archnemesis. Which was beyond ridiculous. I watched her every move throughout the whole day, and she was incompetent beyond belief. That girl could barely assemble a regular letter let alone a threatening one. Not to mention she didn't look like the type of person who associated with shady people. Shady people who would break into my car or set my apartment on fire, I rationalized.

She wasn't my stalker; I was sure of that. Still, that didn't mean that someone else at the firm wasn't.

And that was exactly why I was completing a thorough list of all potential suspects. Naturally, at the top of that list were the coworkers I had been promoted above.

As I did that, my phone rang. It was a photo and a message from Kelly.

In the photo it was her lying in bed next to a man. He was lying on his stomach, turned away from the camera, so all I could see was a massive, tanned back.

Kelly wrote:

I completely wore him down

Shaking my head, I put my phone away without replying. Trying to discourage her from sending such things would only encourage her more, so it was better to ignore it.

Besides, I had more pressing issues than her raging hormones. And that was figuring out who my stalker was.

Following the logic it was someone at the firm, it was safe to assume it was one of the people who were pissed off that I'd been promoted instead of him or her. It fit perfectly when I thought about it. Since the threats started after I'd been promoted.

I will catch you now, you son of a bitch, I thought with renewed energy, feeling like I was finally onto something.

I couldn't refer to my stalker as he because there was a huge possibility my tormentor was actually a woman.

That kind of made sense too because women were known to be sneakier than men. If a man had a problem with you, he would more commonly than not confront you, call you a bitch, and be done with it. Women acted differently, though. They could act as though all was well until they were ready to make a move or strike.

The more I thought about it, the more convinced I became it was one of the associate bitches. It was no secret they hated me, and this was an act of perfect revenge.

The only vexing thing was that I shouldn't have dismissed this thought in the first place just because Grant wouldn't like it.

Then again, I preferred a direct approach when trying to take someone down. Logically looking at things and trying to ignore the fact this was happening to me, I had to admit this tactic was sound as well.

My stalker did promise complete ruination of my life, and this, what I was living at the moment, definitely felt like that. My whole world was crumbling around me, and there was nothing I could do to stop it.

Or was there?

Of course there was something I could do about it. I could compile a list of the most likely suspects and hand it to Detective Sheldon to deal with.

Although I'd been opposed to this at first because I knew Grant wouldn't like having some detective snooping around and harassing employees, I realized I had no other way. I needed to involve him if I wanted this maniac caught. And I wanted that more than anything.

So I decided to implement my most valuable weapon while creating the list of potential stalkers. And that was to pull out my personal files on all the employees I worked with at Grant, Bryant, and Dawson.

I had created these files the moment I started working

for this firm. Over the years I'd managed to accumulate a lot of details on my coworkers. I mainly focused on all their strengths and weaknesses, but a lot of dirt had ended up in those files as well. Some were merely rumors, yet for others, I had concrete evidence. Evidence I used to my advantage each time I needed it.

Looking at the folders, I decided to start with the most obvious candidates, those who were the good associates who'd been overlooked for the promotion.

I had to admit that the best associates, now that I wasn't among them, were definitely Catharine Haze, Morgan Jeffrey Clark, and Dwayne White. However, people who were candidates for the promotion were Caleb Fitzpatrick, Mina Padalecki, and Patricia Miller. That wasn't solely based on their merit, but pure politics. Each of the senior partners had their favorites, so they tried their best to push them forward.

In my honest opinion, Caleb was a pure moron, and Mina wasn't much behind to earn the title as well. They were brats with rich parents who wanted their spawns working at prestigious law firms so they could brag about it to their equally rich friends, and nothing else.

I wrote those names down, focusing on their files.

I was pleased to see I had plenty on each and every one of them, especially on Patricia. They were mostly minor things, mistakes made while we'd collaborated on cases together, because if any one of them had caused a major infraction, I would have made sure they were fired a long time ago.

That was something that wouldn't have worked in my favor. I liked having people around me whom I could control. And people were more easily manipulated and encouraged to do things my way when they knew I could dangle something over their heads.

I'd used everything I had within those files to ensure I got the promotion in the end. And I never felt bad I'd discreetly pointed Grant in the right direction, so he could discover, on his own, how some of his employees were faulty and unfit to be promoted to junior partners. At least not before me.

Besides, I never believed he solely gave me the job because I made sure he knew about other people's mistakes. I was obviously better than anyone else and made no mistakes, which was precisely why I got the promotion to begin with. I merely made sure Grant knew everything.

Perhaps someone learned what I was doing, I began to speculate, remembering those two secretaries in the bathroom joking about me wanting to take down Phoebe.

Perhaps one of the associates learned I had been sharing my displeasure about them with a senior partner and decided to take revenge on me. It made sense. Sadly, that didn't make my search any easier. The more I read, the more I believed they were all in on it in some way.

There was a possibility my stalker wasn't a single person, but a collective of disgruntled associates. They all looked guilty to me. Each had a "reason" to hold a grudge against me. I'd pointed out their faults and still felt no remorse.

It was possible they saw things differently though. They could be blaming me for not prospering at GBD. Weak people could convince themselves of anything to avoid admitting their own faults.

All the same, their reasoning made no difference to me. I believed one of them, if not all, was doing all these nasty things to me. And because they were fellow lawyers, they would certainly know whom to call, whom to hire for specific, shady business that needed to be done, like trashing my car and all the rest.

But even after compiling such a well-thought-out list, I was still no closer to discovering who looked the guiltiest to me. Who hated me the most?

How was I to decide who was doing this to me among such fine candidates? Unfortunately, after racking my brain the entire morning, I realized that I couldn't.

Not on my own. I needed help. And I hated asking for help. I believed that if I wanted things done and done correctly I needed to do it myself. Unfortunately, this wasn't one of these times.

Although I didn't particularly care about working with someone else, I saw no other way. I had no choice. No matter how much the idea felt wrong to me, I realized I needed to take this list and share it with Detective Sheldon. I was sure he would know what to do next. It was his job, after all, to deal with suspects and find the guilty party.

At least that was the hope. That he was competent enough in what he did to accomplish that. Because I really could not live like this anymore, always looking over my shoulder, looking for threats.

I was about to start printing everything when I reconsidered. I didn't want my coworkers to know I possessed such files, so I copied everything on a flash drive and decided to copy everything at home before sending it to the detective.

I was sure he would be slightly irked with me for not mentioning these people the last time we spoke, but I hoped he would get over it fast and do his job. That was what he was paid to do. To find the bad guys, eliminate threats from civilians' lives, not nurse his bruised ego.

I was on my way out, ready to leave early to deal with everything, when my phone started ringing. I groaned inwardly. It was David again. He was constantly checking up on me after the night of the fire. It was irritating. I really didn't need him playing some kind of hero, since I was definitely not a damsel in distress.

I needed him to fuck me every once in a while, when I felt like it. Yet as of late, I didn't want to bother with him. It was too big a hassle, so I decided to ignore his calls.

Bonnie looked at me questioningly, clearly not understanding why I was leaving in the middle of the day.

"Cancel all my appointments. I have to deal with a personal emergency," I said to her in passing.

"Mrs. Bryant wants to see you," my secretary replied with slight panic in her voice.

I really didn't want to deal with Phoebe. Especially since I knew there was nothing important she needed to speak with me about. She only wanted to see me so she could humiliate me some more and put me back in my place. Well, I was having none of it.

"I will see her tomorrow," I threw over my shoulder.

I was waiting for an elevator when Phoebe approached. "Leaving so soon?" she inquired.

"Yes, I have to deal with something."

"Didn't Bonnie give you my message?" she asked, all innocent, looking as though she didn't already know the answer to that question.

"Yes, but sadly that will have to wait till tomorrow. I have to go to the police station."

"About your personal problems?" She said personal as though it were a dirty word.

"Yes," I replied. "It's about my stalker."

"I see," she replied slowly.

It was obvious she was highly displeased. Then again, there wasn't much she could do about it. If she tried to stop me or even punish me in any way, she would be seen as the witch who didn't care about her employees or their well-being.

Sending a polite smile her way, I entered the elevator.

I made a mental note to move Phoebe Bryant to the top of my list. She wasn't an associate, that was true; nonetheless, she absolutely hated me enough to try to ruin me by any means necessary.

20

THE INTERROGATION

The first time I met Detective Sheldon, he came to my office. Now I was sitting inside his. Or more accurately put, to have some privacy, he took me to one of the interrogation rooms.

By the way he was looking at me, the questions he was asking, I was starting to feel as though I was being interrogated, as though I were one of the guilty parties and not a victim.

Although I detested that word, such characterization, I knew I was precisely that in the eyes of the law. *Just a nameless victim...*

Nonetheless, I had to admit I didn't care about such sentiment one bit. Being scrutinized, questioned, and having to justify my every move definitely wasn't my cup of tea.

All the same, I endured, hoping there was a method to his madness, and that all that was transpiring was for the greater good. My good, naturally.

"Is something wrong, Miss Dennis?" he asked, snapping me from my thoughts.

I gave him a questioning look.

"You keep fumbling in your chair, looking around the room," he clarified.

The chair was beyond uncomfortable. If I was guilty of something, I would confess everything just so I could leave this place. "I just feel strange being here," I replied.

He cocked an eyebrow. "Whatever for?"

"Well, as you can imagine, I have been inside this room many times in the past, though it was always in a professional capacity, as a lawyer."

"I see. And you are not liking it as a civilian," he guessed.

"Not one bit."

"Let's go back to this list of yours." He returned us to the main subject.

As predicted, he hadn't looked too pleased when I presented him with the list, but he recovered quickly. Clearly he'd realized this was a good thing because now he actually had something tangible, something he could work with to investigate who had tried to set my apartment on fire.

"I am an open book, so ask anything you want," I urged.

He smiled. "That would be a first," he grumbled, picking up the piece of paper I'd prepared for him, with all the names and short summaries of why I believed they could be my stalker.

I pretended I didn't hear that remark.

"This is a hefty list, Miss Dennis."

I shrugged. "I've been a defense lawyer for a long time, Detective. It's understandable I made enemies along the way."

"These are your coworkers, Miss Dennis. They are not supposed to be your enemies," he pointed out.

"Anyone who is not working with me is against me, Detective."

He leaned back in his chair. "Interesting take on things."

I shrugged again, not really sure what to say to that.

"Let's start with Morgan Jeffrey Clark. Why is he on this list? Why do you think he could potentially be the one stalking you?"

"It's all there in the summaries of why I put them on the list." I gestured to the paper.

"I'm sure it is, but I'd like to hear it from you."

"Very well. Morgan is extremely lazy. His depositions are done sloppily. And he's constantly late. Instead of doing his job, he charms all the female employees into doing his job for him."

Which I found despicable on too many levels. Although to be fair, I didn't consider him solely guilty of that. The women were equally to blame for allowing that to happen. They were stupid for letting him manipulate them with a few smiles.

"The only reason the partners keep him around is because he's the son of a senator." And that was valuable at times.

"Being lazy isn't compatible with taking the time to stalk someone," he pointed out.

"Perhaps he has someone helping him," I replied.

Detective Sheldon nodded. "Is he aware of your opinions about him?" he asked next.

"Those are not my opinions. Those are facts," I insisted. And I was right. I hadn't said anything that wasn't true.

"Is he aware of those facts?" He'd clearly decided to indulge me, and I honestly didn't know what to think of it. Was he mocking me? "Is anyone else?"

"I made sure that those in charge knew about his short-comings."

"In other words, you ratted him out," the detective countered bluntly.

"Well, someone had to. And I do not know if that reached him," I snapped, answering his question.

Although his opinions about what I did and how I conducted business and dealt with my coworkers should not be of concern to me, it still bothered me. Not to mention that the way he spoke irked me.

"In that viper's pit you call a firm, he must have," he grumbled.

I gritted my teeth and said nothing.

"What about Dwayne White? Why is he on your list, Miss Dennis?"

"He is constantly absent."

"What do you mean by that?" he asked.

"Dwayne is a single father. I don't know if he's a scoundrel or if his son is genuinely that sick, constantly, but he misses a great deal of work. And that means others have to do his job for him." And that was unacceptable in my book.

The detective only shook his head, not commenting, and moved on to the next name on the list. "What's the deal with Catharine Haze?"

"She is the type of person who sleeps around, a lot, if it means career advantages." I heard she'd even tried to seduce Dawson, but he'd turned her down. I didn't particularly like Dawson, he was stuck-up, but even I had to admire his standards.

"Ok. Next on your list is Caleb Fitzpatrick. Why?"

"Honestly, I have no idea why Caleb wanted to be a

lawyer anyway. A while back we tried a case together, and I had to do all the work on my own."

"Because you had to or because you wanted to, to look good in front of your bosses?" Sheldon challenged.

For a moment I was taken aback by that question. Was he a detective or a shrink? And to be perfectly honest, the answer to that question was a little bit of both. I had to do most of the work, but I definitely used that to my advantage. Afterward, I got all the credit, and Grant was impressed with how I'd handled it all.

For some reason, I decided to reply honestly. "A little bit of both."

"I knew it," he said with a shake of his head while smirking.

"Knew what?"

"That you aren't as you seem, Miss Dennis."

"Excuse me?"

"While you sit here, judging all your coworkers for their shortcomings, you have the biggest flaws."

"And what are those?"

"You are a careerist. That's made you overambitious and cold," he replied without missing a beat.

"There is nothing wrong in valuing my career and wanting to advance in it," I pointed out.

"True," he agreed. "But apparently you have no problems whatsoever stabbing your coworkers in the back if it gives you an advantage."

"So? It's a very competitive business field, Detective. We were taught from day one at college to win by any means necessary. And I won't apologize to anyone for striving to be the best." Especially when I knew I was the best.

He narrowed his eyes. "Even if it means creating a hostile working environment and making enemies?" he challenged.

I didn't like his insinuations one bit. He was saying I was the cause of all the negative things that were happening. And that was just not true.

"I did nothing wrong, Detective," I insisted.

He gave me a look. "That is highly argumentative, as you would say, Miss Dennis."

I gritted my teeth. "Fine, I did nothing illegal."

"That may be the case, but my point is still valid. You created a lot of unnecessary enemies for yourself, so now it's hard to pinpoint the exact person who is trying to destroy you."

"Perhaps," I hedged. "Nonetheless, if none of them had made mistakes to begin with, I wouldn't have been able to take advantage of them." So, in truth, it was their own fault, not mine.

"True," the detective agreed. "But that kind of behavior is low, even for a defense lawyer," he threw in my face.

I couldn't believe he'd just said that. I was livid. But somehow I managed to rein it all in. There was no way I would let this detective rattle me. That was a matter of pride and dignity.

"As I said, Detective, I have done nothing illegal during the course of my employment at GBD, whereas the person after me definitely has, and quite a few times at that. So you should really focus on him."

Detective Sheldon leaned back in his chair, clearly not liking that I'd managed to turn the tables around. He definitely didn't like me suggesting he was doing his job wrong in focusing on me instead of the person stalking and harassing me.

Eventually, he nodded. "You're not wrong, yet all of this still presents a huge problem for me."

"How so?" I asked.

His open judgment and his snide comments had rubbed me the wrong way. Purely logically, I knew they shouldn't have. He was insignificant, and I should suck it up, because I needed him to do his job, find my stalker. Nonetheless, it couldn't be helped. I wanted to punch him in the face for all the nasty things he'd said to me.

This was worse than being interrogated. This was like being put on the stand, then dissected, obliterated. And I hated every part of it. I couldn't wait to be done with this interview, done with this man, so I could return home to my life.

You mean to the home you don't feel safe in anymore? To a life that was in shambles thanks to that psycho stalker?

But I couldn't allow myself to succumb to despair.

"It's very simple, really." The detective snapped me from my thoughts. "In your professional life you screwed a lot of people over, and I have to assume you've done that in your personal life as well, which means that the list of people you provided is only the beginning. I would have to extend that list to at least a dozen more people."

"First you complain you have no suspects; now you complain you have too many," I countered, grumbling. I was so angry I couldn't stop myself. Although I knew I shouldn't antagonize the man working on my case, he'd started it, so I felt obliged to respond in kind.

"Yes, because your attitude is making my job more difficult."

"Well, I am so terribly sorry, Detective, that threats made

against me are such an inconvenience to you," I snapped back.

"Not the threats, Miss Dennis, only your character."

That felt like a slap in the face.

I stood up. "This interview is over. Call me when you have my stalker in custody." And with that, I turned to leave. I couldn't tolerate being in his presence a second longer.

What an asshole.

"It's going to take me a while, considering you've screwed over every person you've met in your life," he said as I was opening the door.

"Careful, Detective. Now I've met you too," were my parting words before walking away.

I was beyond furious as I walked through the building, toward the exit. I recognized a few police officers, and they recognized me. I ignored their dirty looks. Detective Sheldon's words were all I could think of.

I couldn't believe he'd actually suggested this was all my fault. He believed I was to blame for having a stalker.

So typical. Police officers were notorious for blaming victims, especially male officers. And that was as disgusting as it was infuriating.

That was all the jealousy talking, I realized. I was a very successful female lawyer, and he was nothing but a poor cop, a detective.

I make more money in a day than he makes in a whole month. And I was the problematic one?

At least I am good at my job. And so far, he'd shown me how bad he was at his. I was the victim, and he had treated me like a common criminal.

How dare he speak to me in such a manner? He knows nothing about me, what I've been through, what I had to sacrifice to reach this level of excellence, yet he still dared to judge me. Me? That was preposterous.

I had half a mind to turn around and go speak with his boss, demanding he should be punished for his behavior, but managed to convince myself not to. Despite all the anguish, I needed that man. I needed him to catch my stalker. Nothing else mattered; no matter how much it pained me, that was life. At least until I got my justice. Afterward Detective Sheldon and I were going to have an entirely different conversation.

The list of suspects wasn't the only list I possessed. And with his attitude, that asshole detective had moved to first place on my shit list.

My anger toward him held me even after I got home. So, getting out of my clothes and taking my high heels off, I went to the minibar and poured myself a drink.

I was never a big drinker, had a few glasses of wine here or there, and had the minibar mainly for display, but after my conversation with the detective, if that could ever be called a conversation, I felt like I needed one. And a double, at that.

I still had the brandy Kelly had gifted me, but sadly, that was in my office, so I settled for some whiskey.

I drank it neat, and still, my fury remained. It burned inside me like the alcohol I had just consumed.

I would have the last laugh, not that detective, I seethed.

What if he's right? I had a moment of doubt. *What if all of this is my fault?* That was too depressing to contemplate. Besides, I shouldn't let that detective inside my head. I wasn't at fault here. He was.

As I tried to calm myself, unsuccessfully, I received a text from David.

How are you? Are you safe?

I groaned.

He persisted.

Can we meet?

I didn't even have to think about the answer to that question. I was too riled up for company, especially his company. Knowing my current mood, if he started to whine and demand that we become a real couple, I would snap and kick him out, which was precisely why I decided to ignore him.

It was better to be alone tonight.

That son of a bitch, I thought. It didn't take me long to start raging about Detective Sheldon again.

After a couple more drinks, I fell asleep, in my underwear, on the couch. I dreamt about Detective Sheldon and his judging eyes.

21

MATTERS OF THE PLANTS

My head was pounding. It was a pretty severe, loud banging, echoing all around me, making me nauseous, making me want to sob from the pain.

I really shouldn't have drunk that much. I grimaced, trying to lift my head.

Then I realized the banging wasn't actually coming from inside my head. Someone knocking on my door was definitely heightened by my hangover though.

Why isn't he using the doorbell? I thought, although I was grateful that wasn't the case. I could barely stand the knocking; the doorbell would definitely be the end of me. The mere thought of it made me cringe.

Forcing myself to sit up, I checked the time—just after seven—and groaned. This was the only day in the week when I could sleep in and relax because I didn't have to get to the office until noon, and whoever was trying to reach me had robbed me of that by waking me up so early in the morning.

Bastard.

Realizing I could not ignore the knocking because it was a persistent bastard, I grabbed a silk robe to throw over my underwear, and got up. I felt like crap, and not just because of the alcohol but because I'd fallen asleep, more like passed out, on the couch. It wasn't as comfortable as it looked.

I walked very slowly toward the door as the knocking continued, ready to yell at the person who'd interrupted my sleep. I was very cranky this morning. More than usual. Partly because of all the alcohol, and partially because I remembered the detective's words the instant I was conscious, and that was a terrible combination.

I pitied the fool I was about to unleash all my fury at, not to mention all my frustrations as well.

I finally opened the door, and Allan's smiling face greeted me.

The hot contractor is back, I noted. I also realized I hadn't checked myself in the mirror and had no idea what I looked like. So very discreetly, I tried to brush my hair to the side. During that motion, my silk robe opened a little, and I decided to leave it.

Better to stare at my breasts and legs than at my unpainted face.

"Good morning," he said too cheerfully.

Seeing him cheered me up a little. "Good morning," I returned, nowhere near matching his level of enthusiasm. And why did I sound so hoarse?

Then Allan's whole face fell. "Did I wake you? I'm sorry. I thought we agreed on this time," he said apologetically.

I waved his words away. "I forgot, but it's ok. I intended on getting an early start anyway," I lied.

"You sure? I can come back later if you want to return to bed."

"What do you need?" I asked instead of answering.

"Well, I just wanted to let you know that I've finished working in the hallway. Placed the new carpet, repainted the walls and everything," he informed me.

I was quite surprised to hear that. I leaned forward to see. That was a huge mistake, and my head protested greatly, but true enough, all looked new, and then I smelled the fresh paint. That didn't sit well with my stomach either.

"So soon?" I blurted out before I could stop myself.

The last time we spoke, he'd made it seem as though it would take forever to get the new carpeting since it was custom made or something.

"Yup. I don't like wasting time."

I bet.

"Great work, Allan, thank you."

"All that's left is to repaint the walls inside your apartment. If you let me."

"Now?"

"Yes."

I felt ashamed that I'd asked that. I blamed the hangover for my lack of intellect this morning. I nodded and stepped aside.

Once he was inside with all the materials he needed, he started to make preparations for painting the walls, including covering the floor and all the things around so as not to stain them.

I approved.

"I need to dress, so I'll be back in a minute," I told him.

He absent-mindedly nodded in response.

I rushed to the bathroom and was horrified to see the

state of my face. I had forgotten to wash my face last night, so some of the mascara got smudged, and the lipstick was faded, uneven.

I washed my face thoroughly and applied some light makeup again. As much as I could in the limited time I had, before jumping into some comfortable, fitted jeans and a tank top.

I was going for a casual look that morning. He'd already seen me in my underwear. I wasn't about to overdo it by putting one of my power suits on.

When I returned, he was already painting the wall to the left of the door, as it had sustained the most damage.

"Want some coffee?" I offered since I'd decided to have some as well. Usually, I drank tea in the morning, but the hangover I was sporting demanded caffeine, and a strong dose at that.

"That would be great," he replied.

As I worked in the kitchen, I heard him calling out to me. "Miss Dennis?"

"Please call me Amber."

It was obvious he wanted to say something and hesitated.

"What is it?" I prompted, returning to look at him.

"I noticed that the plants on your balcony have died, so I brought you fresh ones to replant. I hope that's ok?"

It was true that I had various plants in crates framing the balcony. They'd come with the apartment, but since I didn't possess a green thumb, they'd all died. I'd meant to replace them yet always had better things to do with my time than play gardening.

"You brought fresh plants for me?"

"I know that's a bit forward of me," he replied a bit

sheepishly. "But I just thought how sad it all looked." He stopped there, scratching the back of his neck.

He was definitely going out of his way to show me how competent he was.

"You really offer a full service, don't you?"

"I try."

"Well, thank you, Allan. That was very thoughtful of you."

"I can take care of them after finishing with this wall," he offered.

"That sounds perfect. Oh, be careful; you just missed a spot." I pointed.

Perhaps it was a mistake chatting with him while he worked. The last thing I needed and wanted was a poorly painted wall.

"On it," he replied gratefully.

Once he'd finished with the walls and cleaned up after himself, he took everything out, only to return with a huge crate full of all kinds of potted plants. There were ferns, climbers, flowers in full bloom, evergreens, and everything else in between. I could only gape at all the displays he would plant on my balcony.

I would really have to start taking care of them after all the work he'd put into arranging all this for me, I mused. *Or hire someone else to do it*, because knowing myself, everything would die all the same.

As he worked, I thought about his motives. As far as I was concerned, there could be only one reason why he was putting so much effort into this and working extra, staying longer than was necessary.

He is trying to get into my pants, which delighted me more than I thought was possible. I had been contemplating taking him to my bed, and learning it was a mutual thing made everything simpler.

I watched him as he worked, offering suggestions. If he was actually doing this for me, he might as well do it right.

"Would you like some more coffee? It's chilly out here."

"I don't mind," he replied with that easygoing smile of his.

"Once again, thank you for doing all of this," I said, flashing one of my own smiles.

I knew he was paid to fix all the damages. All the same, he didn't have to do this, and I wanted him to know I appreciated it.

And I will show him just how much I appreciate it, if he lets me, I joked.

Allan was really going the extra mile, making my living space more enjoyable, and looking at the paintings on my wall gave me an idea.

"Hey, Allan, would you be available to do some extra work for me?" I asked. "I'll pay your standard fees, of course," I reassured him.

"What do you need?" he asked, looking at me while still kneeling on the ground, his hands dirty from all the planting.

"Well, I recently purchased those paintings." I pointed at them.

It was pure luck that nothing had happened to them in the fire. An expert had come to see if there was any smoke damage, and he'd reassured me they were still perfect, which was a huge relief.

"I completely forgot about the spotlights," I explained.

I hated admitting it, especially to a man I was trying to get into bed. Then again, men adored being helpful. Case in point, Allan was currently on his knees, beautifying my balcony, which was something I hadn't asked of him, basically so he could feel helpful and impress me.

He glanced at the paintings in question. "That sounds easy enough."

"That's great," I replied, relieved. "When will you be able to install those for me?"

He took a moment to think about it, as though he was accessing some kind of mental calendar. "First I have to check what kind of lights you need, order them, and when they arrive, I can drop by to install them."

"And that would be when?" I prompted.

"End of the week."

I nodded. "That would work for me as well." And then something else occurred to me. "Can you make it after hours, since I'll be at work during the day," I added as an afterthought.

"Sure," he replied instantly, and that pleased me.

That confirmed something I'd suspected all along. He was definitely doing all of this so he could stay longer in my company than was necessary. He wanted to sleep with me.

That amused me. All the same, I would pretend I hadn't noticed because it was more fun that way, for me of course. And then I would let him seduce me.

I was also quite pleased with how quickly we'd managed to strike an agreement. Usually, contractors were such divas. Not to mention vain beyond belief, but Allan seemed different.

"What kind of work do you do?" he asked.

"I'm a defense attorney."

"So, are you working for one of those big law firms? If

you don't mind me asking," he asked conversationally, which took me by surprise, but I recovered quickly.

"Why do you ask? Do you need my services?" I joked.

He looked confused, then flustered, as though fearing he'd insulted me in some way, so I chuckled. "Sorry, I don't mind you asking. Yes, I work for Grant, Bryant, and Dawson," I said proudly.

By the blank expression on his face, I figured he had no idea who we were. Most people didn't, and then something would happen, and they would need us.

"Oh. So what does a defense lawyer actually do?" he asked next.

"Well, I don't work for the district attorney. I don't work for the government," I tried to explain.

He frowned like he was trying to understand. "So you work for the other side."

I didn't like the way he said that, the way he phrased it, as though it automatically meant I was on the wrong side.

"I offer representation to whoever needs it," I corrected.

He stopped what he was doing, to look at me. "Have you ever gotten a client who turned out to be guilty?"

I would be lying if I said I hadn't been asked that question a lot. And over time I'd perfected the answer. "Of course, that happens from time to time, as well," I admitted.

"And how does that make you feel?"

I found his question kind of strange, perhaps even too personal for a contractor, one I'd met only twice in my life, to be asking as he was replanting my balcony. Yet I found myself answering anyway. "I'm not proud of that possibility, although I firmly believe everyone deserves fair representation. It's not easy going through something like that while knowing your client is guilty."

"So why do it in the first place?"

"Because I'm a professional, and I have a job to do, like everybody else. Besides, the idea of innocent people being sent to prison or even put on death row bothers me more than one guilty person out on the streets."

"Huh," was all he said in return as he tried to clean his hands of all the dirt, getting up. He had a strange, confused expression on his face, which was clearly a result of my answers. For the life of me, I couldn't figure out why.

And unfortunately, I didn't have time to find out either.

All of a sudden it was like we were being fast-forwarded. "I'm done," he announced. "I have to go."

And in a matter of seconds, he'd cleaned everything up, picked up all the empty crates, and practically dashed out the front door, mumbling something about how he would be back to install those lights for me.

I could only stare after him, wondering what had just happened.

Naturally, I didn't ponder too long about it.

I admired his handiwork for a bit; the flowers looked very pretty, I had to admit. Afterward, I returned to the bedroom and decided to have a well-deserved rest.

All the problems I had would still be waiting for me when I woke up, so there was really no need to rush it.

22

NEW INTERESTS

I had a very hectic day at work. It was supposed to be a co-chair with another lawyer, another junior partner named Frank Galbiati. Though, he'd decided to slack off. He had been a junior partner much longer than me, and pulled some kind of imaginary seniority, which meant I was left to deal with everything pretty much on my own.

I was very much surprised when I saw him in court and participating, glancing constantly at my notes, because he had none. That was probably because he was trying to suck up to our high-profile clients, I realized.

He was trying to take all the credit while having done no work, and that was something I wasn't about to allow.

Overall, I didn't mind the extra work. Partly because having something to do meant I couldn't stress about my stalker or dwell on the fact nothing had happened since the fire, which couldn't be good. And partly because I knew how to cash out in the end.

I made sure Grant knew who was actually winning this case for the clients. In the end, I managed to score a huge settlement. I was talking about dozens of millions of dollars, and that made my clients rather happy. That made Grant happy too because a large portion of that money would go to the firm.

Grant came to me sometime during the day to pat me on the back for a job well done.

"It was easy once our private investigator discovered foul play," I said humbly with a small shrug.

"And how was Frank?"

"Frank was... adequate."

Grant nodded at that, clearly understanding what I meant. I never allowed myself to openly badmouth a fellow coworker, but over the years, Grant had become fairly good at reading between the lines. His next words confirmed as much. "Next time, you'll be able to choose your own partner."

"I would appreciate that," I replied with a smile.

"I won't keep you from your work. Go, make me some more money."

That made me smile. There was nothing Grant loved more than money. Other than perhaps his son.

Actually, golf and David share second place. I wasn't even sure his wives, any of them, ever made it to the top five, I joked.

Speaking of David, I decided I wanted to see him. It had been a while since we'd last seen each other. Come to think of it, the night of the fire had been our last encounter. And I was ready for some action.

So I texted him:

We should meet tonight.

I even snapped a picture of my cleavage, which was showing just a tad of the black lace that was holding my breasts underneath, for additional flavor.

He failed to reply.

I knew he had a job, Grant made sure of that, but I had no idea where or what. That was never of concern to me, so I attributed his lack of response to him actually doing something for a change, being busy.

Then hours passed, and he'd still not confirmed he would be coming tonight.

Why is he not replying to me? I thought, irked, glaring at my phone. And then I realized what he was actually doing. He was playing hard to get; he was trying to make me miss him and need him. It was such a juvenile technique.

I could only shake my head at his poor behavior. It was a true lack of judgment on my part for letting him in my bed in the first place. It was true it was fun for a while, but now it was more of an inconvenience than anything else.

That was precisely why I decided to give him time, until tonight, to reach out. If he failed to get in touch, if he continued playing his silly games, then I would have no choice. I would have to move on in my life without him. It wasn't like I couldn't find someone else to sleep with.

Actually, the prospect of finding someone else to sleep with, someone more mature, more skilled, excited me. More than I had anticipated.

Probably because I already had the perfect candidate in mind. Not to mention, he would deliver himself to my apartment at the end of the week.

Allan was definitely someone I could picture in my bed, so David's behavior made it even easier for me to pursue him. I'd already intended on flirting with Allan a little when he came to install my lights, and now I would step it up a notch.

I really believed he would suit me better than David, anyway. Allan was older, much more mature, and was very handy around the house, which could translate into him being very handy in the bedroom as well. He was definitely someone who would know how to honor a booty call. And not turn into a sniveling brat. I was sure Allan would never try to ruin a perfectly good sexual thing by complicating it with unnecessary feelings.

He was a handyman, after all, and considering the way he looked, so hot and fit, I was sure he slept with his clients all the time. Not that I had any objections, as long as he slept with me as well, whenever I wanted him.

Once my mind was set, I couldn't wait for the end of the week so I could see Allan again.

Luckily, the days passed by quickly enough, and I didn't hear from David at all. I had a lot of work now that I was a junior partner, and in the blink of an eye, it was already Friday, the day Allan would come to install the spotlights for me.

I arrived home about half an hour earlier than normal so I could prepare myself for Allan's arrival. Part of me recognized I was going to too much trouble, but I didn't care. The chase and the prospect of bedding a new man were thrilling. And based on what was happening in my life, I deserved some entertainment.

First, I bathed. I used my special bath oils, knowing how fragrant and soft my skin would be afterward. There was no point in washing my hair since it was still clean and styled.

Once I was done and had reapplied my makeup, I changed into something more comfortable, yet still sexy. I opted for a skirt and blouse combination. Underneath my shirt, the inklings of my lacy underwear were visible, but only at certain angles naturally. I wasn't a slut, only a flirt.

And then I waited for him to arrive.

Luckily, he was right on time, and I was all smiles opening the door for him.

I had to admit, he looked even sexier tonight for some reason, although he was wearing a plain black T-shirt that hugged his body perfectly, and plain faded jeans.

"Right on time," I complimented, letting him in.

"Well, I know how busy you are. I didn't want to waste your time."

"Allan, you could never waste my time. What you are doing is very important to me," I countered, placing a hand over my chest, which was purely intentional. I wanted his focus there.

And I could see it was working.

"The spotlights arrived and are working perfectly. I already tried them out," he told me.

Was it my imagination, or did he say that to distract himself from my cleavage? *How very interesting.*

"The ones with the black on them or purely silver?" I wanted to know since we'd discussed it earlier in the week over the phone. I liked the latter better, but Allan wasn't sure the dealer had a matching set.

"The silver ones."

"Oh, good," I said, relieved.

I didn't like the idea of being forced to endure the black-rimmed ones. I wanted everything inside my house to be perfect, just the way I wanted it to be. Settling was for those who didn't have clear desires inside their heads. I wasn't a settler. In any aspect of my life.

"Do you want something to drink, coffee?" I asked as he started to prepare for work.

He took the paintings down very carefully.

I hovered over them like a mother hen. They were my prized possessions. I couldn't allow anything bad to happen to them.

"A glass of water would be fine," he replied.

"You know, I have wine as well. We can share it once you're done," I offered generously.

I made sure to emphasize the last part. I didn't want him drinking while working, especially since he would be dealing with electricity. The last thing I needed was to be liable for something bad happening to him.

"I don't drink, but thank you," he surprised me by saying.

Did he mean he didn't drink at work or didn't drink at all? *Is he a recovering alcoholic?* God knew this city was full of them, among other things.

I was about to ask when something else caught my attention.

"Could you please not put those tools on the carpet; it's new and white." I'd changed my mind about keeping the wood floors and had just bought the new carpet.

"Oh, sorry," he replied somewhat awkwardly.

"That's fine. I'll bring you some papers or something."

As I brought him his bottled water and a mat to place his tools on, I saw him getting the spotlights out of their boxes.

I approached, frowning. "They are bigger than I expected."

"They won't look as big once mounted on the wall; besides, you have big paintings," he pointed out.

Perhaps he was right. Then again, I didn't want attention on the spotlights, just the paintings. If he'd made a mistake by ordering the wrong ones, I would definitely make him replace them. Naturally, I would give him the benefit of the doubt and see how it all looked together.

"Do you need any help?" I asked.

"No, I'm good. So if you need to go and work, I'm totally fine," he reassured me.

"Could you move them just a little bit higher?" I asked. I didn't like the idea of having them too close to the canvasses.

David moved them.

"That's too high," I warned.

"How about this?" he asked, readjusting again.

"I think that is close enough. I'm just worried something might happen to the paintings." I knew it sounded silly, but I had this worry they would burst into flames if too close to the sources of light.

"You know, these are standard lights for such paintings. Nothing will happen to them," he replied, sounding just a little bit annoyed.

Come to think of it, he'd looked kind of off ever since he set foot in my apartment.

Perhaps he had difficulties at his other job, I mused. Perhaps some other client had annoyed him to death or just refused to pay.

Those were pure speculations, of course. Though it was obvious something had happened to him because he was definitely not his easygoing self. Which was all the more reason for me to cheer him up, I joked.

He tested the lights again, to see if they worked properly, before fixing them on the wall permanently.

"Do they have to be so bright?" I asked. I didn't want my place to feel like a night at the carnival or circus.

"You can adjust the brightness."

"Good. I got worried for a moment that I would be forced to live in a nightclub or something," I said, smiling at my own joke, but I was the only one.

"Ok, I'm done bothering you," I said, still in a light tone. "I'll let you finish your work in peace."

He nodded.

I sat on the couch, watching him install the spotlights while imagining all the work we could be having later in the bedroom.

"All done," he announced about fifteen minutes later.

I was so wrapped up inside my head, the time had flown.

I approached to inspect his handiwork. In the end, he was right, the spotlights were large enough and bright enough. Everything looked as it was supposed to, and once again the paintings took my breath away, especially now when they were finally on display as they should have been from the start.

"Allan, it's perfect," I complimented.

"I'm glad you approve."

I walked toward a small table where my purse was. I needed to write him a check, and added a generous tip so he would know just how much I appreciated all his hard work.

"Thank you for everything, Allan. You've really made my apartment feel like home," I said, offering him the check. "Are you sure you don't want that glass of wine now?" I asked, offering one of my dazzling smiles.

"No, thank you," he said, accepting his payment. "I have to go."

I pouted. I didn't want him to leave. I wanted him to stay and play with me. *How to make him stay? What to say?* I racked my brain.

Was it possible he didn't understand any of my subtle invites? Some men were ignorant like that.

"I hope we see each other again," I said eventually. "I had some thoughts about my bedroom."

He started shaking his head as I spoke. "If you need any further work, Miss Dennis, you need to find someone else. I am booked solid for the rest of the year."

"Oh, ok," I said, somewhat perplexed.

"Have a nice evening." And with that, he left.

I looked at the closed door in utter confusion.

What the actual fuck just happened?

I couldn't believe it. It was like I was dealing with a different person tonight. Gone were the smiles, the flirtiness.

And then it dawned on me. He was only nice, polite and accommodating to score future work. When that was done, all his charms disappeared.

So typical.

His parting words confirmed as much. He'd clearly found another, more lucrative client and didn't have to deal with me anymore.

That was beyond rude. I could only shake my head at that. Then again, it was better I learned now what an asshole he was than after sleeping with him.

So I had only one thing to say: *Good riddance, Allan.*

23

GOOD AMONG THE BAD

It had been ages since I last spoke with Detective Sheldon. And I was really curious to hear if there was any new information about my case. Although, his silence could be interpreted as there being none.

I wanted this man, this lunatic stalking me, caught. Living in fear, constantly looking over my shoulder, stressing over whether he would manage to burn my apartment down next time was not living at all.

So I decided to give the good detective a call. Perhaps if I put some pressure on him, maybe he would actually start doing his job and catch that cretin for me. Because until that maniac was caught, I couldn't do my job properly. Sure, I was still winning cases, but I couldn't work on getting Phoebe's job with my attention so divided. And that wasn't acceptable.

Where did I put his business card? I mused.

As I looked for it, inside my bag, around the office, my phone started ringing. For a second I hoped it was David, which was crazy, but it wasn't him. It was an unknown number. A lot of people called me, seeking professional help, so screening calls served no purpose. "Hello?" I answered.

"Good day, Miss Dennis. It's Detective Sheldon."

Speak of the devil, I thought. "Detective, what a surprise. Are you calling to tell me you have my stalker in custody?" I couldn't help jibing a little, while hoping what I was saying was actually true.

"Sadly, not yet, but I have a lead on the guy who started the fire at your apartment."

That cheered me up. "Really?"

"Yes, and based on your description and the partial picture from the ATM near the law office, I'm pretty sure he's responsible for the phone theft and car vandalization as well," he informed me.

I knew it was the same guy, I thought, patting myself on the back. It was both a relief and a worry that it all was connected in such a manner.

"Who is he?" I demanded.

"He is a local punk kid named Mickey Richards," Detective Sheldon revealed.

I frowned. "Never heard of him," I replied honestly.

"I have. I've dealt with him before. His rap sheet is a mile long, mostly petty crimes, and a few not so petty."

I was guessing torching my apartment belonged to the latter category. *Someone must have offered him a great deal of money to do that*, I mused.

"Well, thank you for letting me know. Are you planning on arresting him?"

"I will be taking him in as soon as I manage to locate him. As you can imagine, he likes to move around the city, but I have a few ways to track him down," he reassured me.

"Great, let me know when you do." I wanted five minutes alone to speak with him.

I thanked the detective again, ready to wrap this conversation up when he said, "Actually, that wasn't why I was calling."

"Oh?"

"I have a question for you."

"Ask away."

"Was Richards ever one of your clients?"

I rolled my eyes. "I just told you I'd never heard of him, Detective; besides, I do not work pro bono." I was sure a character like that could never afford me.

"Can you check that for me?" he insisted.

"Trust me, I would remember him," I countered similarly.

"Humor me, Miss Dennis."

I sighed and went to my computer. Luckily, I had a database with all my clients, and after typing his name in the search engine, zero files came up.

"No, as I said, he was never a client of mine or anyone else's at GBD," I added for good measure.

"Ok, it was worth a shot, thanks."

I didn't agree, but who was I to judge? He was a detective or at least pretended to be. His actual skills were yet to be determined.

"Have you made any progress regarding the list I provided?"

"Some," he replied.

"And?"

"And you were right, they all hate your guts."

"Enough to stalk me?"

"I don't know yet. I need more time."

He needs more time, I repeated to myself, irked. The problem was I felt like I was running out of it. It was just a matter of time before the stalker tried to strike again.

Shortly after that, we disconnected. And I had to admit that speaking with him wasn't a complete waste of time. It was a relief he had a suspect in mind; then again, the fact he didn't have him in custody was disconcerting.

Mickey Richards, I thought with a frown. Since I had never heard of him, I couldn't understand why he was targeting me. Then again, I was overthinking things. He was merely a third party, someone hired to do all the dirty work. The real stalker remained anonymous, just as the detective had said.

I didn't like that one bit. It meant the person behind it all was smart and careful and wanted to remain hidden in the shadows. *Who are you?* I asked no one in particular.

Unfortunately, learning of this Richards guy gave me no clues about who was behind it all. *We need Richards to tell us that.*

Sadly, it wasn't like I could catch him to speed up the process. I had to rely on Detective Sheldon, and I hated relying on other people because, in the end, they all disappointed me, no matter what.

Later that night, as I sat in my home office, finishing some work, I heard a loud banging on the door.

It startled me at first because it was such a fierce knock that broke the silence and filled it with violence. I stood up instinctively to answer it, and then I paused. It was pretty late at night, and I wasn't expecting anyone. David hadn't replied to me, which meant he was dead to me from now on.

Then I started to think something bad might have happened, and I rushed toward the door.

Why does no one use the doorbell? And why didn't Alex buzz my intercom to tell me I had a visitor? I wondered on my way toward the door. The banging was so loud, so savage, it was really scaring me, so naturally, I started to doubt whether I should even answer it. *What if this is my stalker, finally coming to confront me and finish the job with the fire*, I thought and stopped in my tracks.

Calm down, I ordered myself. If I panicked, I wouldn't solve anything. As the person on the other side of my door did his best to wake the dead and scare all the living shitless, I slowly crept toward the door. The plan was to look through the spyhole, to see if whoever was on the other side was a friend or a foe.

I can always call out and see what happens. Despite the thought, I said nothing.

I leaned forward and saw absolutely nothing. *What the hell?* Something was blocking my view, which made my heart race faster. Someone must have covered the hole with something black so I couldn't see out of it.

"Who is it?" I dared to ask, but the banging persisted. "What do you want?"

No reply, only a door that shook from the loud banging. And then the handle started to move. Luckily, my door was firmly locked.

"If you don't stop, I'll call the police," I threatened.

Then the door rattled savagely as though whoever was banging against it had used all their strength, both fists, in their attempt to break in.

Please hold, was all I was able to think about in that moment. Despite my threats, I was unable to move, staring at my door to see what would happen next. I wished Allan had gotten me the metal door like I'd asked, but the building management had refused that request.

Snap out of it, I screamed at myself. In a rush, I grabbed my phone to call the police or even the detective.

And then it stopped. The noise, as unexpectedly as it had started, stopped.

What the hell was happening?

I stood in front of my door, not moving, uncertain of what to do, waiting for it to start again, waiting for something even worse to happen, all the while squeezing the phone in my hands, but nothing happened.

I managed to psych myself up to look outside. I opened the door, and as expected, there was no one there. The hallway looked utterly deserted, and that terrified me. Not knowing was always far worse than knowing because my mind was capable of thinking up all kinds of horrifying scenarios.

On impulse, I went to the lobby to talk with Alex.

He was watching the game on his phone and looked pretty guilty; I'd caught him slacking off.

No wonder he saw no one vandalizing my car, I grumbled.

"Did you send someone up to my floor?" I asked, skipping all the pleasantries.

He frowned. "No, Miss Dennis. Only Mr. and Mrs. Washington passed through here in the last half an hour," he replied, although it was obvious my question had confused him.

"What about through the garage elevator?" I demanded. "Did anyone enter the building that way? Did you see anyone on camera?"

"Yes, of course, there were some residents who did come in, but again, nobody in the last half an hour."

Whoever is using that elevator needs a key card, so a stranger couldn't easily waltz in that way, I mused. *If Alex is so obsessed with the game, my stalker could have come through the front door without him being the wiser,* I fumed. I was sure my stalker had come to torment me. Or they'd paid someone to do it instead. *That Mickey person.*

Maybe I do need to call the detective, to tell him what happened.

"Is something the matter? Did something happen?" Alex asked.

I gritted my teeth, angry, as though Alex were solely responsible for what had happened tonight. "Yes, someone banged against my door like a maniac."

"Who?"

"I don't know; they covered my spyhole."

"Did you call the police?"

"No, I was too scared to do anything," I admitted reluctantly.

"Do you want me to call the police now?" he offered.

"No, there's no point now." Whoever had banged against my door was long gone.

"I'll keep an eye out, just in case they decide to come back," Alex said, clearly trying to be helpful.

I snapped. "I need you to do better than that, Alex," I practically screamed. "You've missed so much already, the vandalism, the fire, now this. If you don't start being better at your job, I will get you fired," I said sincerely before storming back to my apartment.

I had zero regrets for what I had just said. Alex needed to know his incompetence was putting me in danger.

At some level, I knew it wasn't all Alex's fault, but it was easier to be mad at him than stress about the unknown person who was trying to ruin my life.

Reaching my floor, I contemplated knocking on Mercy's door, to see if she'd heard anything, but ruled against it. If she had heard anything, she would have come to see me and asked what was happening. Especially since she knew what I was dealing with.

Besides, it was late. She was probably already asleep, although that was a huge assumption since I didn't know her sleeping habits. There was a chance she was still working. In that case, there was a fair chance she'd heard nothing. She had mentioned that she wore headphones while conducting business, since listening to music helped her concentrate.

I knew too many unimportant details about my neighbor. I should really focus on myself and my problems and not think about Mercy's sleeping habits. *I must be in shock to have such ridiculous thoughts.*

Inside my apartment, I made sure my door was fully locked before going to the bedroom, although I couldn't really say why. I was too riled up to go to sleep and too stressed to continue working.

I felt stuck. This stalker was ruining my life on every level, and I didn't know how to stop him. And all around me, I was surrounded by incompetent people who were doing nothing to help me. Or couldn't help me.

Or wouldn't, I thought glumly.

It was all on me, and I had no clue what to do.

How am I going to save myself?

24

ALL ALONE

After what had happened, I really felt like I needed someone, a sympathetic ear, to listen to me. So I decided to reach out to my only friend, Kelly.

I called her a couple of times, but she wasn't answering. That was so typical of her. I knew she had a certain pattern of behavior. As much as she had good qualities, she had bad ones as well. And this was definitely one of them. Whenever she had a new boyfriend, she totally forgot about me.

When I'd tried to speak with her about that in the past, she acted all apologetic, promising it would never happen again, and then it would. It was like she was possessed or something when in a new relationship, like she was unable to control her hormones and was absolutely obsessed with the man in her life.

Perhaps I was judging her too harshly though. *At least one of us is getting laid*, I grumbled, trying to focus on my work, without much success.

I was dreading going home, alone, after work. I was

afraid whoever had visited me last night would repeat the torment all over again.

Then I will just call the police and be done with it, I thought, trying to appear brave, trying to act as though none of this was bothering me.

That was a lie, naturally, but I still had to try to act normal. To pretend I was stronger than him, unbreakable, because that was the only way I could win this. If I showed weakness, any kind, that would be the end of me. I was sure of it.

All the same, I took my phone and called Kelly again. I hoped we could have a girls' night out, but she didn't respond.

Oh, come on, Kelly, give the poor man some time to rest, recuperate, I whined.

Since she was ignoring me, I called David. And he failed to answer as well. He had been ghosting me as of late. Well, not really. I was ghosting him.

The problem was he was too attentive. Among other things. David was constantly trying to force me to go out on a date with him. I knew I could not relent to that; it would send the wrong message. So I knew I had to be patient and give him time to come to terms with the relationship we had, if one could even call it that, and that it didn't involve leaving my apartment.

Sadly, the boy was too selfish. Thinking only about himself and not about me and what I needed, especially during these trying times. He was also stubborn. But so was I, and I would win in the end because I was a woman with clear goals and with clear wants in life, not a girl.

And the sooner he gets that, the better.

Unfortunately, there was one problem with that. What to

do in the meantime? I needed someone in my life. Someone real. Someone who wasn't as flaky as Kelly or as demanding as David. I needed someone who would be supportive of me and my needs. A true companion, not a boy or a childish best friend.

How to find someone like that? Where to even start the search? *Yellow pages?* I joked. More importantly, who had time for that shit? Especially in my current situation.

Unfortunately, I had to admit, if only to myself, I didn't have many people in my life whom I liked to spend time with. I definitely had no one who could fill that specific role for me.

Perhaps I need to try more. I was never one to be called a people person. Meeting new people outside of business, getting close to someone and opening up, was never easy for me. I preferred my own company, which was part of the problem.

I'd never considered that a flaw, but now I could admit that that way of living had certain shortcomings as well.

Of course, I wasn't complaining. I was constantly surrounded by other people. I had many acquaintances, associates, coworkers, and colleagues. Sadly, that wasn't on the same level as having close friends. Someone I could have coffee with on free days, go to dinners with, spend time with, chat, gossip.

The problem was, I was too focused on my career advancement and making money above all else so I could afford expensive clothes, a nice apartment, a cool car, but now I had to face reality. All that required tremendous sacrifices, and in this case, that meant I had no one in my life I could turn to when in need, no one to rely upon or share my life with.

And for the first time in my life, the lack of a reliable social circle of friends, the lack of a love interest, terrified me.

My stalker had forced me to look deep into myself and realize how much I'd sacrificed to achieve my goals. And although I still fully believed it was all worth it, there was a part of me that wondered if there was another way to achieve all that without being so single-minded, without sacrificing so much. Perhaps I would have had a much better support system now otherwise.

Or any, I grumbled.

It had never bothered me before, but now I found myself troubled by it all. In such a state, I couldn't focus on work, which bothered me too. I ended up trapped in a vicious circle of thoughts, where each one was more troubling, terrifying than the last.

Stop, I screamed at myself, burying my long nails in my palms, forcing myself to calm down. I was spiraling out of control without reason. Nothing was beyond me; nothing was beyond repair. All I had to do was focus and look at the problem analytically until I found a solution.

Luckily, that thought managed to calm me down.

So the solution to all my problems appeared easy enough. Have a stalker, report it to the police. Have no real friends, meet some. Unfortunately, like everything else in my life, it was easier said than done. Still, I refused to succumb to despair. That wasn't part of my personality.

Without realizing what I was actually doing, I grabbed my phone again, but instead of dialing my former, traitorous friend, I dialed my mother. And I couldn't hang up because it was already too late.

"Amber?" She answered in a form of a question. Was she

asking me if I was actually Amber, or was she asking herself? I couldn't tell for sure. "Is everything all right?"

I frowned. It was true my mother and I had a strained, awkward relationship at best, since we never really saw eye to eye, yet this was strange, even for her. "Why do you ask that?"

"Well, you called. And you never call," she said, as though it was a matter of fact.

I was taken aback at that and instantly wanted to argue back, deny it, and then I paused. Was she right? We spoke a couple of times a month, that was true, and looking back, it was always her calling me.

Huh, I thought.

"Everything is all right," I reassured her, by habit. "I wanted to see how you're doing," I explained.

"I'm doing fine, as usual."

"Great. How's work? Did something interesting happen?"

There was a pause on the other side.

"Mom, you there?" I wondered if we'd lost connection. We hadn't. I checked.

"Are you sure you're all right?" my mother asked again, sounding really concerned, once again making it awkward for me.

She always did that. *Why couldn't I chitchat with my mother for a bit, like normal people did, without turning it into an existential crisis?*

"Yes, I am sure. I mean, it's fine," I blurted out before I could stop myself.

What was happening to me? Why was I acting like this? Was I actually that desperate that I was prepared to share some truly personal things with my mother?

Part of me realized the irony of that statement, but

considering my mother and I were not close, this was like speaking with a complete stranger.

Then again, perhaps that was precisely what I needed.

"What happened, Amber?" my mother insisted.

Although I was shaking my head, I started to speak. "I'm sitting in my office, and I just realized that I have this amazing new job, a job that I love, but have no one to share it with apart from you." *And you were never interested in any aspect of my life,* was implied. "And you're right, something did happen that made me feel a little bit lonely." Scared, helpless, angry, isolated, as well.

"Is it connected to that man stalking you?"

"No, not really."

Once again, my mother remained silent. Was she in shock I'd shared all that with her? It was safe to assume she was because I certainly was. I couldn't believe I'd just admitted all that. That was so out of character.

The person harassing me had managed to not only turn my life upside down but my whole being as well.

"I knew this day would come," my mother said eventually, theatrically.

"What do you mean?"

"I knew you would end up alone, lonely, without anything in your life, with only that damn job to cling to."

I made a face. *Why do we never FaceTime?*

"Yes, Mom, you were right, and I was wrong," I countered defensively. "Is that what you wanted to hear? Are you happy now?"

"Of course I'm not happy. I wish you had listened to me."

"Well, I couldn't because you're not completely right. I love my damn job."

"And what good has it brought you?" she countered.

"It brought me plenty of good, especially since I'm doing what I want, reaching my full potential."

Not that it was something she could understand or relate to. If it were up to her, I would have ended up like her, married after high school, with children, taking care of the house and the family, and relying on my partner for everything.

I shuddered in disgust. That was my version of hell.

"That's not a reason to live. That is just a job."

I honestly didn't know what to say to that. This was a mistake.

"No point in arguing about it now, since it's nothing I can change." Or want to change. "My current situation remains the same."

"Well, maybe it could change," she started, much calmer, softer now, "if you would stop pushing people away," she suggested, taking me by surprise.

"What?" I muttered in return.

"You have to remove all those shields and let people in your life get to know you, love you, to be happy."

Her words freaked me out. I wanted to rebel, to negate her words, laugh at them, but couldn't. Was there a possibility she was right?

"Thanks for the advice, Mom, but I have to go."

I hung up before something else happened. Before either one of us said something that would change this dynamic we'd shared for too many years.

I could only stare at my phone as her words echoed inside my head.

Do I really push people away?

25

SAD NEWS

I was going through my morning routine, showering, dressing, having a light meal, preparing for work, milling about my apartment—I could have sworn I could still smell the smoke from the fire—while listening to the news.

I always listened to the news in the morning. It was a good way of knowing what was happening in our small slice of heaven called Los Angeles. Not to mention hearing rumors about potential lawsuits and divorces meant more work for me.

As a junior partner, I had quite a few A-list clients, and it definitely wouldn't be the first time I'd learned something about them, about their indiscretions, via the news.

Then I heard something that stopped me in my tracks.

Did he just mention Kelly? I wondered. I must have heard it wrong. Then again, it wouldn't be the first time she ended up in the news.

I hadn't heard from her in a while and wondered what

she was up to. *Probably got drunk with her new boyfriend and caused a scene.*

I approached the TV, grabbing the remote from the coffee table. I had to rewind a bit to hear the whole segment. They were definitely speaking about my friend since her picture was in the left corner, which was rarely a good sign.

I stopped the rewind and started to watch.

"Kelly October, daughter of Oscar-winning actress and screen legend Anna October, has died at the age of thirty-four..."

What? That can't be right. It can't be.

"The family issued a brief statement saying they are grateful for all the people from around the world sending their condolences and prayers for Kelly, and asked for privacy while they mourn."

I could only stare at the screen as the commentator talked on and on about Kelly and what a wonderful life she had, as each part of my being rebelled against the news she was dead. She couldn't be dead. She just couldn't.

After snapping out of my stupor, the first thing I did was call Kelly's cell. I tried to ignore how freaked I was when she didn't answer. With shaky hands, I rewound the report and watched it again. Still, I refused to accept what had happened.

He didn't say how she died, I noted.

That's because she didn't die. Kelly can't be dead.

I went online to see what others were saying.

No matter how many articles I read, no matter that the voice inside my head was screaming that this could not be happening, I had to admit the truth. Kelly was gone. And to make matters worse, she didn't simply die, she'd killed herself.

Oh my God.

I sat on the floor in front of the TV, listening to the anchorman speak about my friend. He went through her entire life, as much as a three-minute segment would allow, speaking about all her highlights, brushing over what had happened ten years ago, mentioning all her famous past lovers and her excessive use of alcohol and rumors about drug usage as well.

Kelly had never used drugs in her life. She didn't have to, and it irked me this man was speaking about her in such a manner. He didn't know her. Who was he to judge her? I was her friend. I knew her best.

Yet you failed to see the signs she was about to kill herself.

That made me pause. I still couldn't believe it. It felt surreal that I was now living in a world without Kelly. I'd experienced the same feeling when my father died, which was the most painful thing that had happened to me.

Kelly killed herself. She chose to leave this world. *Why would she do that?* She was the happiest person I knew. She lived her life to the fullest, enjoying each moment. So it didn't make any sense she would just choose to die. She was never that type, depressed or suicidal.

Then again, *Would I know the type?* I had a moment of doubt. Of course I would know if she struggled and if she was unhappy in any way. I was her closest friend; she would confide in me.

Would she, if she wanted to end it all? I dismissed that thought. *If she was depressed, Kelly would tell me,* I was sure of that.

Kelly loved life, and more importantly, Kelly loved her life, so this happening made no sense whatsoever.

Kelly's life was as good as it could get, and she was very much aware of that and grateful too. And she never showed any signs of mental illness, I checked. I went online and googled the signs of mental illness.

Sure, she struggled having such a famous mother, yet she was never envious. It was just that her mother was a diva and difficult to live with. But that was no reason to commit suicide, especially not now. She hadn't lived with her mother since turning eighteen.

Why did you do it, Kelly? I asked the heavens. It just didn't make any sense to me. And I was sure anyone who'd met Kelly, even once, shared this same sentiment with me now. Kelly possessed this unique characteristic that always kept her going. She was able to be happy, joyous, and positive even when people around her were clearly miserable. She never let others bring her down.

And now she was dead because she'd killed herself.

Oh my God. I cried on the floor, trying to grasp this new reality, praying this was all a dream, a nightmare I would wake up from, when I noticed the time.

It was time to return to my reality no matter how much it pained me. Getting up from the floor and wiping my face, I went to the bathroom and reapplied my makeup. And then, gathering all the things I needed, I turned the TV off, sending one last dirty look at the anchorman as though he were personally responsible for what had happened, and left my apartment.

On my way to work, I tried not to think about Kelly, knowing how much that would affect me, and I needed to be at the top of my game at work since I was surrounded by vipers.

Unfortunately, I was unsuccessful at that. I couldn't stop thinking about my friend, good and kind, always smiling Kelly.

Why did you do it, Kelly? Why did you leave me? I asked.

Naturally, there was no reply.

A whole day passed with me in a daze. I knew I worked, I saw clients, but what was said, what I did, I had no real recollection of. My mind was still trying to process the information about Kelly's demise.

She killed herself. That affected me more than I could have imagined.

It's true what they say, you start to appreciate what you had only upon losing it. Kelly was a dear friend to me, and I wished I'd spent more time with her. I decided that after work I would go and see Anna, Kelly's mother.

Kelly's father was never in the picture. He was some European nobleman Anna had a fling with, which resulted in pregnancy. Although he was never around, Kelly spent time with him a lot, abroad, and he showered her with gifts, always making sure she had more money than needed. Not that he had to bother. Anna October was beyond rich and never had problems sharing her wealth with her only daughter.

Why did Kelly kill herself? Why now when she was on top of the world and without a care in the world?

Everybody loved her. Even the paparazzi, who were brutal to everyone on this planet, loved her, always wrote nice things about her, and posted the best pictures. It didn't make sense. What possible reason did she have to kill herself?

Kelly was happy. I knew that. I was sure of that. And she had a new boyfriend.

Although it was true, she had ghosted me as of late. That dinner we were at had been the last time I saw her or spoke with her. That picture of her with her new boy toy was the last thing I'd received from her. That made me wonder.

Did that mean she had problems? Did she get into some kind of trouble and thought suicide was the only way out? My mind started to come up with all kinds of crazy theories.

If she was in trouble, she would call me; she knew I would be there for her, to help her, like last time.

Did that new boyfriend of hers do something to her? Did she kill herself because he dumped her? I speculated but then scratched that. Kelly would never allow herself to get too upset about a mere breakup. She knew there was always someone else waiting to be with her.

All the same, I couldn't shake the feeling that her boyfriend was somehow connected to it all. He wasn't mentioned in the news, which I found suspicious.

I don't even know his name, I realized, irked. She'd probably mentioned it to me, but I hadn't been paying attention at the time, too wrapped up in my own drama to care about this new man in her life.

I regretted that immensely. *And now she is dead.*

I can't believe I lost my only friend. I was on the verge of starting to cry again, and I couldn't allow that. I didn't have my makeup kit with me. *Pull yourself together*, I snapped at myself. That worked, barely.

Without consciously making a decision, I grabbed my phone and started reading through our texts. Perhaps there were clues there, claims I'd missed. I could not let this go. I had to know. I had to know why she committed suicide.

What if it wasn't a suicide at all? My mind spun. What if it was a murder staged as a suicide? Although that sounded far-fetched, it actually happened more frequently than people believed.

But then, who would want to kill Kelly? She was loved by all.

I had a chilling thought as I remembered something from years ago. One person came to mind who definitely didn't harbor warm and loving feelings toward Kelly. What if this was connected to what had happened ten years ago?

But then my mind went even further. *What if what happened to Kelly is somehow connected to what is happening to me?* I'd told her about my stalker. Did that put her in danger? *Oh my God.* With such dreary thoughts, I managed to completely freak myself out.

I was reaching, trying to find complicated solutions to very simple things. Kelly killed herself, and it didn't really matter why; she was gone. And there was nothing I could do about it. There was nothing that could ever change that.

All the same, I felt almost compelled to investigate further and learn the truth. And the first step was to speak with Anna. Before that though, I decided to do something else. In the midst of my paranoia, some of the things I thought of still felt worth checking.

And that was precisely why I sent Bonnie to fetch me a very specific case from years ago. It wasn't something I would have kept in my office, since it was ten years old. It was one of the first cases I'd tried in court; however, the firm stored everything in the basement. Grant didn't trust technology that much. Although nowadays we had everything digitized, every case stored on drives, but he preferred hard copies as well.

I knew I couldn't trust the police with this, so I patiently waited for Bonnie to return with the file, drumming my fingernails against the wooden desk, hoping I was wrong, dreading I was right.

It took Bonnie a whole eternity to return with the file I'd requested. I couldn't wait to fire her.

"October case," she announced, putting two huge boxes on my desk.

"That will be all," I replied dismissively before attacking one of the boxes to look at what was inside.

Ten years ago I'd defended Kelly in a serious case. It had been a murder case, and Kelly had been the accused.

That was how we met, actually. I was a green lawyer, just started working at GBD, when Kelly got herself into a world of problems. Despite her lawyer's counsel, Grant, despite better judgments, and her mother's objections, Kelly requested I was her lead counsel.

She saw me arguing with another associate in the hall, thought I was very passionate, and decided then and there I was the lawyer for her. If I could fight with a colleague with such determination and gusto, Kelly was convinced I would do the same for her. And she was right, naturally. Eager to prove myself to everybody, I accepted. And ultimately won.

One night, so many years ago, Kelly was returning home from a party. She was beyond drunk, but wanted to drive herself home. Unfortunately, on her way home, she managed to run over a woman who was trying to cross the street.

It was a really big-profile case, as was expected. The whole country watched what would happen to the daughter of a famous actress. Some argued leniency, since she was a first offender, young, and had her whole life ahead of her. Others demanded the harshest punishments.

In the end, Kelly was found not guilty. And not everyone was pleased with that decision.

I managed to get her off the hook, since the woman in question was jaywalking on an unlit part of the road. I argued Kelly was unable to respond in time due to the woman's careless behavior. I'd had an expert put on the stand who testified how, even if she were stone-cold sober, Kelly wouldn't have been able to avoid such an unfortunate disaster.

The jury agreed with me, and Kelly walked free.

But I just remembered there was something else that happened.

After the reading of the verdict, a young man totally lost his mind. It was the woman's teenage son. He started to cause a scene, threatening to kill Kelly for what she did. He was taken away by the officers of the law, and I never bothered to learn what became of him afterward.

I looked into the files more closely. The woman had two children, twins, a girl and a boy named Bella and Sam. Sam was the one who'd made all those threats.

Is it possible he'd made good on his promise after all this time?

Was it possible Sam was involved in what had happened to Kelly? I wondered with dread. Or did Kelly piss someone else off, which wasn't that likely.

Kelly was a good, kind person, loved by all. And except for that one unfortunate incident, she'd never harmed a soul in her life.

Did Sam kill Kelly and make it look like a suicide? It was possible. Then again, it was entirely possible I was being paranoid and creating crazy scenarios, unable to admit my friend had killed herself.

I pushed all the October files away in disgust. I had no idea what I was supposed to do. I had no idea what to feel apart from sadness and despair.

26

ANOTHER DISASTER AHEAD

My visit with Anna was heartbreaking. Anna was always fond of me, thinking I would be a good influence on Kelly. That only showed that she didn't know her daughter as well as she should, but that didn't mean her pain of losing her wasn't real.

She'd popped so many pills, trying to numb herself, trying to numb the pain, she could barely speak with me. And all the leeches around her—managers, personal assistants, and bodyguards—were enabling her.

It was infuriating and sad to see such a diva in that state. She'd just lost her only daughter. I could understand the reality was unbearable to her. I felt heartbroken and lost, and I was merely a friend. A mother must have been feeling a hundred times worse.

Would my mother feel pain if something happened to me? I thought.

Understandably in such a state, Anna was unable to have a normal conversation with me, which meant I couldn't ask her any of the questions I wanted to, and actually get a coherent answer. All she could do was drone on and on about her precious Kelly.

"I can still remember how happy she looked, visiting me on my movie sets, mimicking all my moves, saying all my lines with me. Even at such a young age, she had the potential to become one of the greatest actresses of her generation," she slurred the words. "Sadly, she was never serious enough to really commit to the craft, and now she never will." She started to sob again.

I held her hands while she cried.

Anna couldn't help me. I was foolish to expect otherwise, knowing what she was like. Although there was no question she loved her daughter, Anna was also very selfish. That was why her pain was all that mattered now.

Seeing no other way, I helped Anna's assistant, George, organize a funeral for Kelly. I kept waiting to see that mysterious boyfriend of Kelly's drop by to offer his condolences to the family, but he didn't come.

"Was Kelly's boyfriend notified of what happened?" I asked George.

He gave me a blank stare in return. "What boyfriend?"

"That's ok. I'll ask Monica."

Monica was Kelly's assistant. Surprisingly, not even Monica knew anything about Kelly's latest boy toy, which I found strange. Kelly usually liked to brag to anyone who was willing to listen about her latest conquest. Why was this man different? Why was she keeping him a secret?

There was a possibility I was blowing things out of proportion, but I didn't think so.

The day of the funeral arrived, and I wasn't surprised at how many people had come to offer their condolences and say a last farewell to Kelly. Yet they were not there because they were heartbroken about Kelly. They were there to be seen. At times, I really hated this city.

The only one who was absent was Kelly's most recent boyfriend, although a few exes did show up, which was highly suspicious. There was no way he wasn't aware of what was happening. Stories about Kelly were all over the news, and I made sure the date and time of the funeral were put into print as well.

I knew how much it would mean to Kelly to have a lavish and most visited funeral, and I did everything in my power to make that happen, making her last wish come true.

It was hard to see all those people acting as though they cared while they gossiped about Kelly's suicide in hushed voices. I wanted to scream at them to behave, to negate she'd killed herself, to reveal she was actually murdered, but kept quiet.

I had no proof for my claims; besides, I didn't want my rash behavior to tip the murderer off that I was onto him. Part of me realized why I was doing this. I was trying to distract myself with crazy theories and nonexistent murderers so I didn't have to deal with the real issue: that my only friend had killed herself.

All the same, it was beyond suspicious Kelly's boyfriend was nowhere to be seen.

I guess it wasn't true love after all, I thought sarcastically, putting flowers on the casket.

Afterward, once all was said and done, I escorted Anna to her car. Many tried to get to her, speak to her, and use this tragedy to get close to her, which was despicable, to say the least. Yet she clung only to me, knowing I was Kelly's true friend.

She wanted me to go home with her as well, but I

couldn't. I had so many things to do, and then I needed to go to work. All the preparations around Kelly's funeral had taken a great deal of time, not to mention energy, so now I was behind.

Not that I was complaining. Someone needed to do all of this for Kelly, because Anna wasn't capable, and I was the best person for the job.

Although I didn't feel like working, considering all the recent events, I still did just that. I had to. Kelly might be dead, but I was still alive, which meant I had to continue living, go to work every day, and do my best to find out who my stalker was. And perhaps convince others that Kelly didn't kill herself.

Although to some that would look like ruffling unnecessary feathers, since I was in jeopardy of being labeled crazy or succumbing to crazy conspiracy theories, I still felt that was something that needed to be done.

Maybe I should ask that detective to discreetly look into things for me, I mused. Even if it was determined in the end that Kelly had actually killed herself, I would feel much better knowing I did all in my power to remove all the doubts.

Life had to go on despite everything, all the problems, all the heartache, and I started to feel angry at Kelly.

How dare she leave me all alone after everything I told her was happening? How dare she leave her mother?

Overall, Kelly had caused a world of trouble for those of us who knew her and cared about her. Killing herself was the most selfish thing ever. And that was typical of Kelly. Despite all the good that was in her, I had to admit she was also very selfish, like the only child of rich parents could be. And I was sure I would need a lot of time to overcome how angry and betrayed I felt because Kelly killed herself.

Besides, being angry instead of sad and worried helped me focus.

Getting to work, ignoring all the things that were coming out of Bonnie's mouth because I already knew my schedule by heart, I entered my office, closed the door in her face, and sat behind my desk.

I took a deep breath, then another. This was the first moment of peace I'd had since learning of Kelly's death. Being here always helped me remember what the most important thing in the world happened to be.

Without wasting any more time, I fired up my laptop so I could draw up a contract my client needed to sign, when something else happened. My laptop was unresponsive. The screen was black, and it didn't respond to any commands.

I tried turning it off and back on. I made sure it had power, yet nothing worked.

"What the hell?" I exclaimed.

This couldn't be happening to me. Not today. I was already at the end of my rope. This had the potential to push me off the ledge. I couldn't deal with my laptop being broken. I just couldn't.

And then a small window appeared at the center of the screen. It was a simple notepad window with one sentence written.

If you want your laptop back, you will have to pay.

There was a link provided that I needed to follow.

What's the meaning of this? I wondered.

Naturally, I did not click on the link, and instead, I called the IT guy who worked for our firm.

He took his time coming, while I was having a mini-mental breakdown.

The IT guy looked exactly as I pictured him, awkward, with a beard, wearing a goofy shirt that was funny only to him, which wasn't appropriate for the office at all.

"I am afraid your laptop has been infected with ransomware," he said after giving it a single glance.

I had no idea what ransomware was, but I could deduce from the context that it was nothing good.

"Can you fix it?" I asked with utmost urgency. I couldn't lose my laptop. Everything of any value was on it. Not to mention all the files with dirt I had on other colleagues.

He shook his head, much to my chagrin. "I can't do that, Miss Dennis."

"Why not?" I exclaimed. Wasn't fixing computers literally in his job description?

"This is your personal laptop, and I'm only authorized to deal with the firm's," he explained.

"Well, you have my authorization to fix it."

"It doesn't work like that, sorry."

"I use this laptop for work," I argued, "when I have to work from home."

"It doesn't matter. It's not GBD's property. I suggest you log into our company's network next time you have to work remotely," he advised.

I gritted my teeth, ready to give him a piece of advice in return, yet the coward gathered his things and excused himself, leaving my office in a flash.

I was furious. I knew those guys from the IT department were useless, but this was a new low even for them. Part of me was sure he'd made that rule up because he didn't want to deal with this.

Perhaps he didn't know how to fix my laptop and found

an excuse so he wouldn't have to try it, I mused. Naturally, I didn't like that one bit because it meant my laptop was in worse shape than I originally thought.

Oh my God, what am I going to do? I panicked.

Should I just pay the ransom? I thought, but thought against it. I couldn't negotiate with terrorists. Who was to say my laptop would be fine afterward even if I did pay what this hacker wanted?

I couldn't risk it. I had to find someone who could fix this problem for me and fast. And then it came to me. *Mercy.* She was an IT nerd techy. I was sure she would know how to deal with my problem.

Gathering my things and grabbing my precious, infected laptop, I left my office early. I felt slightly guilty about that; then again, I was conducting business in a way, trying to fix my laptop, although I was rushing home to do so.

I knocked on Mercy's door immediately, without bothering to go to my apartment first. There was no need for that anyways.

She opened the door, looking slightly confused. It was obvious she didn't expect to see me at her door during the day. "Amber, are you all right?"

"No," I stated, a bit whiny. I pointed at my laptop. "Someone hacked it, and now I can't do anything."

"Are they asking for money?" she asked, frowning.

"Yes. There was a link provided, but I didn't follow it."

She nodded. "Let me see it."

I dutifully gave her my laptop as we went inside. She placed it among her own computers and monitors.

Mercy tried powering up my laptop, getting the same result as I had before. "It's definitely ransomware," she agreed.

"That's what the IT guy said as well, but can you get rid of it?" I asked, actually holding my breath for her reply.

"Sure, but it'll take me some time."

I sagged with relief. "You are a huge lifesaver," I said honestly. "The IT guy at my firm refused to touch it."

"Luckily for you, you have me," she countered with a smile.

Mercy hooked my laptop to one of hers and then started to type furiously, clearly coding something, yet I had no idea what. I was never technically proficient in computer science.

"Can I get you something while you work?" I offered, feeling out of place sitting there, in her mismatched living room.

"No, but you can make yourself some tea if you want," she offered in return.

"That's ok. I already had my morning cup."

"Is everything all right with you?" she surprised me by asking.

"You mean other than being locked out of my own laptop?" I asked sarcastically.

"Yeah," she replied with a chuckle.

"Nothing from my stalker since the fire," I replied. Nevertheless, this got me thinking.

Perhaps this attack was from them as well. They'd promised total ruination. And losing my laptop would definitely mess with my job, ergo my life. Then again, I was sure they wouldn't ask for money. They would just attack my laptop and be done with it.

Part of me was grateful they didn't think of it first.

Yet.

"That's a relief."

"Unfortunately, something else did happen," I heard myself saying.

"What?" Mercy stopped typing to look at me.

"My best friend killed herself."

"Oh my God, that's so sad. I'm sorry for your loss."

"Thank you. I'm still in shock, you know. I had no idea she was having such a hard time."

"That only shows you can never fully know a person or what's in their heart," Mercy said seriously, philosophically.

"That's true," I agreed.

"How are you holding up?"

I half shrugged. "I'm really sad, and I already miss her."

"I felt the same way when I lost someone I cared about," she shared in return.

"How did you get over it?"

"I'll tell you when I do."

I remained silent, hearing that, but not sure what to say. Luckily, Mercy changed the subject.

We continued to chat as she worked, and I had to admit it felt nice having someone to do that with. It took a couple of hours, but Mercy managed to fix my laptop.

"All done," she announced, getting up from her chair and stretching.

"Is it gone?" I asked.

"Yes. I managed to remove the malware without any consequences to your processor's integrity. I'm pretty sure it downloaded onto your computer from an email you must have opened. It happens all the time with these hackers."

"But you were able to get it all off?"

Mercy nodded and smiled at me.

To say I was overjoyed would be an understatement. I was relieved my laptop was fully functioning again.

"And I installed some protection so that sort of thing won't happen again," she added as an afterthought.

I acted on impulse and gave her a small hug. "Thank you, Mercy. I really don't know what I would do without you. You literally saved my life. I don't know how to repay you."

"I may know a way," she replied, with a small smile.

"Name it," I said, figuring she would be asking for money.

I could understand that. Living in this city, in this apartment building, wasn't cheap. I should have offered to pay myself. That was only appropriate since this was what she did for a living.

But then she opened one of the drawers and produced a key for me.

"What's that?" I asked, confused.

"It's a key to my apartment," she explained. "I'm going away on vacation next weekend, and I really need someone to drop by once a day and feed my fish."

I frowned. I didn't even know she had fish, but true enough, there was a huge tank on the kitchen's bar.

"And you want me to do it?" I asked dubiously. I knew nothing about taking care of animals, fish included.

"We do that sort of thing back home all the time, swapping keys with neighbors. That way we can take care of one another. You can give me yours if you want."

That was a lot of information for me to process. "I don't know, Mercy. At times, I even forget to feed myself." And although I'd said it as a joke, that was actually true. "Can I think about it?"

"Sure."

"Thanks for the laptop, again."

"No problem."

27

MISERY LIKES COMPANY

I had just gotten into bed and was dozing off while reading a book when there was a loud banging on the door. *Not again*, I thought in exasperation.

The lunatic banging against my door was a persistent bugger, not to mention they were getting bolder and bolder, as though knowing there was nothing I could do to him.

At first, I was terrified, fearing whoever was on the other side was trying to break in. Since they didn't, although they'd returned night after night, I became pissed off, not to mention sleep deprived.

No matter whom I talked to or how quick I was to the door to try to catch them or how much I threatened them with the cops, they always returned. I tried calling Alex, but by the time he arrived, the lunatic had disappeared. The same went for the police. I'd called them so many times, they'd labeled me a Karen. I called Detective Sheldon as well, but there was nothing he could do about it either, since I had no idea who was doing this to me.

The only way was to open the door and catch them in

the act, and I was reluctant to do that. I didn't want to get murdered or something.

All the same, as I was clearly not thinking straight, I grabbed a lamp from the nightstand, and while they continued the drum solo on my door, I marched toward it. "If you don't stop right now, I will hurt you, badly," I threatened.

I opened the door, but there was no one there.

"Son of a bitch," I cursed loudly. This was the second time this same night that they'd come to torment me.

Frustrated, tired, angry, and so much more, I went to Mercy's door, in my nightgown, barefoot, and knocked, too late realizing how late it was.

I immediately stopped, not wanting to wake her up, when she opened the door. She was still in her regular clothes, meaning she hadn't been asleep, which was a relief.

"Amber," she greeted, surprised.

"Sorry to bother you."

"You're not. I was just about to go to bed. Is something the matter?"

I realized that had become a pattern of ours. I came to her, and she asked if there was something wrong. And I really didn't know how I felt about that. It was depressing, for sure.

"Did you hear a loud knocking?" I asked without preamble.

She frowned. "I can't say that I have."

"It's happening almost every night. Twice tonight."

"You know I wear headphones when I work. Has someone been knocking on your door?"

"More like harassing me," I grumbled in return.

"Did you see who it was?"

"No, they covered the spyhole. And calling the police hasn't worked either."

"You want to come in for a moment? We can talk, and I can make you hot cocoa."

"No, thank you. All I want is to sleep, and this creep won't let me."

"Do you think it's that stalker you told me about?" she asked, making a face, as though frightened to say that, like the mere mention would summon the stalker.

"I don't know. Maybe. Probably." I rubbed my brow. "Sorry to bother you."

"It's no bother at all," she was quick to reassure me. "And I will definitely keep an eye, or an ear in this case, out for them. Maybe together we can catch them in the act."

I nodded. Suddenly I felt too exhausted to carry on with this conversation. "Thank you," I forced myself to say as I started walking toward my apartment.

"You should call Alex; maybe he saw them," Mercy offered.

I turned, leaning against my door to look at Mercy. "I already did, but as usual, he saw nothing. Honestly, I have no idea why we keep paying him. He is beyond useless," I grumbled.

"I hope you manage to get some sleep," Mercy wished.

"Me too," I said, waving to her before closing the door. I felt really tired and wanted to go to sleep but feared they would just come back the instant I did, which would make things even worse.

Seeing no other way, I grabbed my phone and dialed Detective Sheldon, again.

"Your night banger returned, I presume?" he said by way of greeting.

I made a face. "Twice tonight."

"You know there's nothing I can do about it."

"You can be here at night and catch them in the act."

"I don't think camping outside your door would be very productive, not to mention I have real criminals to deal with."

It was on the tip of my tongue to say how unfortunate it was I wasn't a priority, being alive and all. I reined it all in. I couldn't allow myself to antagonize him, because then he wouldn't bother dealing with my case at all. I was that desperate, and I couldn't lose the bare minimum he was putting into it now.

"So what do you suggest? Just let them harass me?" I asked instead.

"Perhaps install some cameras in front of your door."

"There are cameras installed on the floor already," I replied in exasperation.

"And nothing is shown on them?"

"No." I stressed the word.

"Interesting. Let me call you later." He hung up.

I knew he wouldn't call me back. He never did. "Son of a bitch."

Considering the problem persisted, I made a point of calling Detective Sheldon each night so he would know what kind of monster I was dealing with. I hoped that perhaps that would motivate him further to solve my case. Unfortunately, it had had the opposite effect, and eventually, he'd stopped answering my calls.

For a solid week, I couldn't sleep at all because that maniac had kept banging on my door. If I was brave, I would leave the door open to see how they would pester me then. Sadly, I wasn't. In the midst of my madness, in search of a solution, I even contemplated calling David, and eventually ruled against it. I didn't need a man to save me. I was more than capable of dealing with my own problems. And I would, as soon as I figured out how, exactly.

Being sleep-deprived had started to affect my performance at work. I had trouble concentrating and had to reread the same sentence a couple of times to comprehend it like I was a kid with ADHD, not to mention how quickly I lost patience over the most ridiculous things. I snapped at everyone, even Grant, who firmly suggested at some point I should go home and get some sleep.

Or else it was heavily implied, and I really wanted to listen to him. The problem was I didn't want to go home. I knew I wouldn't be able to get my well-deserved rest there because I had a stalker who was doing his best to ruin my life.

And nobody was willing to help me. I was all alone, left to my own devices to deal with that maniac.

Maybe I should install a discreet camera on my door, I mused. Then again, was there something like that for sale, and who would install it for me? The only handyman I knew who proved to be half decent at his job turned out to be a major asshole, so I had no one.

Seeing no other way, I decided with a heavy heart to check myself into a hotel. *Again.* I was desperate to get some rest and knew whoever was bothering me couldn't pull the same stunt in a busy hotel.

At least, that was the hope.

After work I went home to grab a few things, all the while grumbling I was being forced to do this, when I stopped. Although it was out of character, I decided to be a good neighbor, which was a clear sign of how tired I was. Sleep deprivation was making me weak and soft-hearted.

Though, Mercy had helped me a couple of times in the past, so it was time I returned the favor. Picking up the last thing from the bathroom counter that stood by the door, I left my apartment with a small overnight bag and went to knock on Mercy's door.

"Hey, Amber," she greeted, cheerful as ever. Then she sobered up. "Is everything all right with your laptop?"

I patted my bag. "Works perfectly. That's not why I dropped by."

"Ok, so what's up?"

"I thought about what you asked of me, and I'll be happy to feed your fish while you are gone."

"Really? Thank you, thank you." She immediately offered me her key, which I accepted.

"But please leave detailed instructions for me on how to do it."

"Ok, it's pretty straightforward, grab a canister and sprinkle some of the stuff on top of the water," she said, chuckling.

"I will need that in writing."

"Ok."

"And while we are still on the subject, I want you to have this," I said, giving her my key in return.

It felt kind of strange, giving a key to my apartment to a complete stranger, yet Mercy had earned my trust, and I knew she wouldn't let me down. It wasn't in her to betray me.

"Is this the key to your apartment?" she asked, looking at it.

"Yes. I don't have fish to feed. Still, I will feel better knowing you have it."

"Are you going somewhere?" she asked, eyeing my bag.

"I'm checking myself into a hotel for some well-deserved sleep."

"Good thinking. And don't worry, I'll take good care of it," she reassured me, putting my key next to hers. "Water your plants if needed."

"Thank you."

As I was leaving the building, waiting for an Uber to pick me up, I was beyond frustrated the repairs of my car were taking this long. Teslas were expensive, and apparently getting replacement parts took forever. I pondered if I should call Detective Sheldon to let him know I would be staying at a hotel for a few days but ruled against it.

If he needs me, he can reach me on my cell.

Instead, I called David.

"Hello?"

It had been a while since I heard his voice, and it startled me how manly he sounded. I recovered quickly. "Hey, you," I greeted in a light tone. "Want to visit me? Not at my place, I am staying at a hotel."

"Why are you in a hotel?"

"Because I still have problems with that stalker, remember?"

"Are you all right?"

"Yes, I am. I can be even better if you come to see me. What do you say?"

"I can't tonight. I already have plans."

"Cancel them."

"I can't. How about later this week?" he offered instead.

I couldn't believe he was putting me off. I didn't want to

see him later. I wanted him now. "Ok, whatever," I said, hanging up.

I couldn't believe his attitude. Then again, it was his loss. If he wanted to do something other than be with me, then that was perfectly all right. Besides, I should really look at things from the brighter side. I would finally get some sleep.

28

DEAD END

A few days in a hotel did me wonders. I felt like a new me after finally sleeping through the night. Or more accurately, like the old me, fully functioning and ready to take on the problems that were plaguing my life.

I was starting to lose my mind when that stalker kept banging on my door. All that was behind me now though, and I felt terrific. In my current state, I was fully confident I would find out who was trying to ruin my life.

I also realized I'd tolerated the police's incompetence for far too long. I was going to demand full police protection immediately, and they were going to grant it. If they didn't, there would be hell to pay. I would do everything in my power to destroy them as a whole, as an organization. I would go to the press, share my sad story, and tell everybody how the police refused to do their job because they didn't like what I did for a living.

It was time someone taught them a lesson. They couldn't treat innocent people like common criminals. But I was certain it wouldn't have to come to that. One stern conversation with Detective Sheldon's boss would suffice.

And if he refuses, I'll sue them all. I was sure Grant would help me with that and happily. He lived for that kind of publicity. Because he knew that meant more money for the firm in the end.

Feeling quite invigorated, and righteous in my cause, I decided it was time to return home. There was no point in postponing the inevitable. My problems wouldn't magically resolve themselves; I had to do that.

Firstly, I called Detective Sheldon. I wanted to let him know how things would be different from now on. I was slightly surprised when he answered.

"Miss Dennis, I was just about to call you," he said as a way of greeting.

"Oh really, how fortunate we had the same idea at the same time," I replied, not buying into his bullshit. I was sure he was lying. The only time he called me was to ask stupid questions. I hoped he had something better for me this time around.

"Indeed," he added.

"What can I do for you?" I asked, in a slightly mocking manner, certain he hadn't noticed. The nerve on him. He should be asking what he could do for me, not the other way around.

"Are you still having problems with your night visitor?"

I frowned. *Is he mocking me?* This conversation was taking a turn I didn't like. I wanted to speak about my stalker finally being caught. "I honestly don't know. I've been sleeping in a hotel for the last few days."

"Good call," he replied.

It was shocking, infuriating, not to mention devastating

that I was actually having this conversation with a police officer. Instead of helping me fix my problems, he was more than happy I'd found a way to avoid them, as though that would solve anything.

Unbelievable.

"There's a reason I called," I started, deciding to change the subject because I was really starting to lose my patience with this fool.

He interjected, "Actually, let me go first. I have some bad news to share with you."

Bad news? Had my stalker managed to burn my apartment this time around? Did he do something to GBD? My mind started to spin from all the possibilities.

"Tell me," I urged.

"Mickey Richards, the suspect I was chasing, turned up dead."

A strange foreboding washed over me. I was so shocked that I had to sit down. Usually, I liked to walk around the room while speaking on the phone, but now I knew my legs wouldn't support me. "What? How? Why?" I rambled.

"Yeah, it was a hit and run," he replied. Something in his tone caught my attention.

"But?" I prompted.

"No buts. Plain old gut feeling something fishy is going on."

"In what way?" I asked, although I already suspected I knew what he was about to say.

"I can't shake this feeling someone is cleaning house."

Bingo.

"Does that make any sense? My stalker wasn't violent up until this point," I replied, playing the devil's advocate.

"Are you sure about that? He did try to burn you and your boyfriend to a crisp," he said blatantly.

"David is not my boyfriend," I felt compelled to correct.

"Beside the point. My theory still stands," he insisted.

"And what is your theory, exactly?" I wondered because nothing made sense anymore.

"My theory is that Mickey was hired to harass you, steal your phone, and trash your car. He was never the real mastermind behind it all, in my opinion. He didn't fit the profile. He was interested in cash, nothing else."

Based on everything Detective Sheldon told me, I had to agree with him. I had no relation with Mickey Richards, and whoever was harassing me had a personal grudge against me. Or so I'd been told many times since this whole mess started.

"However, things got slightly dangerous when he threw that Molotov cocktail against your door."

"The police got involved more." I filled in the blanks.

"Exactly. And I believe Mickey got spooked, and whoever hired him killed him."

"Why?"

"Because the person targeting you has far more nefarious plans for you than sending you a few threatening emails, and killing Mickey proved that."

And trying to burn me alive was merely the first attempt. A failed attempt. That thought froze the blood inside my veins.

All this time I was taking these threats and what had been happening to me too lightly. Even after the fire, I brushed it all off, because nothing had happened to me; I got out of it unharmed. Now I was realizing what a terrible mistake I'd made. This person, this monster, whoever they were, wouldn't settle for ruining my life. They wanted to take my life as well.

Oh my God, oh my God.

"Miss Dennis? Are you with me?" Detective Sheldon called out to me.

I managed to calm myself down enough to ask, "So what am I supposed to do now?" *How to stop this person from making me his next victim?*

"First of all, don't panic."

That was easy for him to say. He didn't have a huge target on his back. I was the one in danger. This maniac wanted me dead. And there was nothing I could do to stop them. There was nothing the police could do to stop them. They were going to get me and kill me.

Stop it, I snapped at myself, banishing all those terrifying thoughts. I couldn't allow myself to start spiraling out of control.

I can survive this. I can win this. Just like I've won at everything else in my life. I only had to remain calm and approach this problem with a cool head and cold rationale.

"And second of all?" I replied, satisfied with how my voice sounded even, unafraid.

"I need you to list everyone who might possibly have the biggest grudge against you. Big enough to kill, you understand?"

"Haven't we already gone through this before?" I felt like we kept doing the very same thing, expecting different results.

"Yes, but Mickey turning up dead changed everything. So I need you to really think about this. Who hates you enough to be willing to kill? And think broadly, think of everybody."

Without wasting any more time, I started to give him

names. Not of random people, naturally, but people I believed would be capable enough to take steps further than mere harassment. Even without including the clients I'd failed to defend successfully, the list was incredibly, disturbingly long. Some names he had heard before, but others, he had additional questions about.

What had started with me wanting to give the detective a piece of my mind, and threaten if needed to get some justice, had turned into something else entirely. It became a battle against time. The battle to save my life.

And after some thought, I decided to add my mother to that list as well.

"Maisie Dennis," I said calmly.

"Maisie Dennis? Is that your—"

"Mother, yes."

"Why do you think she would do this to you?"

"Because she blames me for everything bad that has happened in her life since my father died twenty years ago."

"All right, I'll look into it."

I was grateful he made no snide remarks on how my own mother could hate me enough to want to kill me. He acted professionally, and for that, I had to give him credit. Even if it was the only one.

"Anyone else?"

"David Grant."

"The not boyfriend?"

"Yes."

"Why do you suspect him now?"

"Because of what you said a while ago. That in most cases the harassers were unfulfilled lovers. And David wanted a relationship with me, and I refused. Many times."

"He was with you on the night of the fire."

"Yes, he was. And now I wonder if he was there so he could play the hero," I said what came to mind.

"Perhaps you're onto something there, Miss Dennis. I just wish you had been up front with me sooner. We could have saved so much time, not to mention a life," he jibed.

"I'm sorry, Detective, I made a terrible mistake. I am aware of that," I replied, deciding to take the full blame.

And then something else occurred to me. Perhaps I was reaching, but based on recent events, I was taking no chances. I decided to be one hundred percent honest with the detective, lay all my cards out on the table, and let him make of it whatever he pleased.

That was something I should have done from the start. I banished that thought since it was counterproductive. Placing additional blame on myself would accomplish nothing. And I needed results, and now.

"Can we meet?" I asked. "There is something I want to show you."

"Sure. I can drop by your place after work."

"I'm still at the hotel for now, Detective. I plan to return home soon though."

"Fine. Text me the address, then."

As agreed, we met that night.

"So what do you have for me, Miss Dennis?" he asked the moment he entered my room, skipping small talk, which I appreciated. This was business, after all.

"I don't know if this is connected to what's been happening to me, but there's something I wanted to tell you."

"And that is?"

"My friend Kelly October died a week ago."

"She was the daughter of that movie star?"

"Yes."

"I'm sorry for your loss."

"Thank you. The thing is, the official report says she committed suicide."

"And you suspect that's not the case?" he guessed.

"Maybe I'm paranoid, but I don't think that's what really happened."

"Tell me what your gut feeling is saying," he prompted.

"I believe her death is connected to what's been happening to me, especially after the death of Mickey Richards."

"Why do you say that?"

"Because she wasn't the type who would just end it all; she had no reasons to do it."

By the expression on his face, I could see I was losing him. He believed I was in denial like any other grieving person.

"She had this elusive new boyfriend who nobody knew anything about, who she kept a secret. And he didn't even bother to come to her funeral."

I understood how it all sounded far-fetched, but something deep inside me was telling me that I was onto something. The question was how to convey that to the detective.

"Did you two have a common enemy?" the detective asked, but it was obvious he was humoring me.

"I believe that we did, actually."

That piqued his interest. "Who?"

I went to the small desk where I kept the October file with the most important piece of information. I removed the file and handed it to him. "Ten years ago, I defended Kelly in a murder case."

"A murder case?" he asked, opening the file.

"It was a hit and run."

He gave me a look, and I knew what was on his mind. It was similar to what had happened to Mickey Richards.

"Kelly accidentally ran over a woman named Susanna Stone. Kelly was drunk at the time, but I still managed to get a not-guilty verdict."

"I'm not surprised to hear you were a formidable lawyer even when first starting up," he said dryly.

"That's not the point. Susanna had two children, teen twins. And I remember how they acted when the jury read the verdict. Especially the boy. He was livid, threatened to kill Kelly, threatened to kill everybody."

The more I thought about it, the more I was convinced it was all connected to that specific case.

On the other hand, there was also a chance I was utterly insane, grasping at straws because I was scared out of my mind. Maybe I just wanted a face and a name attached to my harasser so I would know, once and for all, against whom I was fighting.

"It's understandable they got upset. Their mother's murderer had just walked free," he argued in return.

"You weren't there. This was more than that."

"Perhaps," he allowed. "Then again, ten years is a really long time to hold a grudge. It doesn't mean they still feel the same way."

"Are you sure about that? We are talking about their mother here. They had nobody else, just her."

"You have no proof, only a theory that is pretty shaky, stretched, at best."

"Please, Detective, check Kelly's autopsy report, check out her new boyfriend, check those kids, and if I'm wrong, then I'm wrong. However, if I'm right..." I left the sentence hanging.

Detective Sheldon remained silent for a moment, glancing at the file. "I will look into it, Miss Dennis; all the same, it's a very slim lead."

"It's better than nothing. Besides, you have to admit it all kind of fits."

"It is better than nothing," he agreed, "which is precisely why I'll look into it."

"Thank you."

"I'll let you know what I find out," he promised before leaving.

I sagged with relief, feeling, for the first time in forever, that I had actually managed to accomplish something.

29

THE THINGS WE DO FOR SEX

I was in shambles after my conversation with Detective Sheldon. I was convinced that my stalker, who'd set fire to my apartment and banged on my door night after night, not only planned on psychologically tormenting me, but eventually harming me as well.

I dreaded returning to my apartment, but I had to go home. That was my only option. Although, to be perfectly honest, my apartment hadn't felt like home since this whole nightmare started.

The upkeep for my apartment was expensive, and I knew that staying in a hotel alongside it wasn't feasible. I was running through my savings, and fast, and although I was making a lot of money, it was still not something I was comfortable with, considering I had my future to think of. Sadly, I didn't have a rich parent I could run to each time I had a problem or ran out of money. I had to take care of myself.

The whole day at work, I stressed about going home. I

almost managed to convince myself to return to the hotel although I'd already checked out that morning.

My pride was telling me I should return home because I shouldn't allow some lunatic to chase me from the place I called home, which I'd earned with my hard work. My fear was telling me to run away and hide someplace that they could never find me. They were going about killing people, for crying out loud. And I knew I was next. It was foolish to return to the place they were so familiar with.

I might as well tie a red bow around my neck and call myself a present because I am preparing myself for slaughter.

And then I had an idea. If David was there with me, I would definitely be safer.

You named him as one of your suspects, remember? part of me reminded.

That was true, but I still believed I should give him a call. The way I saw it, it was a win-win situation. If he wasn't the perpetrator, then I would be protected; if he was the one, he would still want to come and be with me because that was his ultimate goal. *Right until the moment he kills you.*

I didn't actually believe he was my stalker. He wasn't that capable. He would need Grant to do everything for him.

Maybe Grant is behind it all. He was definitely ruthless enough and had plenty of resources to hire whomever he wanted to get the job done. However, that didn't really make sense. My fear was making me paranoid.

I decided to give David a call. Grabbing my phone, I paused. I'd called him a few days ago, and he'd blown me off. And that wasn't the first time either. *He's been distant lately.*

Was he really distant, or was it you who pushed him away? I had a moment of doubt remembering my mother's words. Taking a deep breath, I dialed his number.

"Hello?"

"Hey, David."

"Hey, Amber."

"I was thinking we should see each other tonight."

"I don't think I can."

I made a face. "You're constantly saying no, and I don't like it."

"Amber..."

"You said you would be there for me, and you haven't." I pouted. "A lot of bad things have happened, and I really need someone. I need you to talk with, ok?"

"What happened?" he asked in all seriousness.

"A lot of things, David, and I don't want to talk about it over the phone."

"Are you still staying at a hotel?"

"No, I'm returning home tonight, not because the threat's gone, but because I have no other choice."

"What do you mean?"

"I don't want to talk about it, it's embarrassing." There was no way in hell I would share my financial difficulties with him.

"Why didn't you tell me things have gotten that bad?" he demanded.

"I tried, and you kept blowing me off," I threw at him.

"I'm sorry. I figured you only kept calling because you wanted sex, and that pissed me off. And then you started ignoring me."

"David, I kept you at bay because I didn't want something happening to you too. I was afraid. I am afraid."

"I'm sorry, Amber. I'm sorry about everything. Now I see how stupid I acted."

I allowed myself a small victory smile. I sobered up

immediately, knowing this wasn't over. "Does that mean we can see each other tonight?" I sounded just a tad more eager than I should have; then again, that would probably be good for his ego.

"I'll meet you at your place tonight."

"How about we meet in front of my building at eight?" I offered. I didn't want to spend even a second alone inside that apartment.

"Sure," he agreed.

I sighed with relief.

MY TIMING WAS PERFECT, and by the time I exited the Uber that drove me home from work, David was already waiting outside the building.

Not being able to help myself, I kissed him then and there, out in the open, not caring who could see us. Once upon a time, I wouldn't allow myself such an infraction, yet things had changed.

David was the one who broke the kiss first. "Let's get you inside," he said, looking over his shoulder as though fearing someone would spot us.

Welcome to my life. Part of me wanted to point out how the tables had turned, yet the rest was happy he was there because that meant I wouldn't have to spend the night alone.

What about tomorrow night? I thought. *I'll worry about that later.* Currently, I was living one day at a time.

When Alex greeted us as we walked through the lobby on our way toward the elevator, I looked the other way. I was still mad at him for being completely useless and letting the lunatic return night after night.

David looked at me questioningly, but I ignored it.

As soon as we were alone in the elevator, I wrapped my arms around his neck and pulled him in for another kiss.

"I really missed you," I murmured against his lips.

A few heartbeats later we were on my floor and moving toward my apartment. I ignored how nervous I felt going inside. I had this strange feeling in the pit of my stomach as though something bad was about to happen.

That's all in your head. You're imagining things, I told myself sternly.

"You have a new door," he observed as I was busy unlocking it.

"Yeah, everything got sorted out," I replied, remembering how wrong I had been about that god-awful handyman. I couldn't believe I'd actually contemplated getting him into my bed.

Sure, he was hot, but he was also just a contractor. It only showed how distraught I was after the fire that I'd almost slept with someone so beneath me. Luckily, my common sense returned.

And so did David, I joked to myself.

"So the detective still hasn't found who's behind the fire?"

"Unfortunately, he didn't. And the only lead he had ended up dead," I blurted out before I could stop myself.

I didn't want to talk about all of that now. I was afraid enough as it was, and I knew if we continued down that path, my libido would leave the building. And the only reason I'd asked David to come was that I needed a distraction.

And a bodyguard, I corrected.

"I'm worried about you," David said, sitting on the couch.

"I'm worried about me too," I replied honestly, sitting next to him, so close I was practically in his lap.

"I'm serious, Amber," he countered, misunderstanding my words.

"I am too," I insisted. "This stalker is really scaring me, not to mention I was so paranoid I started thinking—" I stopped myself there. I wasn't ready to share everything with him. Besides, if he was my stalker, I didn't want to share the direction the investigation was going. My head was starting to hurt from all the thoughts inside it. *I really need a break.*

"You started thinking what?" David insisted, much to my chagrin.

I sighed. "Can we not speak about this?" I begged. "I really need a night off," I said, putting my head on his shoulder.

"Please, Amber, talk to me; don't shut me out again."

I groaned inwardly. I realized he wouldn't sleep with me if I didn't share everything. *What if he gets mad and walks away?* Then I would be all alone, and I couldn't bear the thought of that.

"I met with Detective Sheldon last night. And we started talking about potential suspects—"

"And?"

"And I started wondering if what was happening is somehow connected to Kelly dying."

"Kelly? Who's Kelly?" he questioned.

"Kelly, my friend?" And then I realized he had no idea what I was talking about. "Kelly October. She was the daughter of Anna October, the movie star."

"Yeah, I know Anna October. I didn't know you two were friends."

"Yes, we were," I said glumly.

I had stopped being angry at Kelly for leaving me. And

now, once again, I was sad she wasn't here anymore. I could really use her company right about now.

"I heard she committed suicide," David said.

"That's the official report, but I have my doubts."

"How come?"

"She wasn't the type of girl to do that," I hedged. I didn't want to tell him there had been a case ten years ago, one that could potentially be the link between us, and what was happening to me, and what had happened to her.

"I think a lot of people who have lost someone in that manner feel the same way."

I moved so I could look into his face. "You don't understand," I snapped, frustrated I was being forced to have this conversation with him. "She wasn't depressed, and she didn't take drugs. She was happy and vibrant, and I'm sure something happened to her," I insisted.

"Did you tell the police?" David asked another brilliant question.

"I did, and I know that won't lead to anything."

"Why do you say that?"

"Because they've been oh so very helpful up until this point. You know I gave a list of suspects to that detective on a silver platter, and still, here I am cowering in fear. He proved to be as incompetent as the rest of them," I ranted, getting all riled up, and I couldn't even specify what had triggered me at this specific moment. Sadly, I had too many triggers to choose from.

"Who are the people on your list? Tell me their names," he demanded.

I actually wanted to laugh at that. "Why? Do you want to go talk to them? Will you be the one catching my stalker?"

"Maybe I should."

"Don't be ridiculous, David. This—what is happening—is beyond dangerous."

He shook his head. "I still think you should at least hire a bodyguard."

The thought of having a man in my life following my every move, just like that stalker, made me want to scream.

Instead of saying what was actually on my mind, I moved, ever so slightly, so I could sit on David's lap. "Now, why would I do that when I have you," I said seductively, playing with his firm pecs.

He gave me a look. "I'm being serious, Amber."

I knew he was, which was part of the problem. I was done with this conversation. I believed I had shared enough, so now it was his turn to provide a distraction because I deserved it.

I looked down. "I know you're being serious. This is all very serious, and I feel like I'm breaking at the seams. So can we please stop, at least for the moment? I... I just need to feel something different, other than scared."

"Amber..."

"Please, David," I begged, and with that, I leaned in to kiss him, and he let me.

One kiss led to another, and shortly after, we were in rather familiar territory, kissing, taking off each other's clothes, passion taking over. It didn't take us long to end up in the bedroom, entwined and naked.

Naturally, as I'd said to him, that was exactly what I needed. I was very pleased he'd remembered everything I'd taught him, and then some, and it didn't take me long to find my release.

Perhaps keeping him around would have its merits, and if that entailed having to endure a date with him, then so be it, I mused.

Surprisingly, once we were both sated and had managed to get our breathing under control, enjoying that post-coital bliss, David got up and started to get dressed. That startled me because I was just preparing myself for round two. It had been a while since we'd had sex, and I was looking forward to making a night of it.

Usually, I had to kick him out, fearing he would want to spend the night, and now here he was, voluntarily putting his boxers on without complaint or a sad face. *Does this mean he is finally getting it?* I thought, full of hope. Then again, his timing sucked because I wasn't done with him yet.

"What are you doing?" I asked slowly, stretching lazily, putting my whole body on display, silently inviting him to come back to bed and play.

"I have to go," he replied, without looking at me.

"Why? Are you going to turn into a pumpkin at midnight?" I teased.

"There's something I have to tell you. I've been meaning to tell you sooner, but we, I, got distracted," he blurted out, and then paused.

I didn't like where this was going. "Tell me now."

"Since we were never that serious, I started seeing someone else."

I could only stare at him. David got himself a girlfriend. So that was the real reason he kept blowing me off.

While I was dealing with a stalker, while I was in the middle of the most horrendous personal crisis, he was fucking someone else. *What a selfish son of a bitch.* I couldn't believe it. After all he'd said, he turned his back on me so easily...

I wondered who his new woman was. I was sure she was

no woman at all, but some girl, stupid like he was. She couldn't possibly be better than me in any regard.

Then I reminded myself I had no right to feel wronged in any way. And I wouldn't allow myself to feel jealous because that was precisely what David wanted.

"Amber, please say something," he pleaded, looking pretty torn up.

I was glad. He should feel like shit.

"It's fine, David," I replied with a small smile. "As you said, we were never that serious, and I'm happy for you."

He looked relieved. "Thank you for being so understanding."

"Always. Please lock the door on your way out," I added, turning away from him, as though preparing to sleep.

"Bye, Amber," he said as he left.

I knew he wouldn't be coming back.

30

WORLD TUMBLING DOWN

I barely managed to sleep after David left. I was beyond furious, although I kept telling myself I had no reason to be, and then I understood why. I realized that despite everything, I counted on David because he'd made all kinds of promises. In the end, he'd gone back on his word like every other man. And that was fine. That was something I should have known would happen sooner or later because people could not be trusted.

Naturally, the next morning, I felt both better and worse. The fact I had finally had sex last night had put me in a better mood. Still, I didn't like the idea of being replaced by someone else.

That son of a bitch. How dare he dump me! I'm the one who does the dumping, always.

Then again, two could play that game, and no one was better at it than me. David was easily replaceable, and I was going to rub his nose with my newest conquest. I merely had to pick someone first.

If I was the vengeful type, I would replace David with his

own father. Grant had wanted to fuck me from the moment I started working at GBD. That was no secret, *so maybe I should let him,* I mused.

Just thinking about the look on David's face when his father introduced me as his new stepmother made me chuckle. *That would be the ultimate revenge.* But would I really do that? I would have to think about it. Grant wasn't in his prime anymore, and the thought of having some living corpse touching me held no appeal to me.

No revenge was worth having to suffer through that. All the same, he'd married countless times. *Perhaps he's good in bed.* I couldn't rule that out. And it would be nice to be with someone who actually knew what he was doing. Even if he could only do it once a night.

With my head raised high, like always, I entered the law firm that would one day soon have my name on the wall. I lived for that day. As I passed my assistant's desk, Bonnie looked freaked to see me. That woman was getting stranger by the day.

"Good morning," I said, hoping that would snap her from whatever unnecessary drama she was going through. It was too early in the morning to be having a mental breakdown.

"Good morning," she practically stammered. "Mr. Grant asked for you to meet him in his office the minute you arrived," she conveyed.

"Fine," I nearly sang in return. "I'll just put my things away in the office."

I was sure Grant wanted to personally congratulate me for my latest victories. I was bending over backwards, despite all my personal problems, to impress him. And I really hoped he would appreciate all my efforts in the right way.

Like adding my name to the wall.

"He said immediately," Bonnie insisted as I walked toward my office.

I rolled my eyes. "A few minutes won't make a difference."

Honestly, did she have to be such a drama queen? She was ruining my mood, when I was working really hard to maintain it.

"Amber, what are you doing here?" Grant demanded, coming up behind me as I was pulling my laptop from my bag. "Didn't Bonnie tell you I wanted to see you?" His tone was stern and cold, which was strange for him.

"Yes, but—"

"In my office, now," he barked. "We are all waiting for you," he added before storming away.

We?

I made a face and continued with what I was doing, placing files on the desk that I would need later.

Naturally, I wondered what had put him in such a foul mood. Did something happen that I wasn't aware of? *Did one of his clients commit mass murder or something?* I hadn't heard anything of the sort on the news; then again, that wouldn't entice such a reaction from him.

Grant was only angry when he was losing money.

What's that have to do with me? I pondered. I was bringing a lot of money in to this firm, and my work was impeccable.

After straightening my blazer, looking at myself in the mirror, and making sure I looked my best, I walked the short distance to Grant's office. Although Grant had said they were expecting me, I was still startled to see all the senior partners assembled in his office.

Dawson was leaning against the wall near a window,

looking grim as always, and Phoebe sat in one of the chairs, looking at me with a strange expression on her face. She looked almost disgusted.

What the hell?

And of course, Grant stood behind his desk, looking beyond furious.

Come to think of it, they all seemed to be in various states of anger. I would be lying if I said that didn't make me feel uncomfortable. Nonetheless, I raised my head high, straightened my back, and stood in front of them all.

"Why did you want to see me, Grant?" I asked calmly.

"Something was sent to me this morning."

"Is it a ransom video?" I only half joked.

He ignored me as he grabbed a TV remote and turned the TV on.

I turned to my left to look at the screen.

As he pushed play, all the blood left my face, and I exclaimed, putting both hands against my mouth so I wouldn't start screaming. Across the big screen, in a video, I was having sex with David. In my bed.

I shut down for a moment, having an out-of-body experience, but then I returned to myself, and all kinds of thoughts rushed through my head.

"Turn that off!" I yelled, moving in front of the TV as though to shield it from everyone's view. Although I was sure they'd already watched it. Their expressions and their somber attitudes confirmed as much.

"By your reaction, I presume the video is real," Grant said dryly, finally turning the TV off.

I was relieved. The office, hosting senior partners, echoing with my moans, was almost too much to bear.

"I'm highly disappointed in you, Amber," he threw in my face.

"Among other things," Phoebe added snidely.

"How did you get that? Who sent it to you? Why?" I started to bombard him with questions.

Grant waved his hand in a dismissive manner. "That's not important."

I jerked as though he had slapped me. What did he mean? That was the most important question. Someone had sent a sex tape to my boss, and they needed to pay for it.

"I can't have my lawyers have sex tapes," Grant continued. "We would become the laughingstock in this city."

"Grant, please, I didn't make that—let me explain," I pleaded as my brain worked a hundred miles an hour, trying to come up with a story that could get me out of this mess.

"There's nothing to explain. I saw everything that I needed to see."

The way he said that almost brought tears to my eyes. I was horrified. I was ruined. I couldn't believe this was happening to me.

Why did David record us? Why did he send it to his father? Why now? Was that some kind of revenge? Against whom, me or Grant? Not that it really mattered right now, the end result was still the same. I was fucked, and in too many ways to count.

"I don't know why David sent this to you."

"Don't get my son involved in this," Grant countered, getting all riled up.

"I know you're surprised by what you saw—"

"Surprised isn't the first thing that comes to mind," Phoebe jibed again.

"David and I are both adults, and—"

"And it's inexcusable what you allowed yourself to do," he said through gritted teeth.

I knew he was overprotective of David, but this was ridiculous. He was acting as though I was some evil witch who had seduced his innocent boy. That was far from the truth.

"There are no rules against it." I stood my ground, no matter how shaky I felt.

I will kill David for doing this to me. First, he dumped me; then he sent a sex tape of us to his father. When did he do this anyway? Why? Why was he trying to ruin my life?

Because he's your stalker.

"I am against it!" Grant boomed.

"Grant, you're blowing things out of proportion."

"Enough, Amber. I won't have you stand here, defending this filth."

"Excuse me?"

"You heard him," Phoebe interjected. "Besides, we didn't call you here to listen to your excuses for such loose moral behavior."

Loose moral behavior? Were we in the sixteenth century? I couldn't believe my ears. Then again, nothing made sense to me.

"Your bad judgment calls are your own, but we can't have our firm's reputation tarnished," she continued to lecture me.

"Precisely," Grant agreed. "This is unacceptable, and I won't tolerate it."

"What are you saying, Grant?"

"You're fired," Dawson said, finally deciding to enter the conversation and be the final nail in my coffin.

I looked at Grant. "Fired, over this?" I forced myself to choke out.

"Yes," he replied sternly.

"No," I rebelled instantly. "You can't do that."

"I can, and I already did."

"I'm a junior partner."

"Not anymore," Phoebe said, and it was more than obvious how pleased she was saying that. She had hated me from the start, and now she had what she'd wanted all along, me gone.

No, no, no.

"I don't want to see you in this building ever again," Grant said before turning his back on me.

That felt like a stab in the heart. After everything I'd done for him, for this firm, he'd so easily discarded me, like I was nothing.

"Grant."

"You disgust me. Get out!"

I ran out of his office, and gathering my things from my office—all that I could in a rush, I left the building. I couldn't believe this was happening to me.

I knew Grant wouldn't like seeing me with his son, but that was cruel even for him. Was his ego so bruised that he needed to fire me? Fire me!

Who sent him that damn video? Why? Why? My mind was in complete shambles.

I sat on the nearest bench, my body shaking like crazy. I'd just lost the most important thing in my life.

I will make sure you lose everything, my stalker warned me.

I started to scream, not caring that I looked like a complete lunatic. He was going to pay for this. *They are all going to pay for this.*

I couldn't be fired. I couldn't lose my job. I just couldn't. I was on the verge of hysteria. There had to be some way to fix things, but how? I couldn't believe this day had started out like this.

Grabbing my phone, I called David. That son of a bitch was going to pay for ruining my life.

"Hello?" he answered calmly, as though all was well in his world. Like he hadn't just single-handedly ruined my career, my life.

"I can't believe you did that to me, you son of a bitch," I screamed.

Some people on the street looked at me funny, and I wanted to yell at them too, telling them to mind their own business, yet I had to stay focused on David. One yelling at a time.

"Did what?" He had the nerve to play dumb.

"You not only made a sex tape of us, you sent it to your father," I said as my voice shook from all the rage I was feeling.

"Sex tape? What are you talking about?"

"Don't try to deny it. I saw it. Grant saw it. And do you know what he did? He fired me! And it's all your fault."

"Amber, I have no idea what you are talking about," he rushed to say. "I didn't do it."

"Your father has a sex tape of the two of us. And he fired me because of it." I knew I was repeating myself, but I was in shock.

"How is that possible? Who made a sex tape of us? It doesn't make any sense," he rambled in return. He sounded genuinely confused and shocked.

I wasn't buying it. He had to be the one. We were the only

two people there. And if I didn't do it, it had to have
been him.

"Why did you do it, David?" I asked, losing some of my
strength. "Was it to hurt me, or him?"

All of a sudden, I felt spent and small. I wanted to crawl
into my bed and pretend none of this had happened. Wait to
wake up from this nightmare.

"Amber, I swear to you I didn't do it."

"I don't believe you."

"Think about it, how could I? We've always had sex at
your place."

That was true. If he had tried anything, I would have
seen it. In the video, we were definitely in my bed. I felt
nauseous just thinking about that tape, which was now in
Grant's possession.

"If you didn't do it, then who the hell did?"

"That is a great question, Amber. I have an idea, and I
don't think you'll like my answer."

31

FROM BAD TO WORSE

I was in the midst of full-on hysteria, having just lost the most important thing in my life. I'd been fired, ruined. I had been mocked by my bosses and chased out of the firm as though I were a complete nobody, yesterday's trash. I went straight home. After my conversation with David, I felt almost compelled to return to the scene of the crime.

Entering the apartment, letting my things fall where they may, I went straight to the bedroom.

David was right. If he didn't do it, and logically he really didn't have a reason for it, not that I was feeling rational at the moment, there was only one person who could do it, who wanted to do it. My stalker.

And for that to happen, they had to have eyes and ears inside my house, my bedroom.

There was a hidden camera inside my bedroom, and I was set to find it, even if it was the last thing I did in this world. And I planned on doing so much more.

I wanted to find this stalker and kill them with my bare hands. They had harassed me, tormented me, and violated me in every way possible, but it ended now. I wasn't going to tolerate them anymore. I wasn't going to stand on the side-lines waiting for the police to actually do something for a change. I would find them.

I will be the end of them.

Without fully comprehending what a hidden camera meant, and what implications it had on the bigger picture, I started to look for it. I could guess the general location of it from the angle of the video taken.

"Do you see me, you son of a bitch? I will find your camera. And then I am going to find you. You are going down. It's my turn to stalk you!" I screamed, clearly out of my mind, as I practically started to tear my room apart.

I was searching for any kind of hidden device, and I was very thorough, looking everywhere. I'd watched enough movies to know to check behind the curtains, inside the lamps, smoke detectors, and so on. Eventually, I found the bugger behind a picture frame. And I knew it was the one because the angle fit. This was the camera that had recorded my sexual encounter with David. That sick son of a bitch had recorded us, then sent it to Grant, knowing he would be furious. I yanked it out of its place.

"Are you seeing this now? Are you scared?" I taunted, half-mad.

I wanted to stomp on it, stick my tongue out at it, but left it be because I wasn't finished. Not by a long shot. I shook from head to toe as I continued with my search. I wasn't done; once I was finished with my bedroom, I planned on moving on to the rest of the apartment.

If this psychopath had dared to put a camera inside my bedroom, it was safe to assume it wasn't the only one.

I tore through everything in search of other cameras. The sick bastard had put another behind one of my precious paintings. After looking at all the most likely places for hidden cameras, I started looking through the unlikely places as well.

"I will find all your cameras, you sick maniac!" I shouted, tearing through my bookshelf.

As I looked about and deconstructed my home, a home I had so carefully arranged and decorated, all kinds of things rushed through my head. When did they manage to do this? How long had they been watching me? What else did they record? Thinking about that made me sick to my stomach; I felt like vomiting. Yet I reined it all in.

There was only one explanation for this. They had to have been here while I was away, to place all those cameras. The question was when? I had stayed at a hotel a couple of times because my place was unsafe or unlivable at the time.

I should have listened to them. Everyone, the police and David, had tried to tell me that I should move, but I didn't listen. I was stubborn, and these were the consequences. There was a sex tape out there of me. And if that maniac had dared to send it to Grant, what was to stop them from sharing it with the whole world? That brought tears to my eyes.

I felt violated on so many levels. They'd been inside these walls this whole time. They were watching me while I read their threats, while I stressed about what they would do next. They watched and gloated, knowing I was afraid of them. They must have felt pretty proud of themself in those moments.

I felt like screaming at the top of my lungs.

"Where are they?" I shouted, looking around me.

I knew they had planted other cameras. I had to find them. I had to find them all because if I didn't, then I wouldn't feel safe ever again. Then they would win. And that was something I wouldn't allow.

Looking through the rest of the house for other hidden devices took the rest of the day. No matter how many things I found, I always suspected there were more that I'd missed, forcing me to start my search over and over again.

"I will find all of them, don't you worry. Or do," I continued, speaking to my stalker.

Even though it was a one-sided conversation, I rather enjoyed it. There was a certain kind of perverse pleasure knowing they could be watching this now, seeing me find and destroy all their devices, knowing they were about to lose that connection to me.

Eventually, I found three more. I had been so crazed in those moments I danced around the room with them like they were some kind of prize, or peace offering to the gods that would deliver me of all my miseries. When I calmed down, I continued.

I was beyond disgusted that one of those cameras was hidden in the bathroom. *Sick fuck.*

The whole day passed, and I still felt watched. Despite finding the cameras, I still felt like I'd missed others. I wanted to rip through walls to make sure that bastard couldn't watch me anymore.

I couldn't live like that, thinking, fearing that they were still watching my every move, which was precisely what they wanted, I realized, to not only enter my apartment, but my head as well.

Feeling exhausted, at some point, I grabbed my phone and called Detective Sheldon.

"Hello, Miss Dennis."

He sounded tired, worn down.

Join the club.

"Detective, the stalker was inside my apartment." I hated how my voice shook, on the verge of hysteria.

"Are you hurt?" he demanded.

"Physically, no."

"I'm on my way," he informed me before disconnecting.

I was relieved. Detective Sheldon was coming, and that meant everything would be all right.

About half an hour later, Detective Sheldon knocked on my door. His facial expression remained neutral as he took in the general state of things around the apartment. "You decided to redecorate?" he deadpanned.

I felt like snapping because he'd chosen that moment to joke but found myself laughing instead. "It was that kind of day."

"Want to fill me in?"

I pointed at the table, where I'd gathered all the trinkets I'd found. "They placed those around my home."

He approached the table to inspect them.

"I don't know if I've found them all."

"I have a buddy who can help with that."

True enough, he made a call and one of his colleagues arrived a while later with a few gadgets and started snooping around my place.

I found it ironic how, once upon a time, I had been against having strangers inside my home, and now everyone was coming and going as they pleased.

But it was all in the name of good, and he managed to

find another camera. I was relieved I'd managed to find everything else myself. I didn't know why, but that felt like a victory, even if it was a pretty small one at that.

He helped remove everything properly, making sure they weren't transmitting anymore. After, the two men spoke in hushed voices as I prepared myself some tea, and the colleague left. I didn't even have enough brain power to ask his name.

"So what's the verdict?" I asked, only half joking, as Detective Sheldon approached me.

"How did you find out your apartment was bugged?" Detective Sheldon asked, ignoring my question. "These things were pretty well hidden."

"In a very unpleasant way," I replied.

Detective Sheldon waited for me to continue.

I sighed, putting down my steaming cup of tea. "A sex tape of me was sent to my boss this morning."

That did earn me a raised eyebrow.

Seeing no reason to keep anything from him at this point, since I'd already lost everything, I told the detective exactly what had happened.

"Do you have anything stronger to drink?"

I pointed at the minibar. He grabbed a bottle of whiskey, which I'd heavily decimated, and poured himself a glass. I didn't comment on the fact he was clearly drinking on the job.

Then, as though an afterthought, he poured a little into my cup of tea. It was disgusting, but I still drank it.

"I can't believe this is my life," I muttered to myself as I drank my beverage.

"You know, these cameras have to be transmitting to

somewhere nearby, as their signal fades out after about half a mile," he informed me almost conversationally.

So my stalker was closer than I believed.

"Have any more good news for me?" I said sarcastically.

"You're not safe here. You can't stay here."

Not being able to take it anymore, I sat down on the couch, or what was left of it, because I'd ripped through the cushions in search of the bugs, and started to cry. I had finally reached my limit. I couldn't take this anymore, this existence.

This fiend had taken everything from me, my job, my friend, and to learn they were also nearby this whole time, watching, lurking, was the last straw.

"Come with me," the detective insisted.

I was so out of place, so defeated, I didn't have the energy to put up a fight, refuse, or stay home. What was the point anyway? My stalker had managed to destroy everything for me. It was all over.

I wiped my tears and grabbed an overnight bag. It was heartbreaking I always had one at the ready. Without a word, I followed the detective out of the apartment without sparing it a second glance. I knew he'd taken all the cameras with him, as evidence, but at that point, I really didn't care. I didn't allow myself to get my hopes up, thinking they would generate a lead.

My stalker was always ten steps ahead of me, ahead of everybody. They'd proved that time and time again. *We will never catch him.* I dismissed that glum thought since it would only bring fresh tears to my eyes, and I was too tired to cry as well.

Detective Sheldon drove me to an ATM and then to a

hotel, and not a nice one at that. I gave him a look, and he explained this would be safer for some reason. He also provided the clerk with a fake name and instructed me to only pay with cash.

"Just to be on the safe side," he insisted.

I shrugged it all off, promising to obey.

He left immediately after making sure I was secure in my room, and I went to sleep, hoping like many times in the past this was all just a nightmare I would wake up from. Sadly, it wasn't. And I didn't.

Sometime during the night, I awoke and realized that while I slept, my mind kept working on this puzzle. There was one piece of information I'd failed to mention to the detective because I'd just thought of it myself.

The front door wasn't broken. I would have known if someone had tampered with the newly installed door, so whoever had installed all those hidden cameras in my apartment had to have a way of entering without me noticing.

And the door was the only way in since I lived so high up. Nobody could come through the balcony door, which was locked from the inside anyway.

That left only one possibility.

My stalker has a key, I thought, shivering all over.

But how was that possible? It was a short list of people who had a key to my apartment.

One of them was the building manager. He held keys to all of the apartments, for safekeeping, just in case something happened.

The other person was my mother. I gave it to her once so she could come during the day and leave a birthday present for me since I was too busy and couldn't go to lunch with her. She never returned it to me.

And the last person who had a spare key, as of recently, was Mercy...

Was it her?

32

THE RETURN HOME

Although I dreaded it and had major second thoughts, I decided to return to my apartment the next day, only because I needed fresh clothes. In my state yesterday, I'd grabbed my overnight bag without bothering to look inside.

This morning when I opened it, I was unpleasantly surprised. It was filled with dirty clothes from my last stay at a hotel, which meant I had to return home to replace them.

I might be jobless and practically homeless since I couldn't live in my apartment anymore, but I still had my dignity. And there was no way in hell I would wear dirty clothes or be forced to wash them in a sink like some laundress in the old days.

I felt pretty confident I would be safe in my apartment during the day. I tried not to dwell too much on the fact I had so much free time on my hands, and failed miserably. I was heavily mourning the loss of my job, but I had to deal with one crisis at a time. And changing dirty underwear felt like the biggest one right then.

With a heavy heart, I returned to my building. Looking at it now, from this perspective, I couldn't believe I'd craved to live here. It was a soulless concrete prison, in which no one really cared about one another. I had so many neighbors, but nobody was there for me. Nobody helped while I was dealing with a stalker.

Would you if the tables were turned?

All the same, my dream of living here felt like a million years away now. My desires for it were long quenched. I detested it now. I saw it for what it truly was, an empty shell for even emptier people who cared only about themselves.

Well, what does that say about you?

My heart pounded as I rode the elevator. And no matter how much I tried to convince myself it would all be all right, it wouldn't listen.

My apartment looked exactly as I'd left it last night, in complete disarray.

I dashed to my bedroom, dumped all the dirty clothes from the bag on the floor, and filled it with clean ones. I also stripped naked, cowering in my closet, feeling like someone was watching me, and changed in haste.

I was on my way out when I stopped. I really needed to find a new place to live, not to mention I needed a new job as well, to afford a new place to live. So I grabbed my laptop and fired it up. The internet in the hotel was absolutely dreadful, so it would be more prudent and efficient if I took care of the search here. Once again, I reminded myself nothing bad would happen during the day, and that helped me relax, a little.

While I looked through the classifieds, there was a huge frown on my face. It was insane what people tried to pass off as livable spaces, and the cost was the most outrageous part.

Then again, beggars can't be choosers, and I was pretty much a beggar at that point. Staying in a hotel wasn't a viable option anymore. Even staying in the dump Detective Sheldon had taken me to last night would eat through my savings pretty fast. And I couldn't afford that. Not now when I was out of a job too.

I couldn't believe they'd kicked me out like I was nothing. *Less than nothing.* And I was sure Grant would try to deprive me of my severance payment because in the contract I signed, there was a morality clause.

Damn it.

While I was signing it, I had considered it a formality, and now I knew that would definitely be used against me. Grant would want to punish me for sleeping with David in any way he could. That miserable old bastard was the worst.

They ask how much for this? I fumed as I resumed looking at properties. *That's not big enough to house my shoes, let alone me.*

My mind kept hopping from topic to topic. I stayed near the door, stooping to listen every once in a while, in fear my stalker would appear out of nowhere to hurt me.

Hasn't he hurt me enough already? I didn't dare answer that.

In the midst of my paranoia, I crept toward the door to look through the spyhole, too late remembering it was still blacked out since the last time my stalker had banged against my door.

Sighing, I returned to my place to finish my search. The sooner I finished, the better. I didn't like the idea of spending more time in that apartment than was necessary.

Oh, the irony...

I had a sudden thought. I should start calling my clients.

I should tell them I was leaving GBD and starting my own practice, reassuring them it would be business as usual, at lower rates, naturally, once I'd set everything up. But I hesitated. What if Grant had already reached them all and turned them against me? It was business, after all, and clients didn't really care who represented them as long as they got exactly what they wanted.

Damn it.

There was another reason I abandoned my plan of speaking with clients if I was completely honest. I dreaded they would all say no if I asked them to stay with me and keep me as their lawyer.

I balled my hands into tight fists. I hated the person stalking me, ruining my life at every turn, with my whole heart and soul. I wanted them dead for all the pain they'd caused me.

I hate them. I hate them, I screamed inside my head as tears started to fall down my cheeks. I was ruined, as they'd wanted.

What was I to do?

You can't sit around crying, that's for sure, part of me pointed out.

Wiping my tears and taking a few deep breaths, I continued with my search. I needed a new place to live. That was the most important thing. And once I'd dealt with that, I would move on to the next problem on my list. Having a clear plan helped with my fragile nerves.

After an hour-long search, I accomplished nothing. There wasn't one place I wished to see in person, let alone rent. *I am doomed.*

Maybe I should stay with Mom. Every part of my being rebelled against that. Staying with her wasn't an option. She would just love to see me like this, begging her for a place to live because then everything she'd kept telling me would prove to be true.

I would much rather sleep under a bridge than ask her for help.

Maybe you'll have to.

If I wanted to find a new place that was actually worth living in, I needed to see precisely how much money I had at my disposal. I wanted to stay clear of my savings as much as possible. I still had my primary bank account. Opening a new tab, I went to my bank's website to log in to my account.

Doing so, I read the balance displayed and then simply stared at it. *That can't be right.* A large sum of money had vanished from my account.

Someone's robbed me!

Without wasting any time, I called my bank to complain.

"I'm looking at my bank account right now, and I'm telling you it doesn't add up. I've been robbed."

"Please, ma'am, calm down," the customer service worker said in an irritatingly nasal voice.

"Don't tell me to calm down when my account has been practically depleted. I have been hacked, or whatever you want to call it."

"Were you hacked or not? You need to be sure."

"I'm telling you I didn't send those payments. The last thing I paid for with my credit card was a hotel room."

After a very tiresome conversation, with a lot of toing and froing, I was told my account was now blocked.

There would be an investigation to verify if my story was true. If they determined my account had been genuinely hacked, they would return the stolen funds to me. All of that was going to take time, though. Time I didn't have.

On the positive side, I got a brand-new account, to which my remaining funds were transferred, and a brand-new credit card would be sent to me, although I had no idea where to have it sent, since I had no residence.

On the negative side, now I was penniless as well, I thought in desperation.

That was an exaggeration. I was far from penniless, since I had my savings. I checked it, and it was intact. And I would fight Grant tooth and nail to give me what was rightfully mine.

That didn't mean I could start spending like crazy. I still had no job and needed a place to live. It was reassuring to know all the money stolen would be returned to me eventually.

At least that was what I was led to believe. The way things were unraveling in my life, I wouldn't be that surprised to get a call from the bank saying the money was gone for good, and there was nothing they could do about it.

My train of thought was interrupted by loud laughter, a female's.

Is that Mercy? I needed to speak with her. I wanted my key back. Although I was sure she had nothing to do with my stalker, I realized I didn't feel comfortable sharing it with her. It didn't matter that I planned on leaving this place, that key should still be returned to me.

And then another voice, much deeper, joined her. I immediately recognized it. *What the hell?*

I got up and opened the door just in time to see David and Mercy kissing in front of her apartment. It was obvious he was leaving, and this was a farewell kiss.

I had received it many times, to know what it looked like. Besides, the general dishevelment of both of them suggested they'd already had a good time together. My mind exploded as I watched the scene in front of me.

"What?" I exclaimed, not being able to help myself. I was flabbergasted, to say the least.

David looked startled and a tad guilty that he'd just gotten caught. On the other hand, Mercy was glowing.

So she was the new girlfriend. I was disgusted. He'd traded me for her. *Her!* And then I realized this was all just a show. He intentionally hooked up with my neighbor to get back at me.

I was furious.

"So this is your new girlfriend," I commented, shaking my head as I approached them. "You are unbelievable."

"It just happened," he replied with a shrug.

"So you would come and have sex with me, then go and be with her? You are a two-timing piece of shit. I can't believe I ever let you in my bed," I ranted.

"Amber, please calm down," he said, taking a step forward, both hands raised high in supplication.

Mercy was grinning like she was enjoying the show.

That only infuriated me more, but it was David that I directed my anger at.

"Don't tell me to calm down. I know I was wrong about the sex tape, but I am not wrong about this." I pointed at the two of them in disgust. "This is pure revenge."

"Revenge?" He jerked as though I'd slapped him. And apparently, it was his turn to get angry. "What are you talking about?"

"It's obvious that since I didn't want to be with you, you decided to get back at me by being with her. Your attempts to stay in my orbit are completely pathetic," I threw in his face.

"Hey, wait a minute—" Mercy started, sounding offended.

"I am not with Mercy because of you."

"Yeah, right. As if you would ever really date a girl like her."

"Are you hearing yourself? That is absolutely insane."

"I am not the insane one here. You are, for stooping that low."

"You know, Amber, not everything is about you," Mercy commented.

"So it's all a big coincidence? You found true love across the hall from me," I mocked. "You are beyond pathetic."

"And you are clearly crazy. I was a fool for caring for someone as selfish as you. You really deserve everything that stalker does to you."

I slapped him. "You take that back."

Gritting his teeth, David looked apologetic at Mercy and then left without a word.

"Don't you dare walk away," I screamed after him. "Take that back, David." That was beyond cruel, even from him. But he didn't.

I turned to look at Mercy. Someone had to feel the wrath I was brimming with. She too had some explaining to do.

"Mercy," I said her name as though it were the foulest word in the English language.

Seeing me approach, she quickly went inside and closed the door.

What a coward!

I started to bang on her door. She wasn't going to get rid of me that easily. "Mercy, open the door. I need to speak with you."

There was no reply.

"Did you know who he was before getting involved with him?" I demanded. She must have known. He came to see me all the time. Besides, there was no other explanation for how they could have met, other than here.

Unfortunately, that coward refused to open the door and answer for her behavior.

"I want my key back. Do you hear me?"

Still, there was no reply.

I screamed out of sheer frustration.

Getting myself under control, still beyond angry by this turn of events, I returned to my apartment and slammed the door with greater force than was necessary.

Mercy and David are together, I fumed.

Well, that was just perfect.

33

THE BIG REVELATION

I poured myself the biggest drink imaginable. Although at that point, in my state, I couldn't understand why I bothered with the glass anyway. I should have just drunk straight from the bottle.

Everyone had turned their backs on me. David included. Mercy included. All the smiles, all the friendliness were just an act. She was nothing more than a sneaky bitch, like the rest of them.

They were never truly there for me to begin with, I fumed. *They were using me like everyone else. The moment I encountered problems, they vanished, they fired me, and they discarded me like I was nothing.*

And that hurt. A great deal.

That was precisely why I planned on getting properly drunk. That was the only thing I had left, at any rate. I had no friends, no family, no job, and no place to live.

I'm all alone in this world, and I'll die alone. It was too scary a thought to consider my stalker was still out there, trying to finish the job. They had already ruined my life, as they'd promised. *And now they will kill me.*

I took another gulp of my drink. It burned my throat, but I didn't care. Better to feel that than the betrayal I was feeling from the rest of the world.

I looked about myself, at the trashed apartment. The mess around me was a perfect representation of my whole life.

What am I going to do?

There was nothing worse than a drunk person trying to figure out her future. Naturally, that didn't stop me from trying.

I was also in no state to get up and return to the hotel. *Should I?* I thought.

Seeing as how a large chunk of my money had disappeared, without a specific date for when it would be returned to me, it was only safe to assume the rest could vanish into thin air as well, especially if I continued to spend like crazy.

I couldn't risk going to a hotel, even if I could. And I couldn't risk renting another place, even if I could find something suitable that didn't look like a complete dump.

I had the perfect apartment already, and I was staying here.

The fact it was ruined and that I hated it didn't enter the equation. I had to face the music. My stalker had managed to trap me here, and quite successfully at that, because I had no place else to go.

I was too pretty to stay under a bridge. Besides, my chances of getting murdered there were equal to my chances of getting murdered inside my apartment. *At least here, I can sleep in my bed*, I joked humorlessly, taking a little bit more alcohol to help me swallow this harsh reality.

I hated my stalker with all my heart and beyond. *What did I ever do to them to deserve this treatment?* I had minded my own business my whole life, so what had I ever done to them? I hated them for making me feel like this, for making me hate.

My stalker, I grumbled. They weren't mine. I didn't want that kind of familiarity with them. It was a lunatic who'd targeted me without reason. Nothing more, nothing less, yet in this case that felt like plenty.

Thanks to that maniac, I had nothing left in my life. They'd ruined everything. Thanks to them, I discovered how cruel and selfish people truly were. I had no job, and I had no place to live, other than here, which wasn't safe at all. Not to mention how difficult it would be for me to see Mercy again. Especially if David was by her side.

I started to cry. I didn't feel like living like this anymore. This was pure torture.

Right in the midst of my pity party, my phone started ringing.

At first, I wanted to ignore it and continue drinking and feeling sorry for myself. I had the whole evening planned, and it didn't involve speaking on the phone. I wanted to be left alone so I could continue to feel miserable and abandoned by all.

Unfortunately, the ringing persisted.

Feeling pretty irked my wallowing in sorrow wasn't going according to plan, I grabbed my phone and instantly let go of the glass I was holding with the other hand, as though I would need both hands for this conversation.

Detective Sheldon was calling me, and I hated how hopeful that made me feel.

"Hello?" Even my voice betrayed me. That greeting was nothing more than a plea for how I desperately needed all my problems to just go away. And that was pretty stupid of me. Detective Sheldon wasn't some white knight who could solve all my problems for me.

"I've done some digging about the Stone twins," he replied without preamble.

In my alcohol-soaked brain, that caused a short circuit. I had no idea what he was talking about. Did he dial the wrong number? "Who?" I asked.

"The kids who lost their mother when your friend Kelly ran over her," he replied gruffly.

I made a face. *Their last name was Stone?* For some reason that sounded pretty funny to me despite the fact that I'd known that. Not that I dared to laugh. This was no time for laughing, which only made me want to laugh more.

Besides, laughing was better than crying. Right? *Not if it's a sign of a complete mental breakdown.*

"What have you found?" I asked, to distract myself from all the unnecessary thoughts inside my head.

"Well, first of all, Bella received a bunch of awards while in school, and then she disappeared for a bit; nothing special about Sam. Second, they both live in your area."

What was it to me if Bella was accomplished in some field of work? I was a great lawyer, not that it mattered to anyone but me and my clients. And it sounded like a coincidence they were living here. It wasn't something that would cause a red flag, at any rate. Many people lived here. It would be more alarming if they lived near Kelly.

"And?" I asked, hoping the detective hadn't called to tell

me something so trivial. They had the right to live wherever they wanted. Or do whatever they pleased.

If he told me Sam had a record and was known to kill people, then that could be interesting, or alarming.

"You told me you hadn't met Kelly's last boyfriend."

I raised an eyebrow. That was a quick change of subject. "No, I hadn't," I agreed. "Come to think of it, I don't even know his name."

Which was something I regretted because I really wished I'd been a better friend to Kelly. Not that she was such a good friend to me. She'd abandoned me when I needed her the most.

"I got his name. John Davidson."

That sounded like a made-up name, I thought for no reason. "Never heard of him."

"Yeah, I got that a lot," he grumbled in return.

"Did you find him?"

"No. But it could be a fake name."

"Really?"

"I spoke with Kelly's assistant."

"How is Monica? Did she manage to find another job?" I asked almost conversationally.

"Miss Dennis, are you feeling all right?"

I was more than all right. I was perfect, especially since I had this nice buzz going for me. Although to be honest, Detective Sheldon was kind of ruining my mood. "Yes, I am."

"Are you drunk?" he asked in a tone I couldn't quite decipher.

Not that I was putting too much effort into it. I couldn't care less what some detective thought about me or my drinking. I had the right to do whatever I pleased, especially while struggling.

"Did Monica tell you anything useful?" I asked instead of answering.

"After some questioning, she mentioned a man who came to pick Kelly up once recently, and he matches Sam's description, but she didn't know if he was Kelly's boyfriend."

Who was Sam again? Oh, right, the twin.

"Is it possible it's the same guy?" I asked, since that seemed important. If it was the same guy, then that would mean I was right. That would mean Kelly had actually been murdered. As I made all these connections, my heart started to beat like crazy.

Calm down; nothing has been answered as of yet.

"I believe so."

Oh my God.

"Do you have a photo of him?" I asked, hopeful. I only had one image of him, which Kelly had sent me, but it didn't really reveal anything, so I hoped there was at least something I might recognize. I said as much to the detective.

"I managed to find a slightly older picture of Sam, with his sister."

Perfect. "Could you please send it to me?"

"Ok. I'll send it to you via email because the files are slightly bigger."

A few minutes later my phone started pinging, notifying me I had received an email. Since my laptop was already fired up, I grabbed it and opened my mail. True enough, a message from the detective with one attachment waited for me.

"Did you get it?" he inquired.

"I'm just opening it," I reassured him, doing just that.

Opening the image, I waited for it to appear on my screen, and that took forever. Then I finally saw the image he'd sent me. Although the photo was clearly an older one, I could see everything perfectly. I gasped.

"What is it?" the detective demanded.

"I know both of them," I exclaimed, horrified, infuriated, and afraid, among other things.

"How?"

"The girl in the photo."

"That's Bella Stone," the detective provided.

"Well, I know her by another name. Mercy something, and she's my neighbor."

"Are you sure?"

"Yes." I stressed the word. "I've been inside her apartment many times, and she fixed my laptop."

Oh my God. As I said that, I started to connect some dots. Was it possible she'd infected my laptop and made it worse when I took it to her? *Oh my God.*

"And how do you know Sam Stone?" Detective Sheldon snapped me back to reality.

"He told me his name was Allan. He was the contractor the building manager hired to deal with the fire damage."

Was that a lie?

"And later I hired him to do some additional work around the apartment."

Sam and Bella Stone had inserted themselves into my life. *Why?* Why were they here? Why did they both lie to me?

Did they kill Kelly? Did they ruin my life?

34

THE CONFRONTATION

All kinds of thoughts rushed through my head. My whole world exploded as pieces of the puzzle finally started to fall into place.

With everything Detective Sheldon had shared with me, I was now one hundred percent sure these twins, these spawns of evil, were my stalkers. They were the ones sending messages, organizing all the attacks, bugging my apartment, and so on. They had done so many bad things that the list of their infractions went on and on. Not to mention I was sure Sam had dated Kelly so he could torment her as well. *What a sick bastard.*

They were both beyond sick. Him coming to my apartment, pretending he was interested in me. And her pretending to be interested in my life, pretending she wanted to be my friend.

I was blind for not making all the connections sooner. Mercy was working in IT, for crying out loud. I went to her for help instead of making her my prime suspect. And even after I found all those hidden cameras, I was sure Mercy had nothing to do with it although she had a key. I was an idiot.

Mercy was Bella, and Allan was Sam. I still couldn't wrap my head around it, but everything finally made sense. Then again, it was natural to have overlooked it. I never expected someone who looked like Mercy to be a threat, which was the point, I realized. I was sure it was all just an act to gain my trust.

That would show me not to underestimate people in my life ever again. They'd actually shown me how vicious, depraved, not to mention evil, people could be while hiding behind masks of kindness and loyalty.

David fits into that category as well. Did he help Bella torment me?

It was a possibility. I wouldn't put it past him to help my aggressors because his pride had been wounded. He was the spitting image of his father.

"If Sam and Bella are the ones stalking you, we need proof," Detective Sheldon warned.

"I already have all the proof I need. I gave her a key to my apartment." That had to be how they'd come in and installed all the cameras. She'd sent the sex tape of me with David to Grant. Probably after sleeping with David herself. I was sickened by the depths of their depravity.

"Remain calm. It's important not to make any rash decisions now."

Why was he speaking so rationally to me at such a time?

"Do you know if Bella is home right now?"

"I don't know if she still is; she was a little while ago." *I can definitely find out.* It was true Bella had a key to my apartment; however, she'd made one huge mistake. Apart from messing with me. She'd given me a key to her apartment in return.

"Under no circumstances are you to go there alone," Detective Sheldon growled, and I too late realized that I'd said everything out loud.

"I need to confront them. I need to know why they chose to ruin my life," I argued.

"That's at least obvious. You helped Kelly escape justice."

I had so many problems with that statement but had other more pressing issues to deal with. I was done with this conversation. I needed to go see Bella immediately. "I have to go, Detective."

"Don't do anything rash. Please just wait for me. I'm on my way," he informed me.

I hung up on him. I had no intention of waiting for him. Besides, watching her get arrested for everything she'd done was the last thing I wanted right now.

I wanted to look her in the eyes and then make her suffer the way I'd suffered because of her.

With that cheerful thought in mind, I got up, went straight to the kitchen, and took the biggest knife I had. *It's about time this bitch gets to know the real me.*

And I was about to show her how neighborly I was prepared to be.

Pretty tipsy, not to say drunk like a skunk, I grabbed the key my lovely neighbor had given me and, still holding the knife in my other hand, left my apartment and walked to Bella's door. It was time I had a heart-to-heart conversation with her about her immoral behavior. And I wasn't speaking about her fucking David. Although that too had been done simply to hurt me.

It sickened me how elaborate their scheme actually was.

They dared to play with me. Me! Me? I will show them. I will show them I am not a person to take attacks against me lightly. Or go down without a fight.

I tried the key, but it wouldn't go in. And it wasn't because my motor skills were compromised due to all the alcohol I'd ingested. The key didn't belong to that lock.

That bitch gave me the wrong key, I fumed.

Then again, at this point, should I really be that surprised? Of course it didn't work. Everything else she, they, ever told me was a lie. Why would this be any different?

What to do now?

I wasn't giving up. That was for sure. I would have my confrontation with Bella, and I would have it now.

The instant I realized the whole swapping keys was a scam, I started banging on her door.

"Mercy, open up!" I screamed, using the knife handle to bang even louder on the door. "Or should I say Bella," I sneered her name.

"Yes, I know who you really are," I said smugly. "I know who your brother is too; now open up," I commanded.

I wasn't leaving until I'd spoken to her. She needed to feel my wrath.

Much to my delight, Bella opened the door. But my victory, my elation, was short-lived. She wasn't alone, and the smirk on her face made perfect sense. Sam was standing next to her, and he was holding a gun. *Gun definitely trumps knife*, which meant I was screwed.

I took a step back, but Sam started tsking at that, backing me in with his weapon.

I made a huge mistake. I just had time for that delightful thought when Bella grabbed me and pulled me inside, taking the knife from my hand in the process.

I was now surrounded by enemies and completely defenseless. It was tragic how I hadn't thought things through. I'd felt so self-righteous, so elated, as I stormed here. But now I saw the error of my ways.

And because of these errors, you will die.

"Sit down," she ordered, giving me a push.

Seeing no other way, I did as I was told. It was sad I hadn't seen this coming. They had planned this together. They had worked together from the start. Of course, they were living together as well.

I was beyond stupid. Yet chastising myself now felt like an exercise in futility. I had other more important issues to deal with. For example, how to get the hell out of there.

I was sure they wouldn't just let me leave. Not when I'd practically fallen into their laps.

Stupid, stupid.

They both looked down at me, wearing the same expressions, with arms crossed over their chests. It was amazing how similar they looked. When stood next to one another, it was more than obvious they were related.

"So you finally discovered the truth," Bella said almost conversationally.

"Took you long enough," Sam mocked.

I opened my mouth to say something like, *Sorry I'm not an evil mastermind like the two of you,* but bit my tongue at the last second. The last thing I wanted to do was antagonize the maniacs further.

"You managed to ruin everything for me," I said instead.

"That was the idea," Bella replied, with open malice.

"And we're not done yet," Sam said with an evil grin while eyeing his gun, his meaning more than obvious.

I almost blurted out the detective was on his way but stopped myself in time. What was the problem with me? Apart from the obvious, being drunk, being scared shitless made me incredibly tongue-loose. I had to prevent that by any means necessary if I wanted to get out of this predicament.

"What are you planning on doing?" I forced myself to ask.

Sam chuckled. "That'll be ruining the surprise."

I didn't like the sound of that. I just hoped Detective Sheldon would hurry and bust inside with the cavalry because I had no idea how much time I had left before they decided to hurt me.

"So after figuring everything out, you decided to come here with a knife?" Bella asked, in a mocking manner.

"Not a smart move," Sam agreed.

"I wasn't thinking clearly. I got upset," I replied honestly, with a small shrug. It was unreal how casually we were speaking about all this.

"What tipped you off in the end?" Bella asked, genuinely curious.

"You're not as good an actress as you thought you were. All the bubbliness showed how uncreative you really are."

That earned me a slap. Half of my face started burning. Bella didn't hold back.

I couldn't believe they hated me that much. Then again, after everything, it was silly to think that. It was more than obvious how they felt about me.

"The key and the hidden cameras," I corrected my answer.

"I figured as much," Bella said. "But no matter. It served its purpose."

Sam laughed again. "And then some. I hope your boss enjoyed the video we sent him."

I felt like scratching his face for that remark. They'd gotten me fired thanks to that, and still had the audacity to laugh in my face. They were monsters.

"I can see you enjoyed my video too. But you can only dream about being with someone like me," I jibed, not able to stop myself.

That earned me another slap on the face. "Don't you dare speak to my brother like that."

Great, now my whole face hurt. *I hope you are proud of yourself, Amber.* I should be figuring out a way out of there, not indulging in futile conversations with my stalkers.

Despite the very sane advice I'd just given myself, I was apparently not prepared to listen to it. "Why?" I asked before I could stop myself. "Why are you doing all of this?"

"Because our mother was murdered, and you all need to pay for it!" Sam yelled at me, instantly enraged.

His mood changed from cold to hot in an instant, startling me. He was totally insane. Then again, I already knew that.

"Why me?" I insisted. That part boggled me the most.

"Excuse me?" they practically said at the same time.

"Why target me? I did nothing wrong to you," I pleaded.

That was the part of the story I never fully understood. I understood they'd tried to extract some kind of revenge, feeling wronged for what had happened to their mother. Although in the eyes of the law, everything was as clean as a whistle. All the same, I'd had nothing to do with her death.

It wasn't like I'd forced her to be there on that road that night. It wasn't like I'd driven the car. I hadn't even been in the ambulance when the paramedics had failed to save her life.

As I said, I played no part in her demise, but all the same, these two people had dedicated all their time and resources to destroying me. *And they'd succeeded.* I had nothing left. And that didn't feel fair to me.

The twins looked at one another before scowling at me.

"Are you kidding me?" Bella was the one who chose to answer.

I got the feeling she was the brains behind it all while Sam was the muscle. She was definitely more levelheaded than him as well, because he was pure rage standing next to her.

They were both mad, that much was apparent, but there were differences in their madness.

"You defended that murderer," she said, getting in my face. "Thanks to you, she walked free as though she'd done nothing wrong."

"I was one of many lawyers."

"Don't try that game with us. We know it was you who came up with the whole trial strategy," Sam interjected.

"It wasn't like that at all," I tried to defend.

"We know you're guilty," he said with eyes full of hate.

I could see in his eyes he wanted to kill me, then and there.

Bella nodded at that. "You deserve to have your life ruined for what you did to ours. You deserved everything we threw at you and so much more. It was beautiful watching you suffer."

"I can't say what satisfied me more," Sam mused. "The expression on your face when your car got trashed, or when you lost your phone. No, no, it was definitely when you thought your apartment went up in flames." He chuckled.

"The best was when she ran out of the firm after getting fired," Bella joined in.

"And then she yelled at poor David." Sam made a sad face, mocking me.

It was a shame I didn't have my phone with me to tape their confession. Not that it would do me any good; California had a "two-party consent" law. Not that that mattered at the moment.

I decided to keep them talking, buying myself time, to find a way out, to give time for the detective to come, save me, whichever happened first. "How did you get into my apartment to hide the cameras?"

"I wanted to do it when I was installing the lights, but you wouldn't leave me alone," Sam said. "You kept watching me like a hawk. Not to mention you bitched about everything I did, constantly correcting and criticizing the whole time."

"So we had to wait until you went to the hotel," Bella said. "Then we used the key you gave me. I connected the cameras to my laptop and set up a live feed so we could see and hear everything."

"How did you make David help you?" I asked.

Bella made a face. "He was so heartbroken; he was more than happy to open up to whoever was prepared to listen."

So they'd tricked him, and he was foolish enough to fall for it, I realized. It was small comfort, knowing David wasn't an active member of this scheme. His betrayal still hurt though.

"Look at her; she doesn't care about David. She doesn't care about anyone other than herself," Sam said, disgusted.

"True. Look how she treats her poor mother," Bella agreed.

"Don't you dare speak about my mother," I snapped back.

"And you don't pretend to be insulted. We know what you did to her, and we know she was on your suspect list because we tapped your phone, and we were tracking you. You are pure evil, Amber Dennis."

"Yet here I am being held hostage, at gunpoint, by you," I countered.

"True," Sam agreed.

I didn't like the expression on his face when he said that. And then he continued.

"And now we're going to kill you," he announced.

35

FEER

Kill me? The words echoed in my head. *Kill me?*
He couldn't kill me. I wasn't prepared to die. I
was too young, with my whole life ahead of me.
There was so much I still had to accomplish... Not that that
mattered right then. I could see it in his eyes. Sam was dead
serious about wanting me gone.

Unfortunately, I had only myself to blame for my current
predicament. I'd rushed in here without thinking, and now
this maniac was going to kill me.

Although I'd done nothing wrong, had simply done my
job, he was blaming me for everything.

Oh God, what did I get myself into?

"Pray to whatever God you think is listening to you
because these are your last moments," Sam taunted.

Every part of my body stopped functioning. I was para-
lyzed by fear, unable to move. I could only stare at him and
pray to the heavens for some kind of miracle.

"Sam, what are you doing?" Bella asked.

"She deserves to die for what she did, so I'm going to kill

her." There was such determination in his voice, it chilled me.

"You can't kill me," I cried out, shaking my head.

Sam chuckled. "Watch me," he countered and raised his gun, pointing it at me.

Bella jumped in front of her brother. "No," she said sternly.

"Bella, get out of the way," he said, sounding bored.

"No, Sam. I will not," she replied, crossing her arms over her chest.

"What do you mean *no*?" he repeated.

"I think it's perfectly clear what I mean." Bella stood her ground. "We can't kill her."

Sam nodded. "You mean here," he replied, motioning around the apartment with his gun.

"What?"

"Why not here?" he continued. "I mean, it's not like you actually live here and have to worry about the bloodstains."

The ease with which he was speaking about murdering me was shocking. It was like I wasn't even there.

"That's not what I meant, Sam," Bella snapped. "I meant not here, not anywhere. We can't kill her."

"Why not? She deserves it," Sam argued.

"Because that's not part of the plan," Bella replied. "We both agreed to ruin her life, not take it."

"Well, plans change," Sam said, and he took a step to the right so he could aim at me again. "Amber, where would you prefer to be shot, in the head or the heart?" He laughed. "What am I saying." He slapped himself across the forehead with his free hand. "You don't have a heart, so head it is."

Once again, Bella blocked his aim. "Knock it off."

Sam glared at his sister. "Get out of the way. I'm serious."

"So am I," she said in return. "We're not going to kill her."

"*We* are not going to do anything. *I* will do it. I will end her."

"No, I won't let you," Bella countered, matching his level of anger. "I won't allow you to become a murderer."

"I'm not asking for your permission; now move, or get out if you have no stomach to witness it."

"What is wrong with you?" she asked.

"Nothing is wrong with me. I just want to end this. Punish her the way she deserves."

Bella shook her head. "Kelly's death and Amber's complete ruination, exposure for who she really is, are enough. That was the plan from the start. And I'm set on keeping it."

"No," Sam exploded. "It's not enough. Nothing will ever be enough."

"Sam, calm down," she pleaded.

"Our mother is dead, and this bitch helped her murderer walk free, party, drink, fuck around and carry on with her life as though nothing had happened. As though we hadn't lost the only person who cared about us in this world."

"And Kelly paid for her crime with her life."

"Because he killed her!" I yelled. I couldn't believe this was happening. "She didn't commit suicide! He murdered her!"

"She needs to pay too," Sam countered, pointing his gun at me.

"We're not murderers, Sam. We're better than them." Bella was clearly ignoring my accusation against her brother.

Sam shook his head. "I don't care about being better. I

only care about punishing them, taking them out one by one."

"Sam, you can't really mean that."

"I do. I really, really do."

"I can't believe you," Bella said. "We were always so united. Us against the world. I will not let you kill her."

I hoped this would be the moment Bella stopped her brother.

He looked at her incredulously. "You're choosing her over your own brother?"

"No, Sam, I am choosing you," Bella corrected. "I won't allow you to become the very thing we despise the most in this world. I'm trying to save you. If we stoop to their level, then it's all for nothing. We would tarnish our mother's legacy if we became like the person who ended her life, who defended the murderer."

"It's not up to you to save me. I don't need saving. I need revenge."

"You're making a terrible mistake. This isn't the way. We got our revenge. It's now time to carry on with our lives."

He shook his head. "No. It's not over."

"It is. We won."

"No. It won't be over until she's not breathing," he insisted. "Now move out of my way, or I'll make you," he threatened.

Bella grabbed his arm. "No, let her go. It's over."

"Let go of me. I'll end her right now," he said in a rush.

"If you harm her, I won't be here waiting for you afterward," she threatened.

"What are you saying?" Sam asked.

"Choose now, life with me or revenge, because I'm done," Bella said. "This is all so very wrong. This whole night turned out wrong. We should be celebrating, but instead, we're arguing, ready to cut ties. Mom wouldn't want that for us."

I couldn't believe that tears had appeared in her eyes. Why was Bella standing up to her brother to save my life after everything they'd done to me?

"You don't know what you're saying." He jerked his arm away from her. "I need to do this."

"Then that means goodbye."

Bella wiped the tears from her face. "Goodbye, Sam." She gathered her fake IDs, some cash, and a laptop, and left without looking back.

Sam stood there unmoving.

I finally saw my chance. I jumped up from my seat and bolted toward the door.

"Stop!" he shouted in desperation.

I ran, glancing back once to see Sam pointing his gun at me. Then he pulled the trigger.

36

THE CHASE

It was pure luck the twins had got into an argument. It had allowed me to escape. I wasn't out of the woods yet. I was sure they would come after me, so I kept running as fast as I could.

I couldn't believe Bella had stood up in my defense. I thought she would have been more than happy to bury me like her brother, but she wasn't. Not that I was complaining. I was all for staying alive.

I ran past my apartment. I knew this reprieve wouldn't last. They would come after me. I was sure of that.

And true enough, mere seconds later, gunshots echoed around me. At times, I hated being right.

He really wanted to kill me! If I had time to stop and contemplate the fact another human being was running after me to kill me, I would be shocked. *Things like this happen only in movies.* As it was, I was too busy running for my life for such trivial thoughts.

I only had one goal, and that was to stay alive. I hoped

Detective Sheldon was close, and that he would be in time to save me.

One bullet made a hole in the wall next to my head, and I screamed.

He is going to kill me, he is going to kill me. Those words were on repeat in my head as I forced my legs to move even faster.

My lungs were burning; it was a struggle to breathe and run at once. I had never been much of a runner, I stayed fit by dieting mostly, but I kept running. It wasn't like I had a choice anyway.

"I'll kill you, you bitch!" Sam shouted after me.

I knew he was close. I wouldn't dare turn to see where he was precisely.

"There's no place you can hide from me," he continued to rage.

Too late I realized I was running in the freaking wrong direction. In my fear, I had moved away from the elevators.

Fuck. Fuck.

Then again, it wasn't like I could use them. It wasn't as though Sam would be kind enough to let me call for the elevator, and then wait patiently for me to enter before resuming his chase.

That madman was set on killing me. Like he'd killed Kelly. I was sure of that. I'd been right all along. I knew she would never voluntarily leave this world. She loved herself, her life, far too much for that.

I had no idea if Bella had participated in Kelly's death, but it didn't sound like it. Based on her reaction, I wasn't sure she knew what her brother had done, but that didn't change the fact Sam was a killer. And I was his target.

What am I going to do? How can I escape this maniac?

I couldn't knock on any of my other neighbors' doors. I was sure nobody would open their doors for me even if I did. I had one option. And that was to use the staircase.

If only I could reach the stairs, I would be safer, I prayed to the heavens.

And then what? My mind raced. Sam could catch me and shoot just as easily there. But it wasn't like I had any other choice. There was no place for me to hide on my floor. And going to my apartment would be a dead end, even if I could double back to it. He could kill me there too; I was sure of that.

So I rushed through the door that led to the staircase and started the descent toward my freedom. If only I could reach the ground level, I would be safe. If only Detective Sheldon could get here in time to stop Sam killing me.

If only... There were a lot of those in my plans. It was better than nothing.

The whole building felt like a ghost town. All the neighbors were probably locked behind their doors, scared to open them to see what was happening because of all the bullets flying about.

"People like you make me sick," Sam continued to rant as he chased me.

He kept shooting at me, and I did my best to stay out of his aim.

How many bullets does that man have?

"I could barely stand being in your presence, pretending to be Allan, while you paraded around in your underwear, offering yourself to me like a common whore."

I'd done no such thing. I wanted to rebel but kept my mouth shut. I didn't want him to know my exact location.

"What else to expect from a woman who defends

murderers and criminals? If you associate with filth, you become filth. It's as simple as that."

No matter how taunting his words were, I knew he was trying to provoke me, make me pause so he could catch me, kill me.

Well, I wasn't falling for it. I continued with my quiet descent, watching my steps while praying like hell he wouldn't shoot me. A bullet hit the balustrade next to me, ricocheting next to my left foot. Instinctively I jumped. He was so close.

I am not going to make it. I started to panic. He was too close. He was going to kill me. I was spiraling out of control, and there was no pep talk good enough in this world to prevent it or calm me down.

All the same, I continued. It wasn't like I had any choice.

Sure, I could stop and accept my fate, but I really didn't want to do that. And not just because I didn't want to die. My pride wouldn't let me yield. I was the master of my fate, not this lunatic. I could not let him win. I just couldn't.

I had to have faith that if I helped myself, the universe would help me as well.

Detective, where are you? I really, really needed his help right about now.

"What? No witty remark this time?" he taunted. And then he started to laugh.

It chilled me to the bones.

"You thought you were at the top of the world. But we showed you who you really are. Nothing. You are nothing, Amber Dennis. Less than nothing."

I snapped. "Who's we?" I shouted back as I turned a corner for the next bank of stairs. "I don't see Bella helping you. Face it, Sam, you've lost your freaking mind. And even your sister decided to abandon you, realizing this is wrong, realizing there's no hope for you."

"Shut up!" he screamed. "Shut the fuck up!" He fired the gun again.

Nice going, Amber. You just antagonized a man with a gun. He was definitely going to kill me now.

"You are the last person to speak about right or wrong. You lost your compass a long time ago. If you had it to begin with, you fucking psychopath." He shot his gun after every couple of words.

Did he just call me a psychopath? Now, that was ironic. Not that I stopped to point out the obvious.

There was a pause in the shooting. Maybe he was reloading. *Thank God*, I thought, and then mentally slapped myself. More bullets meant additional opportunities for him to kill me.

Fuck. Fuck. Fuck.

"You sold your soul to the devil, Amber. And I'll be more than happy to deliver you to him," he said ominously, starting to fire again.

At least now I knew who'd written those crazy, religious emails. Not that that was of huge importance now.

What floor was I on? I had no idea how far down I'd gone. It was hard to concentrate when there was a raging lunatic with a gun chasing after me.

I needed to reach the lobby. That was the only thing that mattered now. I dodged bullets and tried not to listen to his crazy ramblings. His words couldn't hurt me. They meant nothing. His bullets, on the other hand, could definitely kill me. So that was what I focused on. Staying out of his aim, avoiding bullets. I stopped myself from interacting with that lunatic any further.

Sam proved to be much crazier than his sister. Blood thirstier too.

The fact he was chasing after me with a gun, shooting like a maniac, like he was in the Wild West, settling disagreements with bullets, pretty much covered that already.

He fired again, and the bullet zoomed past my head, hitting the wall behind me, and I screamed. He fired again, and a bullet grazed my arm. I screamed again.

The hit caused me to miss a step, and I started tumbling down the stairs.

No, no, no, no, no. I was panicking now. This was how I would die. Alone on a staircase.

And nobody would mourn me.

On the landing, I smacked into the wall, stopping my descent. Every part of my body hurt. It was a miracle I didn't break anything, although it felt like I had.

And my arm was bleeding profusely.

If I'm lucky, I'll bleed to death before he catches me, I thought.

I was a mess. I tried to get up and escape, but it was too late. In the next instant, before I had a chance to react, Sam was on me. He loomed over me like some nightmarish grim reaper in a Hawaiian shirt.

Please God, please, please, please save me. I prayed Detective Sheldon would arrive soon because I was running out of time.

I opened my mouth to start begging, pleading with Sam to spare me, but clammed my mouth shut. My pride wouldn't let me beg. Unfortunately, I was sure that in about a second or two I would change my mind.

Sam had a devilish expression on his face as he aimed his gun.

This was it. This was the end.

"Any last words?" he asked.

"I don't understand; why me?" I sobbed. "Why are you targeting me?"

He looked puzzled for a fraction of a second before getting angry again. "Because you deserve it," he spat in return.

I shook my head. "Why go after a defense lawyer, a nobody who simply did her job, instead of the person who actually killed your mom?" I said, out of my mind crazed, managing to right myself a little and glue my back against the wall. Not that the shift in position changed anything. Sam still had me at gunpoint. He still planned on killing me.

And there was nothing I could do to stop it.

No, no, please no.

"Why?" he repeated, as though I were speaking in tongues.

"Yes, why me?" I asked, to buy myself some more time.

Maybe I could try to escape again. Then again, I had nothing to distract him with this time.

Although my ankle was killing me, I was prepared to start running again if I saw an opportunity. I knew I could survive with a broken foot, but with a hole in the head, not so.

"Haven't you paid any attention?" he replied, fuming.

"I have paid attention," I argued, not really sure why. "I was the only one who received threatening emails. I was the only one whose life was ruined."

That wasn't fair. I wasn't the only lawyer on Kelly's team. And I was definitely not the one who killed his mother. So it made no sense that I was the sole focus of his wrath.

Sam shrugged at my words. "No point in ruining someone I knew I was going to kill."

"What?" I exclaimed before I could stop myself.

"Bella had this whole elaborate plan on how we could torture Kelly, since emails and ruining things wouldn't work on a spoiled brat like her. I knew she deserved nothing less than a noose around her neck."

That had been how Kelly died. Supposedly she'd hung herself. I knew better. I always knew.

"I know you killed her."

"Of course I killed her," he replied, a strange expression on his face, as though I had just said the most ridiculous thing. He waved his gun about, gesticulating to accentuate the words. "She killed my mother and felt no remorse about it. She continued to drink and party like nothing had happened. Like she hadn't destroyed so many lives." He was starting to unravel before my eyes.

"That's not true. She was just a kid at the time—"

"Enough!" he shouted.

"And what about Mickey? Why did you have to kill him?"

He made a face. "Don't you dare pretend you give a shit about what happened to some lowlife kid."

"Why did you kill him?" I insisted.

"It was just his time. And now, it's yours." Sam raised his gun.

I cried, knowing this was it, this was the end, how I would die.

37

STAYING ALIVE

Detective Sheldon busted through the door to my right, his own weapon raised high. "Drop the gun, Sam; it's over," he said in his commanding voice.

Sam looked bewildered. "Go away, or I'll shoot her," he threatened.

He's going to shoot me either way, was on the tip of my tongue.

Without further exchange, Detective Sheldon fired at Sam. The bullet hit him in the chest. As a reflex, Sam's gun fired as well, missing me by an inch. Sam's blood covered me as he fell backward onto the stairs, and I screamed.

He's dead. He's dead. I could see a hole where his heart was supposed to be.

And he thought I had no heart; ha, who doesn't have a heart now? I argued, clearly in shock.

Detective Sheldon grabbed me and dragged me away from Sam's very much dead body. He took me to sit on the sofa in the lobby.

I made it to the lobby. For some reason that felt important, yet for the life of me, I couldn't understand why.

Detective Sheldon furiously, animatedly spoke on the phone before returning to my side.

I couldn't believe Sam was actually dead. *Does that mean it's finally over? Am I free?* And then Bella came to mind. *She escaped.* She was out there. She could still get me.

"Amber?" Detective Sheldon was shaking me.

"What?" I forced myself to ask.

"I asked, are you all right?"

No, and on so many levels. "She'll get me. She'll hurt me." I panicked.

"You're bleeding."

As he said that, my arm started to hurt. "The bullet grazed me."

It was hard to focus on just one thought. They kept popping into my head, multiplying like popcorn. That was silly. Thoughts like popcorn.

Am I in shock? I must be. It's understandable after what happened. I mean, Sam tried to kill me. And then ended up dead himself. Will Grant take me back, rehire me, once he learns what happened?

"I called an ambulance," Detective Sheldon informed me. "Where is Bella?"

That was a good question.

"Amber, focus. Where did Bella go?"

Focus, right. What was the question again? "I don't know. They argued. She tried to stop him from killing me, she ran, and then I escaped, and then he..." *died.* He was dead. Dead as a doornail.

Dead. Dead. Dead.

Better him than me.

"I told you not to do anything rash," Detective Sheldon snapped at me.

Why was he so angry? I was the one who almost ended up dead not him. "Is he dead?" I asked, needing to make sure.

"Very," Detective Sheldon replied. "Their apartment is empty; my officers checked. However, something is telling me she won't be coming back."

I had to agree with that statement. She looked adamant this revenge business was over. Then again, her brother was dead now. That could change everything. For her and for me.

If she was hell-bent on destroying me for her mother, which I had nothing to do with, what would she do when she learns her brother is dead?

But I had nothing to do with it, part of me whined.

That didn't stop her before, I argued back.

Stop it, I snapped at myself. I couldn't break now. I had survived this far. That meant I was strong enough to survive the rest.

"I need you to tell me exactly what happened here," the detective said slowly, as though speaking with a child. It was obvious he was controlling his temper.

Why is he so angry? I wondered again. *I had a near-death experience not him. He only killed a man.*

"Amber, focus."

I nodded. Although it was hard. My mind kept jumping from topic to topic, all kinds of thoughts whirling in my brain, and it was hard to keep it still.

"Once we finished our conversation, I couldn't simply sit still."

I was shaking uncontrollably, yet not from the cold. Detective Sheldon placed a jacket over my shoulders.

"Can I get her some water?" Alex asked the detective.

I made a face. What was he doing here? That useless nobody. He really should be fired after this. I had almost been murdered in my own building, and he'd done nothing to stop it.

"Amber, continue," Detective Sheldon urged, stopping my train of thought while sending Alex away.

Very reluctantly, I admitted how I'd marched over to Bella's apartment to confront her.

"I needed her to know that I knew everything," I said with a shake of my head, realizing how stupid that sounded. At the time it seemed like a good idea. Then again, I had been pretty drunk. But I wasn't drunk anymore. Apparently, I was sober after my near-death experience.

"And then what happened?"

"Bella opened the door. Sadly, she wasn't alone. Sam was there with her, and he had a gun." Then I proceeded to explain how they'd held me hostage, and what they'd spoken about in my presence. "They admitted everything."

"Anything else?"

"Sam admitted to killing Kelly. That was revenge for killing his mother."

"What about Mickey?"

"Him too. You were right. He was taking care of loose ends."

I was supposed to be next. I almost was next. If the detective hadn't arrived in time... I stopped myself there.

"They started arguing about killing me. Bella was opposed. I managed to escape, somehow. He chased after me, and..."

"Do you have any idea how lucky you are I managed to get here in time?"

I closed my eyes for a moment. Sam's looming figure with the gun pointed at my head instantly came to mind. And then him bleeding, falling dead.

I opened my eyes quickly. It was better to keep them open.

"I know."

I was lucky to have survived this, and I was grateful. I had a new opportunity in life, and I wasn't going to waste it. I promised.

The paramedics came and took care of my arm, which stalled our conversation, and Detective Sheldon moved away to give me some privacy while they checked me out. I refused to go to the hospital. The bullet had only scratched me, nothing else, and they were able to treat it on the spot. Looking around, I was surprised to see how many police officers were milling about.

While they were wheeling Sam's body out of the building, I looked away. Was I a horrible person because I wasn't sorry he was dead?

Detective Sheldon approached me again while I was being treated. It was obvious there was more he wanted from me. I was having none of it.

"Are we done?" I asked before he had a chance to say anything.

"Why? You have someplace you need to be?"

I ignored that snarky remark. Once upon a time, I wouldn't. I would fight back and win, but I didn't have it in me anymore. I had no energy.

Call it the new me.

"I want to go home and go to sleep."

I was exhausted, so mentally and physically drained that I felt like I could sleep for a week straight. And then I needed to put my life back in order, but that was a struggle for some other day. Now, I wanted to be left alone so I could rest.

Apparently, Detective Sheldon decided to take pity on me and nodded. "We can finish this tomorrow. Officer Marks will take you upstairs."

"Great," I said, going toward the elevator with the police officer he'd recruited to take me up.

"Try not to antagonize anyone on your way there," he said after me. "I'm done saving you for tonight."

"Funny," I said without pause as Officer Marks held the elevator door for me.

I felt everyone's eyes on me. Naturally, the whole building was alarmed by what had happened. *Now they're here. Where were they when there was a maniac chasing me with a gun?* I thought bitterly. Not that I was bitter. I was happy to be alive.

And tired, so very tired.

Inside my apartment, I locked the door and took a deep breath. I tried to keep my brain empty, without thoughts, knowing that if I started to think about everything, I would spiral again. And that was something I couldn't allow. Not now.

The apartment was a complete mess from when I'd searched for the hidden cameras, but I didn't care.

I went to my bathroom, and after showering, making sure not to mess with the dressing on my arm, I went to bed. I was so exhausted I didn't even need painkillers before falling into bed. My arm was bothering me a little, but not enough to make me get out of bed again.

Sleep, Amber. Just sleep.

Unfortunately, that was easier said than done, even in my state.

Although my stalker was dead, I wasn't calm. I couldn't find peace. And not just because Bella was still at large. I kept thinking about everything, how I had been targeted, why I had been targeted.

And poor Kelly had lost her life because of it.

Eventually, I fell asleep.

As was agreed, the next day I went to the police station to provide an official statement. It was tedious having to recount everything, having to repeat the whole story to the same officers who hadn't wanted to get involved before.

I had to speak with the DA a couple of times about Sam's crimes. Eventually, I put a stop to it all because I didn't like how they were treating me, like a criminal. Of course, some of them believed I got exactly what I deserved, and were not shy to show it.

I tried not to be bothered by it all but failed in that endeavor. It did bother me, a great deal. People actually thought I deserved to be tormented, almost killed, simply for doing my job. It wasn't fair. Then again, many things in life weren't fair.

Even my own mother thought so, although she refrained from saying that out loud. It was implied, and that hurt.

In the days that followed, I tried to put on a brave face. Tried to keep myself going, moving forward. Though it wasn't easy putting everything behind me because it wasn't over yet. One of my attackers was in the wind, and that meant I was still living in fear. I had nightmares that Bella would return to finish the job, to kill me because Sam had failed.

It took me a while to put my apartment back in order and fix things that had been broken during my search for the hidden cameras. I'd decided to move out. I couldn't stay there. Once upon a time, I'd considered that place my prized possession, something I was very proud of. Those days were gone.

The twins had ruined it for me. So I decided to put it on the market and move someplace else, someplace nobody knew me.

And not just because so many bad things had happened within those walls. The sad reality was, I couldn't keep it financially either. I'd lost my high-paying job, and I couldn't keep up with all the payments, not without depleting my savings. I was still trying to get the bank to refund my money, but they weren't cooperating.

Alongside the apartment, I ended up selling most of my assets. I sold my beloved Tesla and the paintings, too, to support myself.

If that wasn't humiliating enough, I sold about half of my closet as well. I got rid of my power suits, well, most of them, and all my high-heel shoes. Since they were in mint condition, I managed to get an impressive amount for it all.

I tried not to think about how much I'd spent on them.

Sadly, that didn't fix my money problems. I needed a job. But I was unemployable in the city of Los Angeles.

Grant made sure of that. So I'd had to accept a massive lifestyle downgrade to preserve my finances. I hated every second of it.

I knew better than to ask my mother for help. She hadn't been there for me when she heard I'd been shot. In her mind, a nonthreatening wound meant she didn't have to act motherly at all. She expressed gratitude that I was alive, and relief that my stalker had finally been identified and dealt with.

Detective Sheldon had expressed more concern than her, but that was my mother all right. Never there when I needed her.

Part of me was sure she was acting this way because it was an opportunity for her to take revenge on me. I had to make peace with that and take care of myself. Like I always had.

David tried calling. He'd learned he'd been nothing more than a tool in Bella's schemes. I had written to him to let him know, but I had no intention of speaking with him ever again. His betrayal made me angry, still.

Although I was glad Sam was dead, he definitely deserved nothing less, my problems didn't end there. He had vowed to ruin my life, and he'd done just that, and now I had no idea how to move on, or what to do with my life. How to fix all that was ruined.

Although victorious, I was still standing when my stalker was dead, I felt like the biggest loser. I'd lost everything despite my best efforts, and now I felt lost. I had no idea how to change that.

38

BITTERNESS

With hard work, charm, and imagination, I managed to sell my apartment almost at asking price. The downside was that I had till the end of the month to leave, and I had no place to move to. So I used all my free time searching for a new apartment, having no desire to live with my mother.

I had just finished packing my shoes, those I'd decided to keep, when someone knocked on my door. My first reaction was fear. But I reminded myself Sam was dead, and managed to calm myself enough to see who it was.

I was still irked that everyone seemed to think the doorbell was purely decorative. It was such a nice doorbell, but everyone chose to knock. I couldn't explain this.

I opened the door to see David standing on the other side. I hadn't seen him since the night he'd kissed Bella in the hall. That still bothered me when I thought about it.

The bastard.

Naturally, he looked good, like always, and that stirred

something in me. To say I had mixed feelings about the man would be a huge understatement.

"David?" I greeted. If it sounded like a question, it was because I was startled to see him. I never expected him to visit after everything that had happened.

"Hello, Amber," he greeted.

"What are you doing here?" I asked, genuinely curious.

"You wouldn't return my calls, so I decided to drop by."

So he'd decided to chase a girl who'd almost died at hands of her stalker recently. That was ironic. Naturally, I didn't say that out loud. "You decided to drop by, knowing I would be home in the middle of the day because your dad fired me," I said, not even trying to hide how bitter I was.

"You know I had nothing to do with it," he instantly defended.

"We were both on that video, David, and somehow only I got punished for it."

"It wasn't my fault, Amber. I tried speaking with him, but he wouldn't listen," he countered, clearly irked I'd brought it up.

"Yeah, I know it's not your fault, David. It's your girlfriend's," I jibed, not able to hide how angry, how resentful I still was.

He had the decency to look remorseful.

Thanks to David and his big mouth, Bella had known where to strike and how to hurt me the most. Thanks to David, she'd gotten the idea to send the sex tape to Grant. If he hadn't complained about me to my enemies, I would have my job. I had been fired because of David, and that was something I would never forgive him for. Willingly or not, he'd helped the twins ruin my life.

"I didn't come here to argue with you, Amber," David

said. He was trying to stay calm; it was obvious he didn't appreciate being held accountable for his actions. He was nothing but a spoiled brat.

"Then why are you here?" I asked, folding my arms across my chest.

"I wanted to see how you were doing," he said with a small shrug.

In other words, he felt guilty and wanted to do something to make himself feel better. This had nothing to do with me; it was all about him. *Selfish bastard.*

"Just wonderful," I said sarcastically and decided not to say anything else. I wouldn't share my financial problems with him. Despite everything, I still had my pride.

He glanced behind me, at the state of my living room, and I knew what he saw. A lot of open space and packing boxes.

"Are you moving?" he asked.

"Yes," I replied.

"Why? You love this place," he said, genuinely surprised.

"Not anymore. Not after everything that happened. Besides, I need the money now that I don't have a job."

He looked at the floor for a moment before looking at me again. "You know, I am sorry, for everything."

I smiled humorlessly. "Doesn't really change anything."

His apology wouldn't help me find a new job or remain in this apartment with its bad feelings and memories. His apology was useless.

Like he is.

"I'm sorry there's nothing more I can offer."

You could if you really wanted to, I wanted to argue back, but held my tongue.

"Do you want to come in?" I offered.

Perhaps the two of us could have one last encounter within these walls so I wouldn't have to leave the apartment with nothing but bad memories and regrets.

"I'd better not," David said, much to my chagrin.

I was too prideful to ask why he was blowing me off. Luckily, he continued.

"I'm supposed to meet my father for lunch. I don't want to be late."

Figured. I was sure that would remain true forever. No matter how much he complained, he would never be free of Grant. And not because he couldn't, but because he didn't want to. Not really. Despite his whines, he liked his life too much, which made him a hypocrite. "So you're still on your father's leash."

His eyes flashed with fury, clearly because he knew that I knew what he really was, a spineless brat, and then he shook his head, as though he had some inner debate with himself and decided not to follow on his anger.

Smart move. I was in no mood to argue; however, I was prepared to give him something worth remembering.

Eventually, he said, "Goodbye, Amber."

"Goodbye, David."

I watched him walk away. If I was being honest with myself, I would have to say I had mixed feelings about it all, about David himself.

During my banishment from the rest of the world, I'd realized I cared about him more than I knew. More than I was prepared to admit, even now. Which was precisely why his betrayal hurt so much. That was also the reason I was sure we would never be together again. Not as an occasional hookup, not as a real couple, and not because Grant would never allow it.

David had chosen Bella over me, and that would always stand between us. That was something unforgivable, at least in my book. I had no idea how Bella had managed to seduce him while pretending to be Mercy, but the damage was done. My heart was broken.

As I thought about Bella and David, I looked toward her apartment. Yellow tape still sealed the door, marking it as a crime scene.

Although nobody had died there, that had happened on the staircase, which I refused to use now, the police treated it as a crime scene because of what had happened to me.

The twins had plotted my demise there. They'd watched me through the hidden cameras, collecting dirt to use against me, so it was no wonder the police were collecting evidence there. Sam was dead; Bella was alive and well though, which meant if she was ever caught, she would be tried for everything. Unfortunately, "if" was the operative word. I wasn't holding my breath they would catch her. The police had been pretty useless when I needed them.

Bella being MIA, free despite what she did to me, gave me nightmares. She was nearly as ruthless as her brother, and I knew I would never be safe, be free, while she was at large.

I literally had nightmares about her chasing me, trying to kill me, and she and her brother were constantly switching forms. I usually woke up screaming as the gun fired, hitting me in the chest, and I hated it. It unnerved me, among other things, that I was so weak. And I didn't want to be weak. I was strong, always.

As though spellbound, I walked the short distance and tried the door. Part of me was surprised it was unlocked, the rest of me was excited, in a strange almost foreboding way.

Opening the door and bending ever so slightly to not disturb the tape, I walked inside.

And I received the second shock of the day. All of her things were gone. And I wasn't talking about the ugly furniture. I meant all her personal things.

I'd had half a mind to put all her furniture on eBay and sell it. Some extra cash would be a good idea. Bella owed me that much. But I would have been ashamed to list her belongings for the whole world to see and mock, which was precisely why I'd abandoned that idea.

As I mused, I walked through the apartment and was pleased to see it wasn't bigger than mine. I was amazed Bella had managed to clear out her stuff without anyone noticing, and right under the police's nose.

If I wanted something done, I needed to do it. I was the only person I could rely on, no one else. I had a feeling even Detective Sheldon had given up searching for Bella, clearly too busy working on some other case.

That filled me with anger, of course. I didn't want to live like this, constantly looking over my shoulder, fearing the day Bella would finally catch me and take revenge for what had happened to her brother.

Although it wasn't my fault he died. It was completely his since he hadn't listened to Detective Sheldon and put the gun down. Sadly, I was sure the truth wouldn't matter to his sister. It hadn't mattered the first time around either.

I turned to leave, realizing I was wasting time, arguing with ghosts, and jumped backward, startled. *Oh my God.*

Bella was by the door, leaning against the wall, smirking at me.

Oh no, no, no.

"Hello, Amber," she greeted, almost pleasantly, as though we were old friends.

My heart started to beat fast. Bella was dangerous, and there was no telling what she would do to me. *She returned to finish the job. She returned to kill me because Sam couldn't.* I panicked.

I frantically looked around, for a way out, how to escape. But there was no escaping this place. Bella was blocking the only way to freedom.

"Relax, I didn't come here to hurt you."

I made a face at that. "Yeah, and I should just take your word for it after all the lies. Right."

"If I wanted you dead, you would be already," she countered, sounding almost bored.

That chilled me to the bones. "That's reassuring. Not," I grumbled, mostly to myself.

"I'm not a killer."

"You are everything else," I snapped, not able to stop myself.

She smiled humorlessly. "I was always fascinated by that ability of yours to judge others while holding yourself in the highest regard. What's that called? Oh, right, a narcissist." She answered her own question.

It wasn't the first time I'd been called that. Naturally, people like her had to blame others to justify their own bad behavior and rotten souls.

She was saying that purely to hurt me, and I wasn't going to allow her to do that anymore. She'd hurt me enough already, she and her brother. *Enough is enough.* Although I was afraid, I decided to stand my ground and not let her see how much this encounter unnerved me.

"Why are you here?" I asked, ignoring her remark.

"The same reason you are, I suppose. To say goodbye."

Fuck. She was about to leave the country, flee. I was afraid of that. If she managed to escape, then the police would never be able to catch her, and that was unacceptable. I needed her behind bars. How to prevent her from leaving? Could I make a citizen's arrest? How did someone do that anyway? I had no idea.

I cursed myself to hell and back that I didn't have my phone with me. I could have ended this once and for all by calling Detective Sheldon, but once again my rashness would cost me dearly.

"I heard what Sam did, and I decided to turn myself in."

Say what? Bella's words snapped me from my thoughts. She'd decided to turn herself in? There was no way I heard that right.

"Finally feeling guilty for all your sins?" I taunted.

"No," she deadpanned. "I just don't want to end up like you."

"What's that supposed to mean?"

Without answering me, she turned around and walked away.

"What's that supposed to mean?" I asked again, raising my voice ever so slightly.

I went after her, but when I reached the hallway, she was already gone. I looked to the elevators, but she wasn't there.

Strange. It was as though she'd never been there. Simply a figment of my imagination. By the time I returned to my apartment, I was sure she'd said all that to torment me, and I was the foolish one for falling for it.

More to the point, I was sure she was bluffing; there was no chance she would turn herself in and suffer the consequences. But I was proved wrong when the DA called me to inform me Bella Stone had walked into the police station and turned herself in.

What a crazy bitch she was. Just like her brother.

The trial that followed, with me having to testify, was exhausting, to say the least, but I still went through it all, needing to ensure Bella got the maximum penalty. My experience as a lawyer gave me the advantage of being prepared for the stand. Eventually, after a few weeks, Bella was found guilty and was sent to prison.

I was finally free.

Finally!

I won!

39

MOVING ON

Two months had passed since the trial, and I had somewhat managed to get used to my new life. I created new routines and got used to a different environment, one I was forced to be part of now, new people, a new rhythm.

While I was a successful lawyer, I'd felt like my life was a fast car, a Formula 1 car. Now it was an old Chevy. And that wasn't necessarily bad, simply different. At least that was what I was trying to convince myself.

At first, I was beyond bitter that everything had been taken from me. However, with time, I realized I had nothing to gain feeling like that. Other people didn't care about my problems, so I had to start all over and let go of the past, which was easier said than done.

True, Bella was in jail, she paid for all the crimes she'd committed, but that didn't change anything in my life. Not really. I didn't live in fear, constantly looking over my shoulder, but that was the only difference. My life was equally ruined after hearing her guilty verdict. I had still been fired from my job, and I'd still lost my apartment.

I got the necessary peace of mind with her safely locked up, but I had to do all the hard work, pick up the broken pieces of my life and move on.

That was exactly what I did, or at least that was what I was trying to do, I corrected. As I discovered, starting over with hardly any money and no one I could actually turn to or rely upon in my hour of need was difficult. Every day was a struggle. All the same, I refused to give up. I couldn't.

I was now living in a modest apartment on an entirely different side of the city; it was all I could afford on my salary. Compared to my old apartment, it was a complete dump, and I didn't like the neighborhood or my neighbors. Not that I met any of them. After Mercy, or rather Bella, I was reluctant to form any kind of friendship with any of them.

I didn't allow myself to look at things from a negative perspective, though, because deep down I knew this situation was only temporary. I was grateful I had a job that meant I could afford to pay rent to begin with.

I worked as a clerk at the DA's office. The job was humiliating and beneath me, but it was the only thing that was offered to me in this city since Grant had poisoned all the best law firms, preventing them from hiring me.

Even the ones owned by people who hated Grant didn't want to touch me, not wanting to go to war with him.

Luckily, the DA couldn't care less, took pity on me and offered me this position. At first, I was shocked he dared to suggest I work for him, and at such a lowly station. My pride urged me to decline and storm out of his office, yet the fear of the uncertain tomorrow made me say yes.

I had to admit the job wasn't that horrible, although I worked for the people who used to be my opponents. All the same, I hoped I would quickly rise through the ranks and become a district attorney myself.

If someone had told me a few years ago that would be my goal, I would have laughed, but life was funny like that, with a strange sense of humor.

I knew I would experience great pleasure in going against my former colleagues and wiping the floor with them in court each time once I'd risen through the ranks. I had vivid daydreams about those moments. I knew all their weak spots, and I couldn't wait for that day when I would go toe-to-toe with them and show them once more, I was the best.

I couldn't say for sure if Grant would ever be my opponent, but that was my biggest dream. Either way, with time I would find a way to make him regret firing me.

Although I had a new job and a new place to live, I was still struggling. My life remained a mess. I had nightmares about what had happened each night. At times, it was Sam chasing me around the building with a gun. At others, it was Bella.

I didn't trust anyone around me, I couldn't. Despite all the difficulties, I somehow managed to pull myself together and carry on. As I mentioned before, I had new goals, and that helped in some small way. My pride was responsible for the rest.

I wouldn't allow myself to break apart and disappear into oblivion. I had scores to settle, people to show I was far stronger, mightier than they could ever imagine. Everyone who'd turned against me would see how superior I was. Those thoughts helped me get out of bed in the morning.

It wasn't like this was the first time I'd been forced to move on after my personal tragedies. I had gone through this when my father died, and I still carried on. But it wasn't like I had another choice, anyway.

Although, there were moments that I wasn't particularly proud of on my road to recovery. During one of my weakest moments, I broke down and called Grant. Predictably, he refused to take my calls. I vowed he would regret that and deeply.

I also called David. I hoped he could speak with his father and get me my old job back. I was prepared to just be an associate again, but he too ignored my calls. Apparently, I'd insulted him during our last conversation, although I couldn't see how. I'd only spoken the truth, and now he didn't want to see me ever again.

I felt betrayed, but I realized I could live with that. It gave me additional motivation to excel at my job and show them all how powerful I was. How powerful I could become.

Coming to terms with the fact I would never return to GBD, never become a named partner, and how that dream was forever lost to me was heartbreaking. But over time, I realized that, perhaps, that was all for the best.

Perhaps my dreams were too small to begin with. And people changed goals, changed career paths all the time. That wasn't as big a deal as I once considered it to be.

I used to think it was that or nothing, and now I could see the error of my ways. I was nothing if not adaptable, and I would definitely use that to my advantage.

Apart from switching sides and working for the "good guys" from now on, I also started taking self-defense classes. Considering the huge pay cut, it was a luxury I couldn't really afford, but it was a necessity for my peace of mind. I needed to feel like I was in control of my life once again, and those classes helped a great deal.

If there was one good thing I liked about my new job, it was that I was always home at reasonable hours. I had more free time to do other things now, like read books, stress about my life. Or speak with my mother.

That was one more routine I had incorporated into my everyday life. I talked with my mother almost every day. It had started out of fear. I wanted at least one person to know what was happening in my life. I wanted someone knowing I was alive, and then the calls continued after I had my life back on track, so to speak.

Despite the fact she hadn't been there for me during all that drama, that she hadn't come to see me after I'd been shot, or hadn't been there in the courtroom while I gave my testimony, I decided to forgive her. She was set in her ways, and I couldn't change her. I just had to accept that she was damaged, limited, and always would be. More importantly, I had to accept that our relationship would always be strained and limited.

Since I was home earlier than usual, I decided to give my mother a call.

Our beginnings were always the same. She asked if all was all right, as though she were prepared to do something about it if I wasn't, when she was not. But we were able to move past that moment and talk about other things.

"Some mold has appeared in one of the corners on the ceiling in the living room," I complained, exasperated. "I don't know how to handle it."

I'd tried scrubbing it off, but unfortunately, it always came back, those black spots, irritating me, worrying me they would cause some kind of illness. The last thing I needed after everything was to get sick thanks to some stupid mold in my stupid apartment.

I also sprayed it with some products I bought that were supposed to get rid of mold, but nothing helped, not in the long run. It was as infuriating as it was frustrating.

"I know just the thing you need. I'll send you the name of the product you need to buy. Make sure to follow the instructions to the letter," she warned.

I rolled my eyes at that. Because if she hadn't warned me, I would drink the stuff instead of putting it on the wall according to the instructions. Sometimes she was beyond stupid.

"Thanks," I said instead of what was on my mind. "I'm afraid it will come back." Fixing that wall looked like a lost cause to me. And that was beyond depressing because it reminded me too much of my broken life. I would always have cracks in me, no matter what I did.

"It usually does," my mother agreed.

Then what was the point anyway? "I can't believe this is my life now, talking, worrying about mold," I grumbled, not able to help myself.

Although I was determined to move on, stop feeling sorry for myself or grieving my former life, I still had relapses.

"If you hadn't sold my house, we would both have a proper home to live in now," my mother snapped in return, her tone bitter, taking me by surprise.

It had been a while since she'd brought that up. Then again, it was to be expected. After all this time, she never missed an opportunity to make me feel guilty about something I did a long time ago.

"I didn't sell *your* house, I sold *mine*," I corrected like I always did.

When my father died, I'd sold the house so I could pay for college and rent a place to live while I studied. And she never forgave me for it.

"I lived in that house years before you were even born," my mother said in return.

"I know. All the same, Dad left it to me. That was what he wanted, to ensure my future," I argued in return. Once he got sick, he'd wanted to make sure I had a future, that I was settled even if he wasn't there to help me himself. That was why he'd left the house to me, not her.

"Your father wanted you to have a home you could always return to if things didn't go according to plan. Not throw me out. And thanks to your selfishness, now we both have nothing."

"Selfishness?" I snapped, but decided to rein it all in.

There was no point in arguing anyway. We always did this song and dance routine, and at the end it changed nothing. I still believed I'd made the right decision. She still believed I'd ruined her life and broke her heart. That was the true reason my mother and I could never be as close as other mothers and daughters usually were.

She hated me. The only reason she kept me in her life was because she had no one else in this world. And the same could be said about me. She was all I had too.

"Dad left me the house to do with it what I wanted, which I did, and I guess we'll never see eye to eye on that subject."

"You took all the money, Amber, leaving me penniless, homeless."

"I needed money for college. Besides, you were hardly homeless. I found you that apartment immediately."

"Yes, and I had no money to pay for it."

I couldn't understand why she insisted on bringing up the past.

"That's because you were a stay-at-home wife, but you got a job, and now I am sure your life is much richer because of it." Besides, I did pay rent for the first two months, but she always forgot that part. It was easier to play the victim that way.

My mother sighed, as though my response bothered her. Seeing how she was in a particularly bad mood that day, I decided to end the call.

"Mom, I have something to take care of," I lied. "Talk to you later." And with that, I hung up.

I couldn't believe her. She always acted as though her life was the hardest. *What about me?* Some really bad things had happened, but I didn't go around complaining, crying on her shoulder. I sucked it up and moved on. Unfortunately, my mother was incapable of that, which was precisely why she was nowhere twenty years after my father died.

Pathetic.

I never wanted to be like her. I never wanted to blame others for my failures or my unhappiness. Despite everything that had happened to me, despite all the heartaches, I was happy. Happy to be alive, at least.

Thanks to Sam and Bella, I'd learned that wasn't guaranteed, that it was something each individual had to fight for tooth and nail. Sam almost killed me, but to me, that meant a second chance in life. And I definitely wasn't going to waste it. I wasn't going to repeat the same mistakes from the past, that was for sure.

There was no way in hell I would sleep with my boss's son, for example. I'd learned that lesson the hard way. Luckily, my new boss had two daughters, so I was safe, I joked.

With a heavy heart, I started going to therapy as well. Once upon a time, I would have considered that a waste of time and money. Not to mention it was a sign of defeat, a declaration of how weak an individual I was. But not anymore.

Since I wanted to move on, and not turn into my mother somewhere along the way, I had only one option. To help myself, I had to seek help from someone else. And I found a therapist I liked, eventually.

It took some time; there were a few hits and misses. I even ended up arguing with one jerk, but eventually I settled on seeing Dr. Elizabeth Connelly.

She helped me with my nightmares, which was a true blessing since I was at the end of my rope, desperate for a night of sleep without waking up screaming in the middle of it.

She was helping me with some other things as well. Thanks to the twins, my trust in people had been ruined. And with Dr. Connelly's help, I was trying to change that. It wasn't easy, but all the same, I was trying.

"Based on what you've told me, you had trouble trusting people even before Bella and Sam entered your life," Dr. Connelly observed during one of our weekly conversations.

"I don't know if that's necessarily true," I rebelled, and then paused. Was she right? No, she wasn't. "I had my job, plenty of colleagues, and a guy I was seeing," I continued.

"Yet they all turned their backs on you because they didn't feel connected, emotionally obliged in any way to help," she pointed out.

At times, I really didn't like how she made me confront myself. "My mother once told me I push everyone away," I confessed.

"Do you?"

"Maybe, yes, probably I do."

"Why do you think you do that?"

"I don't really know. Maybe I'm just afraid, and I would very much like to know how to change that," I found myself saying.

She offered a warm, reassuring smile in return. "That's easy, by starting to trust people, opening up."

Part of me knew she would say something so ridiculous and banal. Still, I said, "I'll try."

I would trust her because she knew what the hell she was saying. Perhaps that was already a step in the right direction.

We shall see...

40

OLD HABITS DIE HARD

My plan was to work, and that was no surprise. I could do everything when I set my mind to a specific goal. And this time, my plan was simple, not to remain a clerk for too long.

And I was successful. I was promoted after a couple of months with the DA's office because I'd helped one of the prosecutors. His opponent was one of the attorneys from GBD, and I was more than happy to offer a few pieces of advice on how to beat him, without breaking any laws, of course. It wasn't a conflict of interest because I'd only offered what I knew personally, from my old files, rather than using something I'd learned from a specific case. That would be breaking privileges, and I ensured my back was covered, making sure I said things that I could, not wanting to get in trouble.

Word got around I was the person to come to if they wanted an advantage against that specific firm, and that delighted me. Shortly after, I was promoted, which meant better pay. It wasn't that big a raise, but it was enough for now, and it was certainly an encouragement for me to continue down that path.

Also, that situation gave me an excellent idea. I needed to start compiling dirt on my new coworkers because it could be useful when climbing the organizational ladder over time. I didn't want to wait years for the next promotion. I was on a tight schedule, after all, which meant I would definitely have to push some things forward to move faster. Or move some people out of my way, as it turned out. It was the same tactic I'd used at my old job, so I knew it would work.

My new goal was to become the district attorney. It was the safest shortcut to becoming the mayor or maybe a congresswoman. *Congresswoman Dennis.* That certainly had a nice ring to it. Governor Dennis sounded even better. And this was absolutely the right time to start preparing for such roles.

Once upon a time, I had been opposed to going into politics. I considered it too dirty for me, but after everything I'd been through and how I had been treated at GBD, I realized playing politics wasn't any different to being a lawyer. I had to make deals and shake hands with a lot of people I didn't necessarily like to get the desired results. And that was something I was definitely born to do.

Realizing that, I had nothing to hold me back when I planned my strategy to achieve my goals and win elections. But I was getting ahead of myself. I had to reach the first milestone, which was to become a county district attorney.

I couldn't wait for that day to come. I would give lavish speeches and go after the wicked and corrupt. And people would praise me for it. I wouldn't only love all the money and power at my disposal, I would relish all the fame as well.

I was somewhat famous in certain circles, although right

now I was more of a cautionary tale, thanks to Grant, but if I played my cards right, I would soon turn all that around to my advantage.

What an original story that would make... Perhaps I would even write a book, I mused.

I had been wrong in my assumptions earlier in life, and I wasn't ashamed to admit that. Now I knew that having a career in politics was the best because it ensured you had the whole trifecta, money, fame, and power. It was the holy grail of careers, and I was going to seize this second chance and make something great out of my life.

I just knew I would be great at politics. I was a natural leader.

Though, for that to happen, I had to be in a position that would get me noticed. And I honestly didn't want to spend years doing this meaningless job, waiting for my chance, that promotion, that might never come.

I had to make it happen. I would get promoted based on my merits; I was adamant about that. All the same, I planned on speeding up the process just a little, because time wasn't something I had in abundance. I was thirty-six already. And if I wanted to be somebody important by the time I was in my fifties, then I had to act now.

That was precisely why it was imperative to create new folders and gather sensitive information about my new colleagues so I could strike when needed.

It was Monday morning, and I'd finished my most urgent tasks when I decided to take a few moments to focus on me, my other job, creating my desired future, and started preparing ammunition for prospective battles. Luckily, as though providence wished it so, I discovered something of vital importance that very morning.

One of my colleagues, a fellow lawyer, had had drug problems in his youth. More accurately, he had been busted doing drugs while a minor. His parents had made it go away, but some form of a record still existed. That was something that could definitely cost him his promotion, not to mention his future career as a public figure, and that was precisely why I was so happy that I'd learned about it.

Without wasting any time, I opened his freshly made folder and started typing. I wanted to get all the information I had out of my head before I forgot something. Once I finished with that task, I would definitely go out and snoop some more. I had one colleague who liked to gossip, and I was sure I could make her talk during our lunch break if I nudged her in the right direction.

As my therapist had suggested, I was socializing more, which would prove pretty useful in my secret endeavor.

I was just about done, finishing my entry, when a pop-up window appeared; someone wanted to chat with me.

True enough, I received a message, but the user's name was unfamiliar. All the same, I read what was written. It was hard not to when it was staring at me on the screen.

You'd better not be up to your old tricks, Amber.

I read as my heart started to beat faster.

I may be in jail, but I am still watching you. I can still harm you if I see you doing something you should not. Behave, turn over a new leaf. B.

B for Bella. I didn't have to be a genius to figure that one out.

I couldn't believe it. Even from jail, she'd managed to send me that message. She was watching me still.

I felt like crying. I felt like screaming.

I started to shake, remembering all the times I'd received similar messages and what had happened afterward. I immediately deleted everything I'd written, all the files with evidence, old and new.

I let go of everything I had against my new coworkers and the former ones from GBD.

Although it was hard, I let go of all my leverage. And I really hoped Bella had seen me do that.

I wondered if I should report her message, but ruled against it.

I can't go through this again.

Maybe it would be better to listen to her. I couldn't go through that hellish existence again if Bella decided to torment me anew. If I listened, I wouldn't have to live with the fear she would do something to me, hurt me, and after what had happened, that meant everything to me.

Life without fear, without the urge to look over my shoulder, was worth sacrificing for, even if it meant doing everything aboveboard to achieve my dreams. I'd have to do it by merit alone. Even if it meant staying in this position longer than I wanted to. I would do it and still get to where I wanted to be in life.

I had learned my lesson.

Bella, you win.

THANK YOU FOR READING

Did you enjoy reading *The Couple Next Door*? Please consider leaving a review on Amazon. Your review will help other readers to discover the novel.

ABOUT THE AUTHOR

Cole Baxter loves writing psychological suspense thrillers. It's all about that last reveal that he loves shocking readers with.

He grew up in New York, where there was crime all around. He decided to turn that into something positive with his fiction.

His stories will have you reading through the night—they are very addictive!

ALSO BY COLE BAXTER

Inkubator Books Titles

The Perfect Suitor

The Betrayal

I Won't Let You Go

The Night Nurse

The Doppelganger

The Couple Next Door

I Will Find You

The Cole Baxter Box Set

Other Titles

Prime Suspect

What She Witnessed

Deadly Truth

Finding The Other Woman

Trust A Stranger

Follow You

Did He Do It

What Happened Last Night

Perfect Obsession

Going Insane

She's Missing

The Perfect Nanny

What She Forgot

Stolen Son

Before She's Gone

Printed in Great Britain
by Amazon

33522520R10209